DEMON KNIGHT

A.B. COHEN & JP RINDFLEISCH IX

This is a work of fiction. Names, characters, businesses, places, events, locales, and incidents are either the products of the author's imagination or used in a fictitious manner. Any resemblance to actual persons, living or dead, or actual events is purely coincidental.

Copyright © 2022 by A.B. Cohen & JP Rindfleisch IX

All rights reserved.

No part of this book may be reproduced in any form or by any electronic or mechanical means, including information storage and retrieval systems, without written permission from the author, except for the use of brief quotations in a book review.

Cover design by Getcovers.com

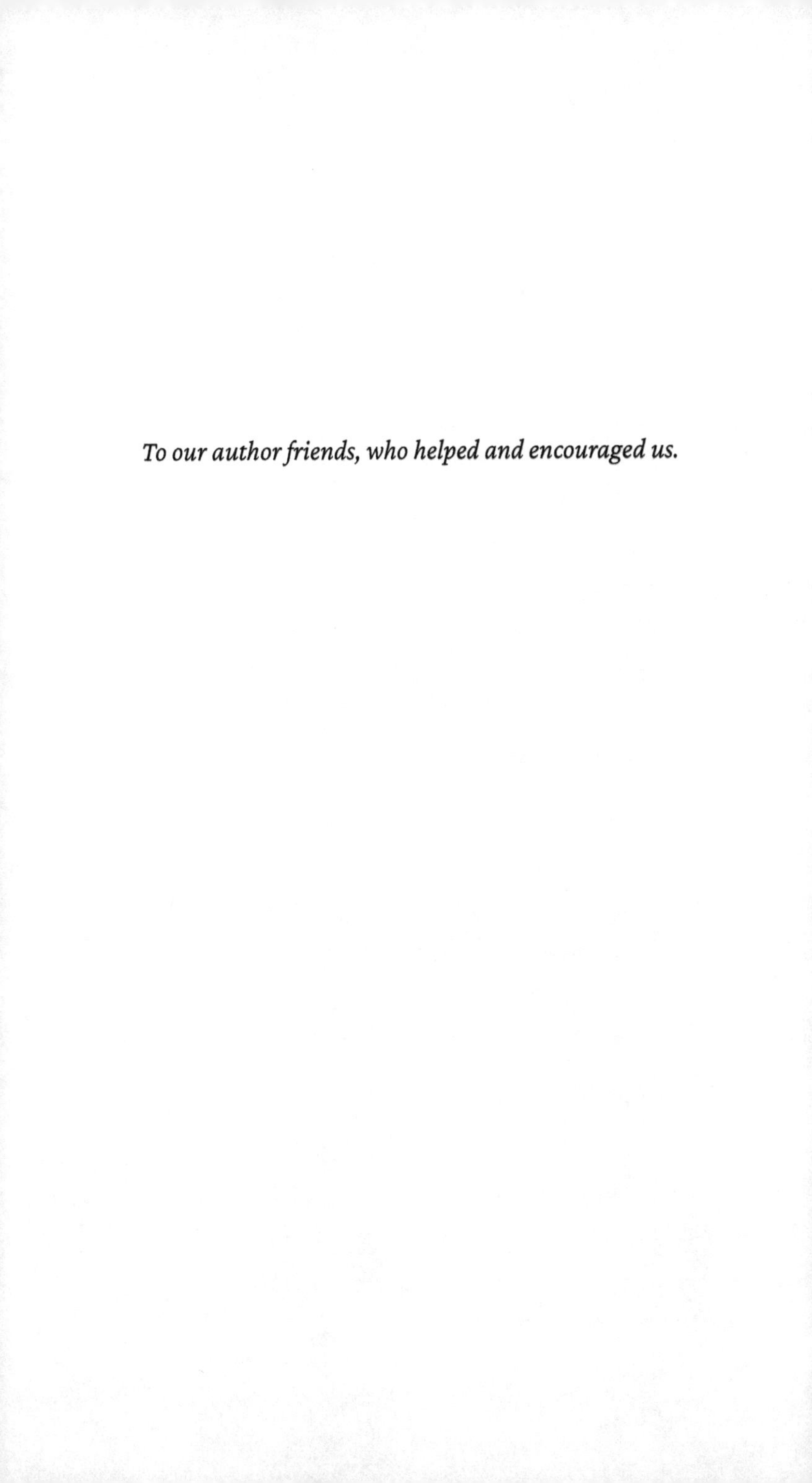

To our author friends, who helped and encouraged us.

Tree of Life

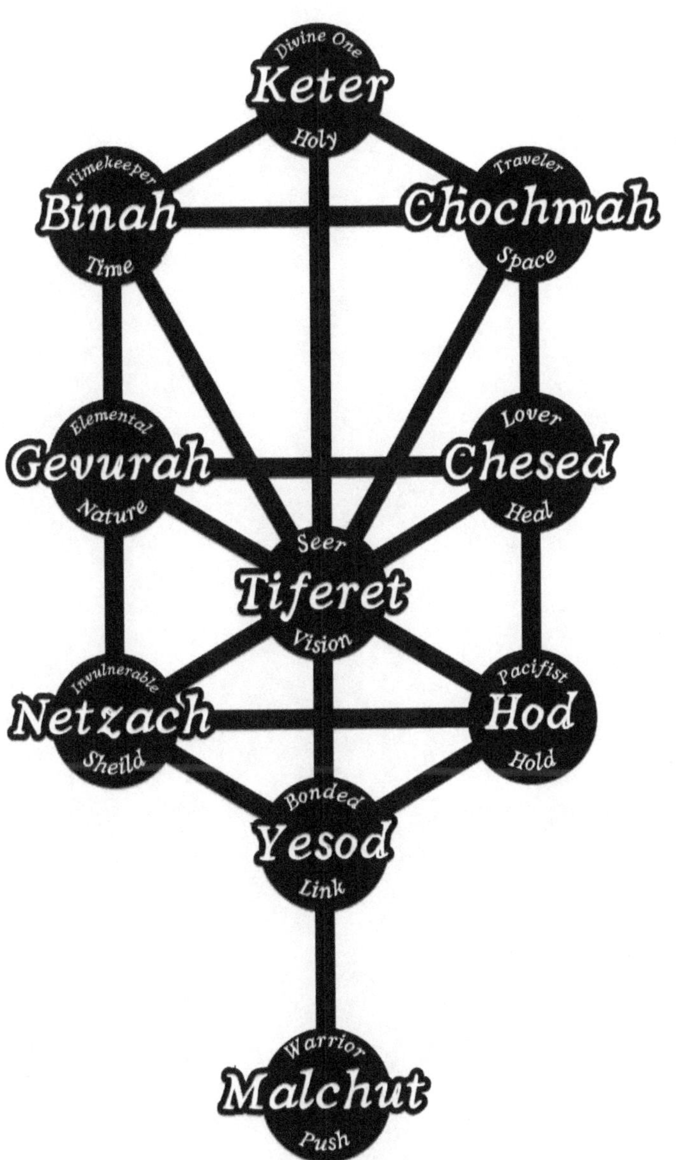

Divine One
Keter
Holy
Timekeeper
Binah
Time
Traveler
Chochmah
Space
Elemental
Gevurah
Nature
Lover
Chesed
Heal
Seer
Tiferet
Vision
Invulnerable
Netzach
Sheild
Pacifist
Hod
Hold
Bonded
Yesod
Link
Warrior
Malchut
Push

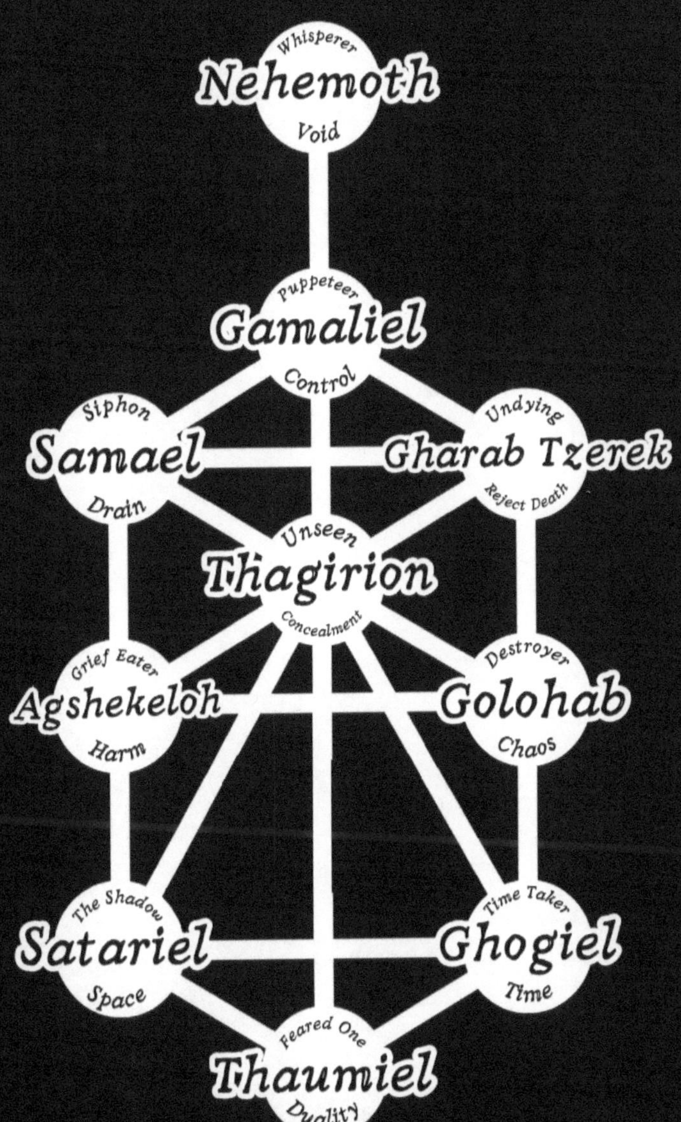

Tree of Death

The Infinity Board

 *King*

 *White Queen*

 *Black Queen*

 *White Rook / Sage*

 *Black Rook*

 *White Bishop*

 *White Knight*

 *Black Bishop*

 *Black Knight*

 *White Pawn*

 *Black Pawn*

 *Square*

CHAPTER I
DEMONS UNDERGROUND

Candlelight stretched across the room, dancing along the buffed concrete floor and tiled walls as Leah's vision focused. The house shook as the squeals of a train sounded overhead. The familiar sweet caramel and smoky pine of scotch filled her nostrils, mixing with a powerful scent of metal.

Leah doubled over and heaved as the smell of blood sent flashbacks through her mind. These visions replayed the day she found her mother on that sofa and her father standing in the living room corner, his hands covered in blood.

A scream cut through her thoughts, pulling her back to the tiled room. She turned and found a body on the floor.

Symbols marked the ground, drawn in a thick red substance she could only presume was blood. An old, naked man lay on his side in the middle of the room, color drained from his face. His bones pressed against his thin, emaciated frame, and white strands of hair sparsely lined his otherwise bald head.

A loud chittering sounded around her, melodic,

reminding her of the spider-like creatures she'd heard once before.

The body jerked, as if pulled up by strings, levitating face down, toes and fingertips grazing the floor. He took in a haggard breath, and the chittering stopped.

He screamed as deep slashes formed on his back, gouges that crossed over one another and cascaded a stream of blood onto the floor.

Dozens of candles lit the corners of the room, yet a thick shadow somehow descended on the man. Another strike as the sound of chains struck his back. He didn't even flinch this time, and Leah wondered if he was already dead.

A low, raspy voice resonated from within the amorphous shadow. "I won't let you go that easily. Her spells can't stop me. You're mine, and you had one job." Another strike. The voice was vaguely familiar, spoken in some faraway dream. "And you failed."

A gloved hand, covered in black leather, reached out from the shadows, palm facing toward the hovering body. As the hand flipped and clenched its fist. The hovering man responded, whipping around like a rag doll, limbs flailing and head dangling back, coughing up blood.

The floating man wheezed and lolled his head before his green eyes flicked to Leah. The corners of his mouth twitched, and he muttered something under his breath in a soft, melodic whisper.

A searing, white-hot pain shot through Leah's arm that echoed through her entire body. Her eyes were drawn to the man, and she frowned. She had sensed his pain, felt it through some strange means, and she wanted to scream. She clutched at her chest, the pressure inside her waking and uncoiling.

"Whispers won't help you now, little Kyjak," the shadow voice continued. Darkness expanded, pressing against the corners of the room, shrouding the man. "If you have something to say, say it."

The man's face contorted, showing his growing rage. He pulled his head up and spat a wad of thick blood into the shadows. "Damn you, Legion."

That rage echoed inside Leah, and the pressure grew from within. Whoever this man was, whatever he had done, it wasn't worth this pain and torture. She wanted to leap out into the shadows and tear apart whatever stood there.

Yet, a strange voice whispered in her head. *Wait, not yet.*

She clenched her fists and pressed her back against the wall.

Shadows snapped back, the candlelight brightening the room once again. Glass clicked from across the room, and Leah's eyes fell on the empty glass next to an open bottle of dark amber liquid on a small round table.

The shadowed figure formed into the blackened silhouette of a man, standing only a few feet from the naked body. He stepped forward and poured an amber liquid into the glass, light recoiling away from the black void standing in the light. "Once so formidable. Feared, even. And now look at you. Too weak. Just like the rest."

The floating body let out a long, labored breath before his head rolled back. His eyes fluttered open and closed, and his chest slowed with every breath. Leah tried stepping forward, tried to race to the floating body and face off with the shadow silhouette so she could stop this agony. Yet her body, wrapped in a cocoon of thick air, wouldn't move.

Legion stepped forward, arms moving as if to roll up unseen sleeves. He held out his right arm, and tendrils of shadows interlaced into thick shadowy chains that clanged onto the floor.

The shadow blurred, and a thick chain flew at the man,

leaving a crevasse of torn flesh across the man's chest in its wake. Legion moved again and again, whipping his flesh, gouging the man's body. A familiar high-pitched shriek and chittering came from the body, one that reminded Leah of the outpost. Blood and flesh filled the air, snuffing out candles and covering the tiled wall in gore.

Leah couldn't keep watching. She couldn't let this happen. The pressure inside her met the pressure holding her. She pushed against it with all her might, feeling her jaw working again and a scream tearing out of her.

"Stop!"

The shadowy figure paused mid-strike and turned to Leah, the tendril dissipating like wisps of smoke. His head cocked, peering at her before summoning the floating man to his side and clapping his hand on the man's bloodied shoulder.

"Well, look at that. You've brought yourself an audience, I see. Ironic. The only one who hears your call is her." He turned to the man and grabbed onto his chin, pulling him close to his shadowy face. "All you've brought is a witness to your death."

The man said nothing in return, his eyes locked on Legion. The shadow pushed him away and turned to Leah, taking a step forward while pointing at the man. "Do you even know who this is?"

Leah continued to push against the air that held her in place, feeling her legs move like wading through thick gelatinous water as she took a step forward. "I . . ." She paused and looked at the hovering man. She didn't know who he was. Did that even matter?

Legion let out a high, piercing laugh. "Well, I hate to spoil the surprise but, different meat suit, same monster who killed your parents."

She stared at the pitiful man, his skin flayed to shreds

and his green eyes not the same as her father's. Something familiar flickered behind those eyes. Something she thought was dead.

Leah whispered, "Asmodeus."

She shook her head, tears forming in her eyes. *Alma killed him. Took him with her when she died. He can't be here. He can't tear apart another family.*

Legion tilted his head. "Shall I keep going then?" He stepped away from the two and headed back to the scotch on the table, picking the glass up with one hand while summoning a tendril of shadowed chains with the other.

Leah lowered her gaze to the ground. Could she watch this, even if it was Asmodeus? She squeezed her eyes shut, willing herself to wake. The smell of scotch and blood still singed her senses.

The ground shook, and another squeal of brakes sounded above. Asmodeus reached out a shaky hand toward her, and her arm tingled. She jerked back, the barrier holding her gone as she pressed up against the wall, looking at him in disgust.

"I take that as a yes, then? Excellent." Legion stepped away from the table and whipped his chain toward Asmodeus, wrapping him tight like a spider wrapping its prey. "Even now, you can't even save yourself. You're better off being a part of me."

Legion contorted and shifted where he stood. Bones popped and cracked as the shadow grew larger, overtaking the room.

Leah pressed against the wall, wishing what she saw and heard would end.

Asmodeus raised his head, and his eyes widened. "No, please, not that!" He breathed rapid, short breaths. "Kill me. Kill me! Please, I beg you, PLEASE!"

Silvery teeth protruded from the darkness as a massive

snout formed. "The time for talk is over," the voice said, clamping down on Asmodeus's legs.

He screamed and reached desperately for Leah.

The fear in his eyes, the terror, cut into her. He was the worst thing to have happened to her, and she dreamt of the day he got what he deserved. Yet here, in this moment, she saw his fear, and she pitied him.

She couldn't stand there and do nothing. She reached her hand out, trying to pull him back away from the enormous set of sharp teeth. Their fingers interlocked, and she pulled. His eyes locked on to her, pleading for help. He gripped his other hand around her arm, and she felt a warmth in her arm as she pulled.

Legion yanked on his prey, tearing Asmodeus away from her grip. He ripped Asmodeus apart, biting again and again as he screamed. Leah saw the light in his green eyes fade before the blood splatter snuffed out the candles, casting the room into darkness. The last thing Leah heard was the sound of tearing flesh and cracking bone.

CHAPTER 2
A WARM WELCOME

The bus jostled from another bump in the highway and pulled Leah out of her trance. She blinked, peering out into the dark sky with only a small hint of a sunrise off in the horizon. When she pulled away from the window, she came face to face with large bright green eyes.

Leah jumped back, bouncing her head off the window hard enough to see stars before the rest of the green-eyed boy filled her vision.

Isaac O'Conner, a short, thin boy—the owner of the green eyes—said, "Oh, sorry! I didn't mean to scare you. You alright?"

Words fumbled in her mouth, a mix between the dream and a new bump on her head. "Why were you so close to my face?"

Sarah Turner's tight-curled black hair peeked out from the seat in front of her, and Leah's other best friend turned around. "He's worried. You kept moving around and kicking the back of my seat, muttering nonsense."

Leah rubbed the sleep from her eyes and yawned. "Sorry. I had another nightmare."

Isaac leaned in. "Do you want to talk about it?"

Leah stared at him, recollecting her dream, and images of blood flinging through the air filled her mind. She scratched her arm and shook her head. "No. It was just a bad dream. One I'd rather forget." She turned back toward the window and spotted skyscrapers lining the horizon. "Where are we?"

"We passed the border into North Carolina last night before we stopped." Isaac nodded toward the skyscrapers. "We only started moving again an hour ago, so I'm guessing that's Charlotte. Or maybe Raleigh."

Leah's memory crept back in. Three days on the bus now. They'd packed up and left the Black Hills outpost right after burying three Knights and her teacher, Black Bishop Alma, who'd sacrificed herself for Leah. Her father's body was also there, serving as a puppet to Asmodeus for months as he tracked her down. But he was free now, buried in a Jewish cemetery that Leah may never visit.

Her uncle Eric was the first to tell her about this secret society of Mystics, bringing her to the Outpost after Asmodeus killed her mother. He'd nearly died too, protecting her friends. Now, he sat in the driver's seat of a bus, transporting a bunch of teenagers across the country.

She looked in the rearview mirror and focused on his face. He had his sister's same honey-colored eyes—Leah's mother's eyes—but now dark circles and heavy bags sat under them. There were secrets behind those eyes. Secrets about her mother's past life as a Mystic of the Infinity Board. Secrets that she hoped to get out of him soon.

From what little she knew about Eric, she knew he would have driven straight to the academy if he could, no matter how many hours it took. Yet, the wounds from Asmodeus, the wounds she sensed from the bond forged between them to save his life, were still healing. Instead, he had to pace himself, parking the bus twice now after driving all day and sleeping through all the whispers and chatter from the Black Pawns.

Black Pawns. The kids were no longer Squares, but members of a secret order they knew nothing about. They were headed now to get their bonds and become White Pawns, the first step as full members of the society. If they made it, Leah and her fellow Pawns may even eventually become Knights or Bishops, depending on if their skills leaned more toward combat or knowledge. Leah doubted any of them had the smarts and political skills to make it to Rook status and become part of the council that oversaw the Infinity Board. Except maybe Isaac, who always stuck his nose in a book and could recite the Infinity Board's history almost word for word.

A loud crack broke Leah from her thoughts. She whipped her head around and saw one of the bus windows had blown open, shards of broken glass still dangling from the frame.

The bus swerved and Eric yelled, "Black Pawn Douglas! If you use *Malchut* on this bus again, I'll pull over and leave you stranded on the side of the road!"

"Sorry!" Harry shouted back while Buck giggled quietly next to him.

Harry and Buck were inseparable and unable to stop themselves from crossing over the line into sheer idiocy. Especially now that Harry had one thing on his mind, which was getting Emma to notice him. It didn't help that Buck enjoyed egging him on.

In front of that duo, Gabe buried his nose in a book —*The Art of War,* again. A tall, ashen-haired boy who had a knack for cooking and had always been kind to Leah since her first day at the Outpost.

Harry faced the back of the bus, peering out toward

Emma and waving for her attention. Emma, however, focused on Serena—Buck's twin sister—and the queen bee, Paige. Each of them lounged on their own seats in the back of the bus, their bare feet dangling in the center aisle.

Paige, a tall, blond beauty who was a carbon copy of all the rich girls Leah knew from her previous life made even this bus ride a living hell. As the day passed, Eric had occasionally pulled over at rest stops, handing out change so the students could grab something from the vending machine or, if the rest stop had it, fast food. Yet Paige insisted they stop at three different rest stops for her to find something she would eat. After that, Eric ignored her pleas, and Paige suspected, out loud, that he didn't care if she ate at all.

Another bump in the road, and Sarah winced as her chin bounced off the back of the seat. "Can't the Queens teleport or something? Isn't that a one of the wells? A *sefira*? Why couldn't they just teleport us all to where we need to go?"

Isaac thought for a moment. "I mean, does a Queen care about saving a handful of Pawns from hours on the road? If they actually *could* teleport, they'd end up like a taxi service if they just ported everyone around. Besides, ten people, plus them . . . that would expend so much energy. *Malchut* takes a lot of energy to even knock over a dummy. It clearly gets better with time and practice, but the other *sefira*? I'm sure doing it would put her in a coma."

Sarah huffed and rolled her eyes. "I guess you're right."

Isaac and Sarah laughed, and a warmth filled Leah. She didn't know what she'd do without these two, who'd saved her in more ways than they could imagine.

They talked as the sun crept up from the horizon and skyscrapers melted away into trees.

The bus slowed to a stop, and everyone peered out the windows into a densely packed forest surrounding them.

Erik unbuckled and stood up, clutching his side. He winced, and with it, a pain shot into Leah. The bond between them was new, but his pain was clear. She stood up and raced to him down the aisle. "Everything okay?"

He tested his footing and smiled. "Yeah, we're here." He looked past Leah, down the aisle. "Stay put. We're at the gates. They'll want you to line up outside when they call." He nodded for Leah to head back to her seat while he hobbled down the bus stairs.

Buck turned to look at Emma and Paige and took the opportunity to over-exaggerate a stretch while saying, "Finally."

After several minutes of waiting, Eric lumbered back onto the bus and into his seat, and he proceeded through the ornamented white metal gates. The bus weaved up a curvy driveway, through the forest until it broke into an open, well-manicured field leading up to a beautiful set of brick buildings.

The main structure that centered on the driveway had columns lining its entrance, reminding Leah of the pictures of Columbia University on her wall back home.

David Ackerman, her father, had graduated from Columbia with a degree in engineering. He'd hoped Leah would follow in his footsteps, so he'd pinned it to her wall the moment she started her freshman year of high school. Memories surfaced in Leah's mind. His smile also reminded Leah of her mother's smile, all of it tainted by the mark Asmodeus had left. They were dead. Gone, along with their house, reduced to rubble. All because of her.

A pain surfaced in her chest, feeling like an uncoiling of knots and a pressure that followed. The serpent was ready to strike. Ready to take in the energy from the Tree of Life, or the Tree of Death. She breathed through her nose, focusing on the grassy field while shoving that pain back into the hole it came from.

A sudden sense of calm poured over her, and that serpent inside her vanished in an instant. She looked in the rearview mirror and caught Eric's eye. He flashed a half smile at her, and she realized what she'd felt wasn't her but him sending reassurance through her bond. It felt wrong, almost forced, and she wondered if she was ready for this new bond.

The bus stopped, and a tall man with short black hair and a square jaw stepped onto the bus. He stood at attention and peered down the aisle. "Attention!"

Everyone sat up straight in their seats—including Paige, who understood that, in this society, not adhering to certain rules meant taking on extra duties that no one wanted.

The man nodded and smirked. "I am Black Knight Ian Kim, second in command of this academy's security force. Follow me and form a single file line along the bus." The man turned and stepped off.

They obeyed, sliding out of their seats and stepping off the bus one by one. Paige and her groupies pushed past Leah and Isaac, making them the last ones off the bus. Leah squinted at the bright blue skies and took in a breath of fresh air.

Ian joined the group of men and women dressed in pristine jackets of either black or white, mimicking the uniforms the Black Pawns had on, but cleaner and more form fitting. Various silver and gold buttons lined the jackets, which Leah figured were various medals notating achievements.

A slender woman stood at the front of the group with long black braids and dark eyeliner that stressed her eyes. She adjusted her white uniform, which was a stark contrast to her dark skin, and took a long drag of her cigarette before dropping it to the ground and snuffing it out with her white boots.

She peered out at the Pawns. "Attention!"

Everyone behind her moved quickly, standing up straight again and staring forward. A second later, Alma's training took over, and the group of nine took the same firm stance.

She frowned and pursed her lips. "I am White Knight Amana, but I prefer you use my first name, which is Nykima. I'm the head of logistics and security at Maimonides Academy." She paced down the line. "You've come late, and the other students are well ahead of you, but one of our Queens has asked us to accept you." She paused in front of Eric, an eyebrow raised. "Do not expect special treatment. We don't plan on giving any. We will bring you up to speed, and our trials will remain on schedule." She looked away from Eric and to the nine Pawns. "First order, remain still while we scan you." She stopped in front of Leah, looking into her eyes. She paused, her eyes softening before turning around.

A woman with dark blond hair, large grayish eyes, and a thin white cane stepped forward. She tapped the cane back and forth in front of her. Another woman, older with olive skin and a hijab, wrapped her arm around a younger man who sported a short, clean-cut black mohawk. They approached the first person in line, Paige, and gestured her to step forward.

They didn't speak. Instead, they circled her. Paige turned her head back and forth between the two, but the moment she opened her mouth, she froze.

Hairs stood up on Leah's arm as a tingling sensation rippled through the air. The two continued their pacing around Paige, their eyes glowing with a faint yellow light.

"She passes." The woman with the cane spoke.

"Little corruption, but good potential," the other woman said.

They gestured Paige back and moved on to the next, Emma, doing the same to her before passing her back into line.

When it was Buck's turn, he muttered, "Like what you see?"

The woman with the cane whacked his ankle with it for that, and Nykima cleared her throat and eyed Buck. "Remarks like that get you cleaning toilets for a month. Care to continue?"

Buck shook his head, leaning back with eyes wide.

Nykima turned her head and raised her hand to her ear. "What was that, Pawn?"

"Ah—No, White Knight Ama—Nykima!"

Nykima gave a slight nod, and they carried on with the rest of the line one by one. Leah noted that, as the woman continued to scan, the tapping on the cane and the dependency on the man grew more prevalent. Whatever they were using to scan them impaired their vision as they continued using it.

They came to Leah and gestured her forward. Electricity passed through her as their eyes glowed, and she shivered. Both women shielded their eyes, as if they'd stared into the sun. The sensation vanished, and they stood on either side of her.

Nykima stepped forward, her eyes flaring a golden hue while a tingling sensation washed over Leah. She knew the Knight could see something she couldn't. Nykima's glowing eyes trailed past Leah and followed an invisible line toward Eric. The sensation vanished, and Nykima blinked several times before saying, "You two, with me. Now."

CHAPTER 3

MEETING THE DEAN

Nykima escorted Leah and Eric as they walked up the gravel driveway and to the marbled stairs that marked the entrance to the academy. They passed massive white pillars that framed two large red wooden doors.

Inside, Leah found herself in a bright foyer. She spun around, noting a large door leading to a cafeteria on her left, and a tall corridor entrance to her right. On the wall beside the corridor entrance was a large, framed piece of parchment hanging from the wall. Scrawled in small letters were names, and next to each name were sets of numbers, both positive and negative, as if whoever had written them were keeping a score.

Eric cleared his throat, and Leah turned, realizing both Eric and Nykima were already on one of the two enormous staircases that led up to the second floor. She raced to catch up to them, peering up at the second floor and noting that the stairs lined the sides of the walls from the second floor, leading up to a third floor. Red and green light shone through a large stained-glass window depicting a pomegranate tree shown from the second floor to the third.

Leah followed Nykima as she stepped up onto the left-most marble staircase. Another member of the academy, a woman with a stern face all dressed in all black, walked up beside Nykima, drawing her into a whispered conversation.

Leah leaned in toward Eric. "Why did she pull us from the others like that?"

"It's the bond. You're not supposed to have one."

"But wouldn't the Queen have told them? If we just explain what happened . . ."

Eric shrugged. "The Infinity Board Queens don't meddle with Pawn affairs. Aside from that, traditions keep us going. Even if it were to save a life, some members may not find it justifiable to break our protocols. We just need to be careful with what we say next. I've already got one person against us." He scratched the back of his head.

"Who?"

He nodded to Nykima. "Nykima and I, uh, sort of had a thing together. And it didn't exactly end well."

The woman having a hushed conversation with Nykima broke away before Leah could ask any more questions.

They reached the second level, turned left, and walked into a hallway lined with doors on both sides. They stopped in front of the only door with a different color than the rest, a rich red wood, the same shade as the front doors.

Nykima knocked, and a voice sounded from within. "Come in."

She ushered them in and closed the door behind her.

Bookshelves lined the room—far more than Alma's office, with space enough for a window in the back of the room that drew in light. The desk, a deep cherry-red wood, barely fit in the space, with a laptop and stacks of papers cluttered on top of it.

A man stood in the center of the room, adjusting his white tie and gray three-piece suit. His brunette hair was brushed with a touch of gray, and he had sharp blue eyes and a smile that melted her nerves away.

Nykima bowed her head, looking to the desk before she spoke. "Dean Wright, this is Black Pawn Leah Ackerman, and I suppose you already know Black Knight Eric Mizrahi. They're bonded, as Black Queen Nielsen noted."

"Ah, yes. Please, take a seat." He spoke with a smooth British accent and gestured for them to sit while Nykima stood at the door. "I am White Knight William Wright, Dean of this academy." He looked at Eric, those bright blue eyes piercing into him before looking at Leah. He steepled his fingers. "Right, well . . . where do I begin?" He eyed the ceiling before he continued. "Black Pawn Ackerman, I presume our Knight here hasn't told you much about the workings of this academy. Perhaps our late Bishop provided you with some information, but let's ensure you are up to speed." Dean Wright leaned back in his chair and crossed his arms. "An academy's goal is to prepare the *Yesod* Bond for inducted Black Pawns. They train over six months, explore their connection to the Tree of Life in a safe and controlled environment. This process is slow, helping you grow your energy and explore any affinities you might have with a specific well, or as we call it, *sefira*. I'm assuming you've all been studying all the wells, yes?"

Leah nodded. "Yes, ten in total. First is *Malchut*, then second, *Yesod*, the bridge to all the other wells."

He leaned forward. "Excellent. With *Yesod* activated, a Mystic has the potential to access up to the seventh *sefira*. Yet, with the bond open, but not formed, this is only a taste of what a Mystic can do, making it safe to manage and understand."

Alma had gone over much of this with Leah and the others already. Leah opened her mouth to tell him as much before he interjected her thoughts.

"To quantify your progress, you will take part in three trials. These exams will score you on your performance and determine your placement for the scouting Knights and Bishops. That, or expelled from the academy if you don't reach the minimum threshold to pass the trials. I'll explain more about it during your induction ceremony; all you need to know for now is that there are rituals and traditions for each phase, including a final one to bond you to your new master and set you off to work within the Infinity Board."

He grabbed a glass off his table, filled with dark liquid, and took a drink. Leah glanced over at Eric, who shifted in his seat. Leah wondered what it would be like to bond with someone else. It already felt so strange, knowing he was just as uncomfortable as she was. And yet, they were family, albeit estranged, but it was comforting, nonetheless.

William eyed his glass before looking at Eric. "So, you see the predicament we are in with you two. Our traditions keep us protected from the Tree of Death's chaos and corruption. Severing is painful if the bond has settled, but of the few who have severed early, I hear it is little more than what it feels like to break a bone." He smiled at Leah, like a father to a child. "Then you could proceed in your studies with the proper safety precautions and on an equal playing field with your classmates. My sources tell me you've got quite a talent with *Malchut*. I can only imagine how you might fare with the others."

Leah couldn't believe what he was saying. *Sever the bond? But why? Why would it matter so much if she and Eric had bonded already?*

Nykima stepped forward. "Dean Wright, I—"

The dean waved his hand. "The administration and I already discussed this to great length and determined it was the best mode of action. We must uphold tradition."

Nykima shook her head. "Yes, but I checked the bond

myself. It's already progressed beyond the point it should have. Severing it wouldn't be the same as severing a new bond. She could be out of commission for weeks."

"So, what do you suggest, White Knight?"

"She doesn't belong here. The disadvantage from the other students facing off against her is too high."

Eric glared at Nykima. "And what else should she do if she can't stay at the academy? She has a lot to learn before you throw her out into the wild."

Nykima spoke through gritted teeth. "That is not my concern. My concern is with upholding the traditions of this academy and keeping everyone—"

Dean Wright stood, his back straight, and stared past Nykima. Silence filled the room, and Leah looked back to the doorway where Black Queen Nielsen stood. Nykima turned on her heel. Eric clamored out of his chair, and Leah followed suit.

Helen smiled and nodded at Leah. "At ease." A beige blazer hugged her frame, and a light blue skirt matched her crystalline eyes. She had groomed back her short blond hair, accentuating her sharp cheekbones and nose. She stepped into the room, and one of her guards closed the door behind her.

"My apologies for being late. I had other matters to tend to. William, this academy's library has grown since the last time I was here. Your collection on poltergeists matches no other. Fascinating beings."

"Thank you, Black Queen Nielsen. My last trip to Cairo was a great breakthrough."

"We've known each other for long enough, William. You can call me Helen. And Cairo had minimal casualties, I hope?"

He nodded. "They didn't even notice we were there."

"Fantastic. I'd appreciate a debriefing later today. I also

recently procured another book you'll find most interesting."

William raised an eyebrow. "I would love to see what you have."

Helen smiled and stood behind Leah, resting her hands on the girl's shoulders. "How are you holding up?"

"I'm better. Thank you."

"Wonderful. I was worried about this bonding of yours." She turned to Eric. "And you, Black Knight? How have you been healing?"

"Fine. Nothing a warm bed and a glass of whiskey won't fix."

Helen stared at William. "Very well. So, where were you?"

"We were discussing the bond."

The queen furrowed her brow. "Is that so? And what of it?"

"Three of us detected the bond. It is stronger than we predicted. The administration was looking to sever it but—"

"Sever?" Helen said, cutting off Nykima. She turned to William and tutted her tongue. "Why were you discussing severing the bond?"

William sighed. "We feel like this bond puts other students at a disadvantage against Miss Ackerman. You had called us about the bond so we would have time to deliberate and determine the next steps."

"I did no such thing. I informed you of the bond and instructed you to make arrangements for these two with the rest. The bond our late Black Bishop Alma performed was old magic, and not something I want us to dabble with until we have a better understanding of what she did."

Nykima frowned and cocked her head. "But why should

Pawn Ackerman take part in the trials? She'd have an upper hand."

Helen pursed her lips. "I have already taken your concern into consideration. Perhaps if you would let me speak to the dean of this academy, instead of questioning my authority, we would have already come to an agreement."

Nykima dropped her gaze and shifted on her feet. "Yes, my Queen. Apologies."

A wave of giddiness struck Leah, and she fought back a smile. Then she frowned, trying to figure out why this made her so happy, until she looked over at Eric who was also stifling a smile behind a smug look. He was enjoying this as well.

Helen nodded, and her face softened. "Your concerns are fair, and I do not take them lightly. I do not want them severed, but you should be happy to know that we have been able to discern from the ritual Alma performed that physical distance should slow the bond from settling."

Dean Wright rested his hands on the back of his chair. "Then, given the nature of the *Yesod* bond, it is imperative that we keep these two separated."

Anger crashed into Leah, and before she could stop herself, she blurted out, "Why?"

"The bond between you two grows stronger even now," Black Queen Nielsen said. "In the first few months, physical proximity plays a role in how quickly the bond settles. This ritual Alma performed seems to do the same, but faster. Traditions of the Infinity Board are the foundation of our society, and our best mode of action now that you've already bonded is to separate you two as much as possible until after the trials."

Dean Wright clapped his hands together. "That is that, then. Pawn Ackerman will undergo the trials with the others, kept under close watch to maintain fairness among the others. And Black Knight Eric, you will take part with the Knights and Bishops, first on missions to keep you off premises until the trials begin, then you'll observe and compete with the rest of them. Understood?"

"Yes, sir," Eric replied.

Helen added, "Given the advantage, we may need to consider the strength of her opponents. I strongly recommend a re-evaluation after each trial to avoid an unfair advantage or disadvantage. By the time the trials end, we'll have a better understanding of the way our former Bishop produced this bond. If Black Pawn Ackerman does not score high in at least two of the trials, I suggest we sever their bond and consider all options."

"Yes, my Queen." Dean Wright nodded with a grin.

Eric leaped to his feet. "Severing the bond? I don't think I can. I can't—"

Helen raised her hand. "Knight Mizrahi, I understand your concern, especially after what transpired with your last Pawn." She paused, waiting for him to slow his breathing and calm himself before she continued. "We will keep you separate, ensuring the bond does not strengthen any further. If Black Pawn Ackerman is worthy, then the bond shall remain intact."

Dean Wright cleared his throat and settled back into his chair. "I agree Black Queen N—Helen. It is only fair that this Black Pawn partakes in the trials like everyone else and proves she deserves the title of White Pawn and the bond."

Leah swallowed and sat back down, her lips dry and her palms clammy. Tossed into the fire, forced to prove herself again. And if she wasn't good enough, she'd wind up hurting her uncle too. "What happens if I fail?"

"The trials altogether?" William asked, his eyebrow raised. "You would be bondless, and we will remove you from the academy and transfer you to a different sect of the Infinity Board."

What the hell does that mean? Leah could feel the fear coming off Eric in droves. The threat of the bond being severed hit a nerve in him, something Leah didn't understand quite yet. She knew Eric had had a Pawn before her, one he didn't like to talk about. *Jade.* Could he handle going through the same thing twice?

Leah looked at the ground and shook her head. "Why does this come off more like a punishment for saving Eric—I mean Black Knight Mizrahi's life? Alma did it to save him."

A small vein popped out on Dean Wright's neck, yet his face remained calm and collected. "Tradition maintains order. An order that the late Black Bishop Sachs knew about and still broke. Her cause was noble, but we will maintain tradition as much as possible with this decision to keep your bond. Be thankful. If I could, I would sever you right now and solve everything."

Black Queen Nielsen turned toward Dean Wright and clasped her hands. "But you won't." Her head tilted, and her voice became more constrained. "While you may have final say here, I suggest you remember where your funding and your bylaws come from."

Dean Wright winced and clenched his jaw. "Indeed, Helen. Maimonides Academy welcomes these two to take part in the trials then. We will accommodate to ensure fairness in competition between Black Pawn Ackerman and the other students."

Black Queen Nielsen nodded. "Thank you, Dean. I look forward to the outcome of the trials. I hope to see some strong White Pawns coming from this term." She turned, her eyes falling on Leah. She patted her shoulder and mouthed the words, *good luck,* before passing her and leaving the room.

The dean checked his watch. "Well, best to get Black Pawn Ackerman to the rest of the Pawns. I'd like to have a word with Black Knight Mizrahi."

"Yes, Dean." Nykima opened the door to his office and waited for Leah to follow.

Leah glanced at Eric, towering next to her, as she got up from her chair. A feeling of grief washed over her, and she realized this may be the last time she would see him for a while. The only bridge between her old life and this one, maybe even the only member of the Infinity Board with some authority she could trust.

He smirked and nudged at her shoulder. "You'll do just fine. Keep your head in the game. Oh, and uh, stay out of trouble."

Leah smirked, turned to the dean, and stood at attention. "Thank you, Dean Wright."

CHAPTER 4

LOST FACES

Muffled voices sounded from inside the dean's office the moment Nykima closed the door. Leah followed Nykima down the hallway, still processing what had happened. Her first day here, and they'd already sent her to the dean's office. More than that, they'd threatened to strip away her bond, and she'd lost any chance to learn about her mother's past life as a Mystic from Eric. At least for now.

Nykima's voice pulled her out of her thoughts as they reached the first floor. "From here on out, all the other Mystics will judge you. The ones who came to make a bond will build a case for you to have yours severed. Best to steer clear of conversations unless in a group."

Leah frowned. "Thanks, White Knight Nykima. But why offer me that advice?"

"You have something to lose that the others don't. Consider it my one and only act of kindness."

At that, Nykima turned. Leah followed, walking past to a large door just below the start of the stained-glass window, and stepped out.

Leah had thought the training course at the outpost

was large, but the academy blew that out of the water. Multiple courts the size of football fields lined her vision. One looked like it was straight out of an army movie, lined with wooden towers, climbing ropes, and mud pits. Next to that, a regular grassy field was surrounded by a track. To her right was a field of sand. The only thing that seemed out of place there was a moveable rack of weapons, filled with axes to spears.

A small crowd stood on the grassy field, and Leah immediately recognized them as her fellow outpost peers. Nykima led Leah across the field and stood in front of the man with the black hair and square jaw that had stepped on the bus. "Ian, this is Pawn Ackerman, the last one from Black Hills."

He stood at attention before motioning to the group. "Get in line, Pawn." He turned and started across the field.

Leah joined Sarah and Isaac, and Sarah whispered loud enough for Isaac to hear. "So, what'd you do now?"

Leah shrugged, while Isaac reached behind Leah to smack Sarah.

Paige edged closer to Sarah, staring forward, but her eyes shifted toward them, clearly trying to eavesdrop. Remembering the advice Nykima had just given her about being careful with what she said with certain people around, Leah shook her head and whispered, "We'll talk later."

Ian gestured to the second building, separated by a pathway from the main. "This building houses most of the White Pawns, Knights, and Bishops who come for the trials or are the subordinates to anyone in administration or high-ranking security. It is off limits to Black Pawns, and that is all you need to know."

He headed toward the main building without another

word, entering through a side entrance into a massive corridor.

He gestured to the wooden doors at the end of the hall. "In there, you'll find the library. Dean Wright takes great pride in the collection he has constructed over the decades, most of which will be off-limits to Pawns. However, there are a great number of other texts to aid you in your studies."

They continued down the hall, and Leah spotted the main foyer up ahead.

"To your left is your classroom, and to the right is the infirmary."

A woman wearing a long black coat stepped out of the infirmary. She'd styled her gray-streaked dark hair in a short bob that framed her face, and wrinkles surrounded her dark eyes. Beside her was the man with the black mohawk that Leah had seen when she exited the bus.

Ian placed his hands behind his back. "Ah, students, this is Dr. Toppen, our local medical practitioner. We're lucky to have hired her on as a consultant. Right, Black Bishop?"

The man with the mohawk eyed Ian and nodded.

Dr. Toppen scanned the students before smiling at the Black Bishop. "Thank you for your help today, Sid. I have some work to do at the hospital. I'll come back tomorrow to check on Miss Andra."

"What about her eyes? Can we salvage them?" Sid asked.

"No," Dr. Toppen said, her voice low. "Her vision is gone. All we can do now is make her comfortable. You know how to contact me in the interim if anything changes."

Sid started toward the infirmary.

Dr. Toppen stared at Ian. "Pleasure to meet all the new students. If you'll excuse me, I have some supplies to get." She walked past him and left without another word.

Ian gestured behind them, toward the classroom. "Go on. More to see."

Photos lined the walls, featuring groups of youthful faces clustered on the front steps outside the academy. Images trailed back from color, to black and white, to sepia, covering the wall from top to bottom.

"We keep a record of all who have come before. Unfortunately, we'll need an addendum to this year to include all of you." He stepped off to the side, toward the foyer and out of the way of the photos. "This academy was the first, after the war that separated us from the International Mystic Society. We set the precedent for all other established academies, pushing our students to their limits, ensuring we prepare future generations to maintain the balance."

Harry scratched the back of his head. "Uh, Black Knight Kim, I have a question."

Ian looked at his watch. "Wasn't looking for questions. But fine, go ahead."

Harry's cheeks turned red. "Well, this academy is just so big. If the Infinity Board is such a secret society, then how does it stay secret with places like this?"

Ian nodded. "The Infinity Board has many fail-safes in place to protect us. We select private, well secluded land to keep out any prying eyes. That includes several miles of surrounding woods. Most wanderers turn around well before they get to the gates. Sometimes someone will come too close, but nothing a small *Malchut* push on their memories won't remedy."

Serena frowned and chimed in. "But what about the skies? I mean, satellites, planes, and drones."

Ian took a deep breath. "We take care of that too. The Infinity Board is everywhere, in everything. That includes the different governments and private sectors to ensure no plane travels above and all satellite images get doctored.

We're always a step ahead." Before any other students could speak up, Ian looked at his watch and said, "Let's carry on. More to see."

Leah paused, catching something strange in one picture on the wall. She took a moment to look closer and noticed a burned-out face. When she stepped back, she noticed other images had it too.

Isaac nudged her. "What is it?"

Leah pointed to the burned-out faces. "Do you see that? Someone burned out their faces, like they wanted them erased—"

Ian cleared his throat behind her. "You know, being a tour guide is not a profession I care to keep for much longer. Especially when I expect people to follow, and they choose not to listen."

Leah turned around, noting that everyone had stopped to stare at her and Isaac, including Black Knight Kim who stood only inches away from her.

Leah fumbled for her words as his eyes bored into her skull. "Sorry, Black Knight Kim. I was just wondering why some images had burned-out faces."

Ian's eyes shifted toward the photos on the wall. He scanned them for a moment before saying, "Some people can't handle the pressure of the academy and trials." He pointed to the most recent image with a burned-out face. "No doubt you'll hear about this one. Theodore Roe. He couldn't take it anymore, so he ran away in the middle of the night about two weeks ago. We have no use for cowards here, and no need to remember them." He stepped between Leah and the photo, facing all the others. "Let this be a lesson that the trials are difficult. We will push you to your limits, but you are already members of the Infinity Board. We don't reward weakness, so if you can't take it, then best to follow in Mr. Roe's footsteps."

CHAPTER 5
SETTLING IN

Ian stepped into the foyer, and everyone followed in silence. He pointed to the opposite wall, toward doors with square windows that showed a massive room with small tables scattered about. "Those doors lead to the cafeteria. The bell for lunch will go off in a half hour. Until then, I'll leave you all in your dorms."

Their bags were all lined up against the wall at the main entrance. Gabe brushed against Leah's shoulder as they reached for their bags. "This is definitely different from the outpost."

She hefted her bag over her shoulder and stood up, grabbing an eyeful of his ashy blond hair and freckles. They both started toward the stairs, peering out the stained-glass window. "Yeah, it's missing that whole run-down cabin in the woods vibe."

He chuckled. "I bet the kitchen is the size of the whole outpost put together. I can't wait to see it."

Sarah turned on the stairs in front of them. "Hold on. You're excited about the kitchens when they showed us the most uppity boarding school I've ever seen?"

Gabe shrugged. "I like to cook."

"Of course you do," Sarah said.

Leah stared at Ian's back. Something settled in her gut. A weight she couldn't let go of. "It's all nice, but don't you feel like we're not welcome here?"

"Oh yeah. Have you seen the looks he's been giving us?" Gabe whispered, nodding at Ian. "It's like they all know what happened at the outpost and they blame us."

An ache twinged in Leah's chest at the mention of Alma, even indirectly. She tried to breathe, but the pain crept in, something she'd been trying to push down. It was her fault she'd died, her fault her father had killed Alma, her fault her father had killed her mother.

A warm hand gripped her shoulder, pulling her out of the dark. Gabe's eyes peered into hers. "I'm sorry. Too soon? I didn't mean . . ."

Leah found her breath and shoved that pain back down, back into the abyss where it could stay forever. "It's fine." She lifted her head and continued up the stairs. "We just need to show them what we can do. For Alma. No doubt we annoyed them because Helen—I mean Black Queen Nielsen —went over the dean's head and sent us here."

They stopped at the platform on the second floor, and Ian turned and faced them. "Girls, wait here. Boys, with me."

"Guess this is goodbye, for now," Isaac said. Before anyone could get another word in, Gabe pushed Isaac along, and they disappeared behind two heavy wooden doors.

Leah eyed the door as it closed. "I hope he'll be okay."

"He'll be fine," Sarah said. "The other guys will keep an eye on him. Gabe will see to that."

Ian emerged from the boys' dorm a few minutes later and led the girls to the third, and highest, floor. They stepped through another set of heavy wooden doors.

Inside, couches of all colors and styles clustered around the center of a massive room. Several girls dressed in all black occupied the sofas, staring at the new arrivals. Along the walls were doors. A few were open, revealing smaller rooms with bunk beds.

Ian brought them over to a bulletin board with a poster of an overhead view of the girls' dormitory. Beside it were notes and notices, including one note that made Leah chuckle. *Boys in common space? Okay. Boys in your room? No way.*

"Check for your names; you've all been assigned rooms already. We couldn't keep you all together, and assignments are final. Settle in and wait for the lunch bell." Ian turned and walked out the doors, closing them behind him.

Leah traced the map until she spotted her name.

Room 4
　Leah Ackerman
　Paige Jones
　Emma Mitchell
　Sarah Turner

Leah glanced over at Sarah and shrugged. "At least we're together."

"Ugh!" Paige shouted, her finger tapping on the board. "Can we swap one of you with Serena?" She glared at Leah, dropping her bag and crossing her arms.

Sarah cleared her throat. "Can we swap you out? I don't think I can handle your snoring for another night."

Emma raced to Paige's side and narrowed her eyes at Sarah. "Shut up and swap already."

Serena whimpered at the board and looked down at the ground. "He said all assignments are final."

Paige pushed past Emma and wrapped her arm around Serena. "At least I don't smell like some wild animal. Have you ever heard of showering?"

Leah glanced at the couches, noting all the eyes on them, excited to watch the cat fight between Paige and Sarah. She wondered how long it would take for Paige to find something to complain about.

Sarah balled her hands into fists. "Just shut up, Paige."

"Oh, I see how it is. I insult you, and you're ready to start a fight with me?" Paige shook her head and leaned into Serena, whispering. "Didn't know she was such a drama queen."

Leah scoffed. "You know what? Maybe if you stopped being a complete selfish bitch all the time, you would have actual friends instead of people groveling at your feet for your approval."

Paige turned and glared at Leah; her eyes locked on her like a viper. "What did you call me?"

A voice sounded behind Leah. "I think she called you a bitch."

A girl with dark wavy hair and a fistful of silver necklaces atop her black uniform stood behind Leah. The girl eyed Paige. "Although I don't even know you, and I'd say you're more of a cunt."

Paige sneered, and her two lackeys mimicked her. "And who the hell are you?"

The girl locked eyes with Paige, tilted her head, smiled, and shot out a hand with scratched black nail polish and black wristbands. "Joanna Morales, pleasure to meet you." She dropped her hand before Paige could move to take it. "So, you're the Squares from Black Hills Outpost?"

Leah cocked her head. "Black Pawns, and yeah."

Joanna rolled her eyes. "Rumor has it you all let your Bishop die so you could skip the final exam. That doesn't make you Black Pawns, not to the rest of the people here. Even if you got a Queen involved."

That weight inside Leah dredged its way out from the abyss again, carrying with it the fear and memories she tried to lock away. Fear that she couldn't push back. Fear that brought her back to that night. The sounds of popping and breaking as her father's body transformed and turned into a monster.

The light left her eyes. She was sinking, falling into the abyss, when a shout from her side brought her back.

"You bitch!" Sarah said. "You don't know what we've been—"

Leah pulled Sarah's arm and stepped up to face Joanna. She didn't push that fear back down, didn't hide the weight inside her. She turned it on Joanna, a hunger and a rage that rose to the tip of her tongue. "You missed the part where a demon chased me from Chicago, tearing apart Knights like they were nothing and cutting us off from the rest of the world when it showed up at the outpost. If it weren't for Alma, none of us would be here." Leah stepped in closer, that hunger fueling her words as she took in a long cool breath. "So, who's the actual cunt now, talking about things they know nothing about?"

A chill grew from Leah's arm, and she swore the room grew colder. Joanna stared, expressionless, into Leah's eyes for what seemed like an eternity. No one else moved. The only thing on Leah's mind was the loud thrumming of her vein pulsing in her temple.

Joanna smiled. "I like you." Then she turned on her heels and walked over to one couch in the center of the common area, plopping down and crossing her legs. "Welcome to Maimonides."

CHAPTER 6

LUNCH BREAK

Leah and Sarah left the other three to mourn the "loss of their sister" and walked along the doors until they found room four.

Sarah sighed. "Of all the luck, we get grouped together with those two. I was hoping we'd get more space from them."

They opened the door to a room smaller than the one at the outpost, with two bunk beds and two wooden chests at the end of each bed. The walls were a stark white, and gray carpet covered the floor. A large window overlooking the front lawns was the only feature giving the room any character.

Sarah eyed the top bunk, so Leah tossed her bag on the bottom bunk, then placed her hands on her hips. "Well, it's no five-star hotel, but I suppose it's better than being trapped in a room like this with that Joanna girl. At least Paige gets bored if we ignore her. I'm pretty sure this new girl would cut you in your sleep."

Sarah chuckled. "True." She cracked open a chest and dropped her bag inside, next to a pile of neatly folded black uniforms. She lifted a shirt and inspected the slightly stretchy fabric, which looked to Leah like embroidered athletic wear. "We know what we are dealing with when it comes to Paige. I was hoping they'd be a little less dramatic after what happened. But no, they're still bitches. Yet, that ice queen trick on Joanna might make both her and Paige think twice, if you keep it up."

"Ice queen? What are you talking about?"

Sarah crossed the room and leaned up against the bedpost. "Come on, whatever that cold thing you did was. It was like you went all creepy dark mode."

Leah sat down on the bed and frowned. Had she used an energy back then? It hadn't felt like *Malchut*, but anger had filled her enough that it could have been. She'd thought it was just the tension in the room, but the room did seem colder. Leah shook her head. "I don't even know what I did, if I even did—"

Paige barged into the room, her hand to her mouth and tears forming in her eyes as she threw her bag at the bottom of the other bunk bed. Emma raced in after her, claiming the top bunk, her face paling.

Sarah rolled her eyes. "Oh geez, get over it. She's just in a different room."

Paige glared at her. "It's not that, you cow." She peered out the window.

Leah eyed Sarah, clenching her fist, ready to maul Paige. Leah cleared her throat. "Is it what Joanna said?"

Paige straightened her back, wiping away her tears. "I'm not . . . I don't want to be this way. I don't want to be the bitch everyone thinks I am."

Leah raised an eyebrow. "Well, you kind of are."

"It's all I know," Paige said, looking up at the ceiling.

Sarah pushed herself off the bed post and glared at Paige. "Well, I'm not about to have a pity party because someone called you names." She turned to Leah. "Come on, let's go wait for lunch somewhere else."

Leah's stomach grumbled at the thought of food. She looked at Paige, words failing to form, before joining Sarah as they left the room.

They had just made it to the couches when a loud bell rang through the hall.

Sarah winced and rubbed her ears. "This place really takes the school thing to heart."

The girls on the couches got up and headed for the doors, and Leah and Sarah followed. They joined a line from the boys' dorm that snaked through the cafeteria doors. Spices and scents that made Leah's stomach growl filled the air. Fresh basil topped plates of lasagna and breadsticks topped with buttery garlic sat in a basket next to a massive salad bar. After weeks of surviving off mostly frozen food that Gabe had done his best to season, and the last few days living off questionable vending machine food and fast food, Leah had to do everything in her power to not claw her way to the front of the line.

She counted at least forty students in line with her, all in the same black uniforms Helen had given them back at the outpost. Others joined the line too, not in uniform but wearing clothes that were black or white. Based on what she knew so far, she figured these were Knights, Bishops, and White Pawns who either worked at the academy or were here to observe and take part in the *Yesod* bonding.

Sarah untucked her oversized shirt, attempting to match some of the other girls in line. "Maybe they'll give us some better fitting clothes. The sweaters at the outpost were much more comfortable."

Leah noticed how well the other uniforms fit the other students in line, while she and her fellow Pawns from Black

Hills stuck out like a bunch of deflated black balloons. "Hopefully they will."

Sarah leaned in close to Leah and prodded her side. "So, you gonna tell me what happened with you and Eric?"

As they grabbed food, Leah filled Sarah in on what had happened in the Dean's office. They found an empty table in the cafeteria's corner, and Sarah set her tray down across from Leah. "That's bullshit. You had to bond with Eric. He was going to die otherwise! Why are they punishing you for saving him?"

Leah shrugged and stabbed her food with her fork. She started with her best impression of Dean Wright, terrible British accent and all, "'It goes against tradition' but after Helen convinced him, I just have to not get cut and keep my distance from Eric until after the trials if I want to keep the bond."

"Well, do you?" Sarah asked before digging into her food and filling her mouth full of lasagna.

Leah shoveled the fork into her mouth. Her taste buds went into overdrive, tasting the cheese mixing with the tomato sauce with a hint of sweetness from the ricotta between the noodle layers, just like her mom used to make. She nodded, her mouth still full. "I do, I think. He's my uncle. Who else can we trust?"

Sarah raised an eyebrow. "You said Helen was there, right? She's a queen. Why didn't she just tell them you can skip the trials? I mean, you have your bond. What's the point?"

"Technically, you need to pass the trials before getting bonded. Helen convinced the dean not to sever the bond. Apparently, that is all she can do. She has no authority over students at the academy, and per tradition, I have to go through the trials."

Sarah tore off the end of her breadstick and dipped it in the sauce on her plate, soaking it up. "Trials and grades. Exactly what I needed." She rolled her eyes. "You'd think, being a Black Queen and all that, she'd have more power. Guess not."

"Yeah, who knows?" Leah turned her focus to the salad, which was more like a plate of vegetables with a small amount of lettuce bedding. It had been weeks since she'd had fresh vegetables, and she bit into a carrot like it was a cheesecake, savoring every moment. "Oh, my God this is so good."

"I know, right?" Sarah paused halfway through chewing and peered out into the cafeteria. "Um, any idea why everyone keeps looking over here?"

Leah followed Sarah's gaze, catching others as they looked toward them. Not only Black Pawns, but everyone seemed to stare at them. As her eyes crossed the room, one person didn't look away: Ian, the Black Knight. He stood at the entrance to the cafeteria, arms folded, his eyes staring and not blinking.

Before she could say anything, Gabe stepped into Leah's vision and waved, his blurred smile and tray of food coming into focus. "Hey, mind if I sit with you guys?"

Sarah slid over to let Gabe in. "Sure, Leah and I were just admiring how much attention we seem to get."

Gabe let out a chuckle and dug his fork into his food. "Yeah, same. Definitely noticed the other guys gawking as we settled in. They're all on edge or something."

Leah glanced back over at the doorway and enjoyed a moment of relief when Ian wasn't standing there looking back. Unfortunately, Paige, Emma, and Serena were there instead. Leah watched them as they grabbed food, spotted Leah, and claimed a table at the opposite end of the cafeteria. Serena waved her arm over at the crowd of boys, spotting Buck and Harry, who cut through the crowd to sit with them, Buck stumbling at the last minute and launching his breadstick off his tray and into Serena's lap. Harry found a spot next to Emma in all the commotion, a wide grin on his face.

Sarah's voice cut through Leah's focus. "So, how's Isaac? I haven't seen him come down yet."

"I don't know. They assigned him to another room," Gabe said.

Leah frowned. "But there were four of you."

"Ian wasn't with us long, but he sent Isaac to a room with three guys and told the rest of us we're roommates."

Sarah left her fork standing on the last piece of food on her plate. "But why didn't Isaac just room with you guys?"

Gabe shrugged. "The assignments were final. I don't know how they would've fit another bed in our room, anyway. We're pretty sure they converted a storage closet into a bedroom."

Almost as if he'd heard his name, Isaac raced into the cafeteria and slid in next to Leah, short of breath and glancing toward the entrance.

Leah moved at the last second to prevent him from colliding with her. "Whoa, what's got you spooked?"

Isaac looked at the empty table in front of him and shook his head. "I don't want to talk about it."

Sarah frowned. "What is it? Are you already getting picked on? Don't tell me you got roomed with a bunch of jerks."

"Just leave it, okay?" Isaac hunched over the table, clasping at his elbows. "I said I don't want to talk about it."

Gabe pushed his half-eaten tray over to Isaac. "Here, have the rest. I wasn't all that hungry. Not after that breakfast burrito I ate from the gas station."

Isaac nodded and picked up the fork, taking in the food in small bites.

Leah bit her lip. Sarah and Gabe had the same look on their faces, worried. Her fists clenched at the thought of one of her friends being bullied. "Just tell us who they are and what they did."

Isaac stared at the line, then back at his food. Leah followed his gaze to the three guys, laughing and shoving each other. One was scrawny, with dark and greasy hair. Another looked just like any other football-playing jock Leah had seen before, with a large, muscular build and perfectly sculpted brown hair. The last one, and the apparent ringleader of the three, was only slightly less muscular, with dull ginger hair.

Isaac cleared his throat. "Those are the ones. Remember the pictures you asked about? The burned-out faces? Well, Brandon, the ginger over there, says the most recent one is his brother. Said he went missing a couple weeks ago, and the school just burned out his face and moved on. Then we showed up, and I got assigned to his brother's spot."

Sarah tutted her tongue and glared at the guys in line. "How is that your fault? They said he ran away."

"He seems to think his brother wouldn't have run away. He thinks someone took him. At least, that's what they said before shoving me out of the room."

"But why would the school burn his face out and move on? That doesn't seem right," Leah said.

Sarah looked down at her plate. "They said he was a coward, whatever that means."

Leah shifted in her seat, remembering all the faces that were burned out. Were they all cowards? Would her mother be one of the burned-out faces?

Isaac crossed his arms. "What does that have to do with me? Why am I being punished?"

Gabe scratched the back of his head. "I'm sorry, man. I can see if Ian will let you room with us."

Isaac shook his head. "He won't. I tried. I either sleep in that bed, in that room, or I sleep on the floor in the hall. No exceptions."

Sarah cracked her knuckles. "Maybe we send a message to your new roommates. Leah, do you think you can go ice queen on them?"

"Uh, ice queen?" Gabe asked.

Sarah grinned. "Well, some girl picked a fight, and Leah somehow made the room an icebox. The cold freaked the girl out enough to back down. Freaked me out too."

Gabe smirked and met Leah's eyes. "Sounds like if the central air ever gives out, I know who to go to."

Leah rolled her eyes. "Ha ha, hilarious. Maybe you should run away and pursue a life of stand-up comedy."

She looked at the three boys, then scanned the cafeteria again. She met Ian's gaze and realized he was staring at her again. Goosebumps rose on the back of her neck. He was clearly keeping tabs on her, and the last thing she wanted was a reason for them to kick her out.

Isaac grabbed her arm. "Leah? You there?"

Leah shook her head, pulling herself out of her trance. "Yeah. Sarah loves to play up what happened. It was nothing. Either way, I don't think it's a good idea. Do they really deserve it? We'd be stooping to their level."

Sarah crossed her arms. "And they don't deserve it? They're bullies."

Isaac shook his head. "You shouldn't be picking fights on our first day. Just ignore it."

Sarah tilted her head, her eyes locked on the boys in line as she stood. "No. Why let them get away with it?"

"Because his brother's missing? Leah said.

Gabe leaned over and wrapped his arm around Sarah's shoulder. "We all know you could take all three in a fight, but I'm with these two. Don't start anything."

Sarah pushed herself out of her chair and looked down at Gabe. "Who said anything about fighting?" She turned and jerked her head.

A shout came from across the cafeteria, and Leah spotted Brandon midair, his leg flailing as if it has slipped out from under him.

He landed with a thud, his tray of food spraying across the floor.

Sarah sat back down, hiding her face as she laughed.

Brandon brushed chunks of food from his uniform and scanned the room with murderous eyes.

"That was really immature, Sarah," Leah said.

Sarah's face changed as she looked at her friends. None of them shared her smile, and her face paled. "That was really stupid, wasn't it?"

Isaac rested his head in his hands. "Just don't do anything else. Please?"

Sarah looked down and shook her head. "I'm sorry."

An awkward silence filled the air, then Gabe said, "How did you do that? You barely even moved."

"Practice," Sarah said. "I still can't get a candle to blow out without knocking it over, but stuff like that, piece of cake."

A tray of half-eaten food dropped on the table, and everyone jumped as Joanna squeezed in between Sarah and Gabe.

Sarah glared up at her. "Um, what the hell are you doing?"

Joanna ignored her at first, settling in and stabbing some fruit with her fork and popping it into her mouth. A smug look stretched on her face as she eyed Sarah. "Saw what you did. Pretty subtle, other than standing. Doubt anyone else noticed, but I've got the eyes to spot something like that."

Gabe leaned back and frowned. "And you are?"

"Joanna Morales, from the outpost just outside Blue Ridge." She smiled and batted her eyes at him.

Leah looked around the cafeteria. Joanna was right. No one else had noticed Sarah's little stunt. Especially Brandon, who was picking chunks of cheesecake from his clothes. They'd been lucky, at least for now.

Sarah grabbed her tray and stood again. "And what? You want to be our friend now? Come on guys, let's find somewhere else to sit."

Joanna rolled her eyes. "Look, I won't call you Squares anymore. You two proved you're not already, okay? I just figured you'd want to hear the inside scoop before you get your ass handed to you."

Leah pondered for a moment and looked at Sarah before saying, "Fine, just don't tell anyone what Sarah did."

Sarah gave Leah a half smile and sat back down, crossing her arms and glaring at Joanna.

Joanna cut into her food and took a bite, savoring the moment before continuing. "It's not your fault, but you guys coming in unannounced, two weeks after Theo disappeared—Theo is Brandon's—"

"We know," Isaac cut in.

"Oh, so you're the roommate. Good luck with that. That room was full of douchebags even before Theo disappeared. Anyway, it put everyone on edge. Brandon swears someone took him, but the faculty keeps telling us otherwise. They don't even hide the fact that they aren't looking for him, they just keep pushing us toward the trials, like cattle, making sure we're primed and ready for the highest bidders."

Gabe leaned forward to catch Joanna's attention. "So, if he didn't run, then how'd he disappear?"

"They'll have you believe that all the runaways can't take the heat. There are rumors about what happens to people who get cut from the trials."

"Cut?" Asked Gabe.

Joanna crossed her arms and stood up straight. "Yeah, they cut the weak links after every trial. I heard someone say they get their memories wiped and they end up in some asylum. Others say the Infinity Board breaks all your connection to the Tree. I even heard someone say they executed you out back in the woods, but I don't know about that one."

"Oh, well, none of those sound good," Isaac whispered.

Gabe crossed his arms to mimic Joanna and frowned. "Those all sound like rumors meant to scare you, Isaac."

Joanna shrugged. "Might be. But the administration keeps tabs on all of us. I've seen it, and if they're worried that runaways could start a cult or something, then they'll intervene. Which makes it even weirder that Theo ran away and they won't give us answers." Joanna glanced back over her shoulder at Brandon, who'd sat down at one of the center tables among several others.

Leah cleared her throat. "What was odd about it?"

"He was good with the tree," Joanna said. "Really good. After the ceremony on his first day, he could perform *Netzach*. Saw him take a sledgehammer to the chest and didn't even flinch. Not even a bruise. The Knights and Bishops had their eyes on him. Then, out of nowhere, he's shouting about how he can't take it. That night, poof."

"If he was so good, then why'd he run?" Sarah asked.

A loud ding sounded over an overhead speaker, jolting

them out of their conversation before a voice crackled to life. "Attention, Black Pawns to Field One. I repeat, Black Pawns to Field One. Five minutes."

Joanna shoveled in another bit of food before pushing herself up from the table. "Your guess is as good as mine. Come on, don't want to be late."

CHAPTER 7
OATH CEREMONY

They followed Joanna as Black Pawns jogged past them, running in unison like small military groups. Leah looked around, spotting everyone but them and the others from Black Hills rushing to the field like they were in boot camp.

Joanna, however, walked slowly, ignoring the glares from the others as they passed by. She couldn't care less, and Leah wasn't sure if that was a good thing or not. Either way, Leah warmed up to her indifference.

At the field, Joanna turned to them. "You'll need to form two lines of five and four with your outpost." She broke off with them and joined a line of straight-backed Pawns who weren't shy about staring.

The other Pawns already formed perfect lines of six, leaving the Black Hills Outpost to fend for themselves.

Buck broke away from Paige and the others, bumping shoulders with Gabe. "Any clue what this is about?"

Leah shook her head. "No, but we need to get in line, just like them."

Buck waved for the others to come over. Paige waited until the last minute, after everyone else left her, and rolled her eyes before joining Leah and Sarah. They formed two lines, Paige and her crew of five in front with Leah, Sarah, Isaac, and Gabe in back.

The doors of the academy opened, and Nykima, William, Helen, and three more people Leah had never seen before stepped out and headed to the field. They formed a line facing the Pawns.

"Attention!" Nykima shouted.

Each of the Pawns straightened and placed their hands behind their backs.

Other Knights, Bishops, and White Pawns filed out from the academy and stood behind Queen Helen and William.

Once everyone stood still and in an attentive stance, William nodded. "At ease!"

The Black Pawns widened their stances in unison, keeping their hands behind their back.

William stepped forward and paced the front row, eyeing each Pawn as he walked by. "To our recent additions, the Black Pawns from the Black Hills Outpost, I want to welcome you to the Maimonides Academy. I am your dean and White Knight, William Wright. Through unforeseen and rather unfortunate circumstances, we have allowed you to join us here, outside of standard procedure. To our current students, show them the ropes and bring them up to speed. The success of one . . ."

". . . is the success of all," the other Pawns finished in unison.

William nodded. "And the success of all is the success of the Infinity Board."

His gaze stopped on Leah. His smile was infectious. This was not the same man she had seen in the office, stern and unforgiving. This man was warm and kind. Leah felt like she would take instruction from this man in a heartbeat, ready to fight if he said so.

He outstretched an arm behind him. "I'd like to introduce our new students to the administration. They are the heads of the academy body in charge of your training and trials. First, we have White Bishop Constance Berkenshire."

The oldest of the three stepped forward with a small but tight-lipped smile. Her dark black hair had several large white streaks held together in a perfect braided bun. She looked decades older than Helen, which wasn't helped by the high-collared plain white woolen dress.

"She's been here almost forty years now, serving as the voice of wisdom and counsel for many generations of students," William said.

Constance stepped back into line, and the man beside her stepped forward. He appeared as old as William, with a gray-peppered beard, a bespoke three-piece black suit, and pristine black cane with a golden crow head topper.

"Black Rook Reginald Platt, our advisor and direct line to the Infinity Board's council. He oversees the missions and directives that come to this academy from the Infinity Board."

Reginald took a bow and stepped back into line. A young woman with dark brown skin, not much older than Nykima, wearing a bold red pantsuit with a large white belt around her waist, stepped forward. Of the three, she was the only one who took the liberty to wear as little white or black as possible.

"White Bishop Grace Johnson, our third and newest member of the administration. As a reminder to all of you, you would do well to hear and follow her advice. She has moved up the ladder of the Infinity Board to the position she has today."

Grace smiled widely as she looked at the faces from the Black Hills Outpost before stepping back in line in one swift motion.

William stepped beside Helen and cleared his throat. "Of course, we also have a special guest with us today: Black Queen Helen Nielsen. She has asked that I first introduce the administration to the new students, as to not take away from tradition in this ceremony. That alone should tell you about her character, putting others before herself. I advise all students to honor her presence and take note so you might even learn an iota of what it takes to be a leader in the Infinity Board."

Helen took a step forward, like the others, and gave a slight smile, her eyes scanning each of the Pawns before landing on Leah. Her smile broadened, and she stepped back into place.

William clasped his hands together. "Now for the Opening Ceremony. Our new Pawns, please come to the front."

Leah and the others stepped forward, while every other line moved back to make room for them. Once settled, William went into a speech that sounded like something he'd given hundreds of times before.

"This ceremony is the first step in preparing you to bond and promoting you from Black to White Pawns. As you know, we all share a direct connection to the Tree of Life, and the potential to harness the energy of the ten wells, or ten *sefirot*, as they are properly called. *Yesod*, the Bonded, is the bridge between *Malchut*, the Warrior and first *sefira*, and the next five *sefirot* on the tree of life. They are:

Hod, the Pacifist
    Netzach, the Invulnerable
    Tiferet, the Seer
    Gevurah, the Elemental

"Each provides abilities that propel you forward on your path as a Mystic, but only if you work hard and learn how to activate, control, and master them. With *Yesod*, we bond to our teachers, and to the lineage of the Infinity Board, so we may grow and learn together. Your trials and aptitudes to the tree will unfurl your future, either as a Knight, Bishop, or as something else. Perhaps some of you may even make it to Rook, and if we are lucky, a new Queen may be amongst you."

He held out a hand to his side. Ian stepped out from the crowd and raced up to William's side, dropping a small scroll into his hand.

The White Knight nodded, and Ian remained at his side, at attention. William said, "When I call your name, please step forward. Buck Baccus."

Buck approached William, who guided him in front of Constance, Grace, and Reginald. Constance and Grace rested their hands on his shoulders while Reginald raised his hands, muttering something under his breath.

A warm breeze swirled around Leah, carrying with it a tingling sensation and the scent of fireworks. She kept still but looked around, curious if anyone else could feel it too.

Reginald lowered his hands onto the top of Buck's head, and Buck's back straightened. A current of electricity shot through the air, an unseen charge that surged through Leah and caused her left arm to ache.

Buck wavered on his feet and stepped back, blinking several times before William guided him back to the line.

William named off the rest, and everyone from the Black Hills Outpost stepped forward. Reginald planted a hand on each of their heads, and the same wave of energy burst from the ritual.

Leah noted the names were called in alphabetical order. But he had skipped right over Ackerman, making her wonder if William would outright ignore her.

William's voice broke her train of thought when Sarah rejoined the line. "Leah Ackerman."

Leah's palms grew cold and sweaty. Were they just going to do the same thing to her? They couldn't, right? Alma had already bonded her to Eric. So, what was the point?

She stepped forward, standing in front of the three administrators.

Constance and Grace smiled as they rested their hands on Leah's shoulders. Reginald eyed her, his face unchanging.

"I understand you already have a bond." He spoke in a low, gruff voice that reminded her of her great-uncle, Moses. His eyes flashed yellow for a second, and he nodded, resting his hands on either side of her face. "Yes, there it is. Well, consider this piece of advice. Others will try to break you and prove you are unworthy of this bond, peers and prospective mentors alike. Prove them wrong. Show us why the Black Queen holds you in such high regard."

He lowered his hands and held one out, waiting for Leah to place her hand in his. A warmth spread up her arm, and his face turned into a smile.

He let go, and she turned, joining the others in the line.

William cleared his throat. "Now, in terms of the trials, there are three, each designed by a different administrator. The grades are numerical, scaling from one to a hundred. If you score under seventy points, you fail the standards of Maimonides Academy, and you will be cut. We track your performance and discipline prior to each trial on the scoreboard in the foyer, which serves to either help or hinder you in the upcoming trial. If you fall too far below zero before the next trial, you're cut. Each trial grade is independent from the others, and you start back at zero after each trial. So, even if you score well on the first two and fail the last trial, we will dismiss you from the academy. Life as a Mystic is hard, and these trials reflect that." He paused and peered out at the Pawns for a moment. "Which brings me to my last point: our new Pawns will feel the effects of the *Yesod* bond awakening inside them. It comes on different for everyone, but they will need to rest. I've postponed today's training and lessons until tomorrow morning. New students, prepare yourselves for the next few months. What you are about to endure will determine your future with the Infinity Board."

He paused as if to consider his next words. "You will be pushed to your limits, but remember; strength, knowledge, and tradition are our foundation. You are dismissed."

CHAPTER 8

SPARRING

The first week blended into a malaise of mental and physical strain. From the moment the sun rose to the moment it sank into the horizon, they were either training or sitting in a lecture hall. Leah couldn't decide which made her more tired.

Grace and Constance drilled the History of the Infinity Board into the students' skulls every day. From memorization of all past Queens and their contributions to listing off the major points in the society's history to keeping every student in the classroom late into the evening until each one could state the treaties the Infinity Board still had today. After that came an hour of meditation practice, where Leah received several thwacks to the back for not sitting straight. The information never stopped, and Leah's head was nearing the point of exploding. Perhaps it was the mental exhaustion which proved more difficult to handle.

Before, during, and after lessons, Knights and Bishops trained them on martial art forms from Krav Maga to Judo. They also practiced with weapons like medieval maces and swords. By the end of the week, they were jogging the few miles out to the dock house and learning to fire and properly handle handguns.

Sarah turned over the gun in her hand and looked at Nykima. "Why do we need this? If we can pull energy from the Tree of Life, that would make this kind of pointless."

Nykima raised an eyebrow as she lowered her handgun and shouted so everyone could hear her. "And what happens when you are all out of energy, or you step into a trap that saps your connection? Sometimes subtlety and power are best paired with common sense."

The Black Pawns who weren't a part of Black Hills all chuckled or rolled their eyes at Sarah's question. It had been that way since their first day. William's request to support the new outposters, or even offer a little help, seemed to have gone unheard. Mainly, everyone else ignored the Pawns from Black Hills Outpost and never told them where to go or what to do.

Everyone from the Black Hills Outpost was nervous when Nykima handed Buck a loaded gun, wondering how he'd screw up and end up in the infirmary. He turned out to be one of the best shots, his marksmanship only second to Karen, a bulky girl with short black hair and a piercing in her lip, who avoided them and Joanna like the plague.

As days passed, it was clear that in terms of outposters vs the others, Isaac had it the worst. Yet, he wouldn't say a word if Sarah or Leah pointed out a new bruise.

Leah hoped this would somehow bring the Black Hills Outpost group closer together. Instead, Paige flipped between making her little group of friends sit near Leah and the others one day and finding the table farthest away the next.

Saturday—their only free day—came, and Leah hung out in the library with Isaac, Sarah, and Joanna, catching up on homework.

Sarah spun in her chair, spotting Paige at another table. "Why would anyone want to be on the same team as Paige? I mean, look at her. Her face looks so punchable."

Leah stretched in her chair. "I can't blame you. Not after how she was back at the outpost. But you have to admit, she's acting different. Like she wants to be nice but doesn't know how."

"From what you two have said, you're better off without her. A snob like that, she'd ruin my vibe," Joanna chimed in.

Sarah scoffed. "What vibe? Goth with a side of anger issues?"

Joanna looked at her black-painted fingernails and grinned. "Something like that."

Something moved in the corner of Leah's vision. A pale, nearly translucent face of a young guy peeked out from a stack toward the back of the library. She turned to get a better look, but he disappeared before her eyes set on him. Leah frowned, pushing back her seat and standing.

"Where are you going?" Isaac asked, looking up from a massive tome.

"I'll be right back. I thought I saw something."

She headed right for where she saw the face, walking down the aisle and coming to a pause at a dead end.

What the hell?

She turned back, looking up and down the stacks of books, as if the pale boy might have somehow crawled through a section of shelves. Yet, books covered every inch of shelves, coated in a fine layer of dust like they'd been forgotten for decades.

"Looking for some light reading?" Joanna asked, pulling a book from the shelf and blowing the dust off.

"No." Leah said before sneezing.

"Gesundheit." Joanna flipped through the pages, stopping at a rather gruesome hand drawing of a dissection, turning the book for Leah to see. "I just figured you might want to know that you're in the restricted section. The Bishops don't like it when students sneak down here. It also may or may not be a make out spot."

"Oh, I didn't know," Leah said, her face flushing as she pushed past Joanna and headed back to her seat.

"What was that all about?" Sarah asked as Leah sat down.

Leah eyed the stacks. "Nothing. I thought I saw someone down there, but I guess I imagined it."

"Where?" Isaac asked, turning to look at the stacks.

Leah pointed past Joanna, who was emerging from the same spot she'd seen the ghost. Joanna smirked and whispered, "So you saw it, then? You saw the ghost?"

Leah frowned, but before she could say anything, Sarah asked, "Ghost?"

Joanna found her seat and leaned forward, whispering, "Yep. Some Pawns keep seeing something in here. Rumor has it a Black Pawn got murdered in the stacks and now haunts the library. Right down there."

Cold ran through Leah as she glanced at the empty stacks.

After a few seconds of silence, Sarah snorted. "First demons, now ghosts? What's next? Leprechauns?"

Joanna rolled her eyes. "Laugh all you want; but Leah saw him, judging by her face."

Leah looked away from the stacks and shook her head. "Maybe? I . . . I don't know."

Isaac flipped open another book with a loud thud. "Well, as much as I want to talk about ghosts, can we continue? Unless the ghost is going to help us with the homework, I don't see how we'll be able to finish this."

The following Monday came, and although it had only been a little more than a week, it felt like months. Aside from the aches and pains, Leah enjoyed it. Every minute of every day kept her away from that night back home, back when her mother was last alive. Away from the night she'd faced Asmodeus.

A voice cut through her thoughts. "Attention!" Nykima shouted as she stood in front of them, outside on the sand field. The scorching morning sun crested over the trees. Normally, mornings with Nykima began with a five-mile run around the boundary, but this morning, she had two others with her: Sid and Ian.

In unison, the Pawns clicked their feet together and clasped their hands behind their back.

Nykima paced the front of the line. "At ease. We're resuming sparring this morning now that the new Pawns have caught up enough. Black Knight Kim and I will referee, and we have medical if needed. I'll pair you off. Martial arts only. Winners will receive three extra points toward their first trial. If I spot any of you using *Malchut*, I will deduct two points. Got it?"

A resounding, "Yes Knight Nykima!" echoed through the Pawns.

Nykima continued, "Good. Pair off when I call your names, then wait for my whistle."

She called them one by one in quick succession. They paired Isaac with Gabe, Sarah with Joanna, and so on.

"Ackerman, you're with Fogle."

Leah met the green eyes of Miranda Fogle, a smaller girl with big red curly hair who was almost always the first to raise her hand in class and the first to nail down any movement they'd done in training the week before. The girl smiled, eyeing up Leah like a wolf hunting down its prey.

Everyone spread out on the field, facing their opponent.

Nykima stood in the center and raised her hand. "Ready! Set!" Then she blew her whistle.

Miranda leaped forward with a low kick to Leah's shin.

Leah barely dodged it, her eyes locked onto Miranda's shoe as it grazed her leg. Her focus was down, and she completely missed the fist that was planted firmly on her jaw.

Stars blossomed in her eyes, and she stepped back, tasting blood pooling in her mouth.

Miranda smiled, a murderous look on her face that sent Leah back to that night, back to her father's twisted grin.

Then Miranda was on her again, a fist aimed at Leah's stomach. Leah blocked it at the last second with her left forearm.

The force of the punch threw Leah back, more strength than Miranda should have been able to muster. Leah's arm ached with a pain that shot up her arm and rang in her head.

With Leah stunned, Miranda raced forward, another fist aimed at Leah's side.

Leah moved instinctively, sweeping a kick to Miranda's ankle, hooking it, and pulling her off her feet.

A whoosh of air flew past Leah's face, as if an invisible force had flown by.

Miranda lunged at Leah again, wrapping her arms around Leah's waist and tackling her to the ground.

Air left her, and she strained to get her lungs working again.

Miranda clamored on top of Leah and struck her over and over. Leah bucked Miranda off her and pinned her down.

Leah landed a few solid punches to Miranda's ribs with her right hand while holding her down with her left, before Miranda landed a punch to Leah's shoulder.

It felt as if her fist were a sledgehammer, containing strength that far surpassed what someone like Miranda should be able to do.

Nykima's whistle distracted Leah for a second. "Penalty, O'Conner!"

Miranda used the distraction to spin and wrenched free from Leah, rolling back and to her feet before Leah could process what happened.

Leah stood, her focus back on her target. She dodged a sweep of Miranda's legs, but an invisible wall rammed into her own legs, knocking her back onto the ground.

She opened her eyes to the blue sky and ringing in her ears. Was this really just from training? No. She had dodged the actual kick, but something else tripped her.

There was only one thing it could be. "You're cheating with *Malchut!*"

Miranda flicked her eyes to Nykima, who had her back turned to them, and grinned. "Cheating only counts if she spots it, and she doesn't use *Tiferet.*"

Realization hit Leah, and her eyes widened. She glanced around the field, keeping one eye on Miranda while she noted that no one from the Black Hills Outpost was winning. By the looks of it, others were using *Malchut* the same way Miranda did.

"Ready to give up?" Miranda clenched her fists and hopped on the balls of her feet. "I could go for hours."

Leah shook her head and spit out a wad of congealed blood. She rose to her feet and shifted her stance to ready for Miranda to attack.

Miranda charged forward, her feet pressing off the

ground with the added energy of *Malchut* propelling her forward.

Leah slipped down out of her stance at the last moment, avoiding Miranda's punch as she balled her hand into a fist and punched upward into Miranda's gut.

When her hand connected, she let out a small bit of *Malchut*, feeling the serpent in her chest unwind and strike quickly into her fist.

She had let out only a sliver of energy, yet when her fist connected, it lifted Miranda off her feet. Leah heard a couple of her ribs cracking along the way, but she couldn't stop it now. Miranda hovered in the air for a second before slamming, hard, onto the sand.

Leah panted and smiled. "Got you!" She took in a few more breaths, her lungs begging for more and more air while she could. She crouched, waiting on Miranda.

Miranda didn't get back up. She lay there, a few feet from Leah, a crumpled mess.

A voice shouted from over Leah's shoulder. "Medic!"

Nykima rushed over to Miranda's side and pressed her fingers to her neck. "Don't move." She looked up at Leah and glared. "How in the hell do you think using that much *Malchut* was appropriate?"

Sid crossed the field and dropped his hands to Miranda's head, closing his eyes. "Some internal bleeding, broken ribs. We can move her in a couple minutes, once I . . ." His voice trailed off, his focus now on Miranda.

Nykima's eyes didn't leave Leah's. Words fumbled out of Leah's mouth. "I . . . she was . . ."

Sarah, sporting a massive bruise on her cheek, shouted from behind Nykima, "That's not fair. You didn't tell us we could—"

Nykima whipped her head around and spoke through a

clenched jaw. "One more word, Pawn Turner, and I'll drag you out of this academy myself."

Sarah turned pale and nodded.

Others rushed out from the academy with a small stretcher to Miranda's side. They waited for Sid's command before moving toward her.

Nykima stood and glared at Leah before nodding off to Ian.

"Take her out of my sight. I'm sure Dean Wright will be happy to hear about this."

CHAPTER 9

PUNISHMENT

Ian escorted Leah to the second floor without speaking a word. They traveled down the hall and back to the familiar doors of the dean's office.

After a knock and a brief pause, the dean's voice called from within. "Come in."

As they entered the room, Dean Wright closed a small black book and stacked it atop a pile of papers, sliding them to the far side of his desk next to his computer before leaning back in his chair. "Pawn Ackerman. Didn't expect to see you here so soon."

Ian shut the door behind them and said, "Knight Nykima found her using *Malchut* during a sparring session. The other student required medical attention and is currently being attended to."

William nodded. "I see." His face was unchanged by this news, and Leah jumped into the conversation.

"Permission to speak, sir?"

Ian gripped Leah's shoulder, digging his thumb into her back. She did everything she could not to flinch. "You will speak only when asked to."

William waved Ian off and eyed Leah. "Stand down, Black Knight. I'd like to hear what she has to say."

Ian let go, and Leah bowed her head. "Thank you, Dean Wright. White Knight Nykima gave explicit instruction about using *Malchut*, but my partner used it first. I used it in return in self-defense. Everyone but the Black Hills Outpost Pawns were using it. I just needed to meet her at her level to protect myself, but—"

"But you took it too far?" He looked at his computer monitor. "They already updated the report. Looks like Miranda has a few broken ribs. If you were meeting her on her level, then why are all your bones intact?"

Leah's face warmed. "But she did it first! I was just protecting myself. I didn't mean to—"

William tilted his head and said, "Yet you are standing here, and she is in the infirmary."

"They have also informed me that your close friend, Black Pawn Turner, caused some trouble in the cafeteria on her first day."

"How did you . . ." Leah blurted it out before holding her tongue and looking down at the floor.

William stood, turning away from Leah to look out the window behind him toward the practice fields. "We're here to gauge how well each of you perform. You wouldn't think we'd be watching every move you make? The two of you are a bad influence on that other friend of yours, Pawn O'Conner."

"Bad influence? Sir, she defended Isaac after they assigned him to a room full of bullies."

Ian cleared his throat, catching William's attention. "Black Pawn Turner also spoke out of line, trying to justify Leah's actions. It may seem that they both could use a little reminder."

Leah balled up her fists. She wanted nothing more than

to turn and punch him square in the gut. "Everyone else was using *Malchut*. Why didn't you report them?"

William raised his hand and turned, facing Leah. "Enough! *Black* Pawn Ackerman, because of your inability to manage *Malchut* during sparring, resulting in the severe injury of a fellow pawn, I've deducted five points from your first trial."

Leah drew in a sharp breath, ready to speak out. Instead, William's eyes bore right through her, and she kept her mouth shut.

He waited, seeing if she would have an outburst. When it was clear she wouldn't, he continued, "Atop that, you, Black Pawn Turner, and Black Pawn O'Connor have a week's worth of evening detention. None of you are above the rules, and using others to pick your own fights is just cowardice. The three of you will report here after training. Is that clear?"

Leah shook her head. "Please sir, the others did nothing. Why include—"

"The question was a formality, not an opportunity to state your case. You will do as you are told. Any more outbursts, and you can add on another week."

The vein in Leah's temple pounded, and the pressure in her chest grew. She wanted to tear this room apart, give in to the dark, and watch as they stared in horror. Her arm ached, and she took in a slow breath, the tension inside her subsiding as she nodded.

"Good," William said. "You're dismissed."

Leah left the dean's office without saying another word, leaving Ian behind. Her fingernails dug into her palms, and her jaw ached from how hard she clenched it.

Her mind raced, thinking about how much her opponent had gotten away with using *Malchut*. Miranda had hit her hard enough to jostle a few of her joints if not bring her bones to the brink of breaking.

Clearly, Nykima and the others didn't care if they used *Malchut*. That wasn't the point of the exercise. Instead, they were supposed to use as little *Malchut* as possible, adding an upper hand to their usual sparring while remaining undetected. Yet, she remembered pulling on only a sliver of her energy. Only a sliver did way more damage than it should have. *I can't spar with Malchut. Not if that happens when I barely use it.*

Footsteps sounded behind her. As she turned to look, Ian raced by. He muttered as he passed, "Don't forget to tell your friends."

She thought about pushing him down the stairs, but the thought vanished as she looked out the back stained-glass window and noted that the fields were empty. Instead of following Ian down the stairs, she walked up to the third-floor common room and spotted Isaac and Sarah laying down on the couches.

Luckily for them, the rules allowed Isaac to stay in the girls' common room as much as he wanted, which seemed to make him feel more at ease, not having Brandon or the others nearby.

Sarah spotted Leah and groaned. "So . . . sore. Just kill me."

Isaac shuffled up onto his elbows. "How'd it go?"

Leah prodded her jaw, pushing against a large welt and sparking a jolt of pain. She winced. "Miranda got me good."

"But the dean, Is everything okay?" Isaac asked.

"Yeah, I guess. I got five points deducted, and we've got evening detention for a week."

Sarah sat up and slammed her hand down on the couch cushion. "Fuck that! Everyone else was using *Malchut* too. I mean, no one else threw their partner ten feet into the air, but look at your jaw, it's—"

"Wait," Isaac interrupted. "You said 'we.'"

Leah nodded. "Ian has it out for all of us, so the three of us have detention after nightly training."

Sarah let out a groan. "Oh no. Are you serious? Why?"

"They know what you did in the cafeteria to Brandon last week. And they said Isaac needs to fight his own battles or some bullshit like that."

Isaac fell back onto the couch. "Cool, I'm being punished for having bullies. Well, good to know this place is no different from an actual school."

Leah hopped onto Isaac's couch. "I'm sorry, guys. I feel like this is mostly my fault."

"It's not," Isaac said. "They're just doing this to us because we're the outcasts here."

Sarah emerged from her attempt at smothering herself to death. "At least we're in it together, right? I'll take any time I get outside of that room" She eyed their dorm room, which was propped open while Paige, Serena, and Emma were inside, laughing about something.

"Same with mine," Isaac agreed.

Leah hugged her knees into her chest. "Still, I'm sorry."

Moments passed until Isaac cleared his throat. "We just need to be more careful. They have their eyes on you, Leah, and they are going to take every chance they can to get you —to get all of us."

"What's got you three looking like someone killed your dog?" Joanna asked as she came barging into the common room, pulling a red-faced Gabe behind her.

Leah stared at Gabe's shocked face and raised an eyebrow. "Nothing. What are you two doing?"

"Nothing," Joanna said, crossing the room and squeezing between Leah and Isaac.

"How's Miranda?" Leah asked.

Joanna shrugged. "Fine. It's not the first time that's happened. Constance will heal her up in no time. She's practically a sage with healing."

Sarah frowned. "Wait, it's happened before? They acted like Leah had attempted murder. What happened the last time?"

"Brandon broke a few of Omer Sediki's bones. He got a slap on the wrists and was told not to do it again. I'm guessing they just have it out for you."

Isaac stared up at the ceiling and sighed. "Us. They have it out for *us*."

CHAPTER 10
MYSTIC LESSON

Leah found her seat in the classroom shortly after lunch, sitting between her friends, and waited for either Nykima or Grace to enter the room.

During the previous week, Nykima would come in and take them outside for another round of training in the fields. When Grace showed up, they'd run through lessons on historic battles and discuss strategy.

Instead, Constance entered the room, her streaked hair tied up in a bun, wearing another woolen dress that made Leah instantly think of a teacher from the 1950s. "Good afternoon, class."

Everyone stood at attention beside their desks and said, "Good afternoon, White Bishop Berkenshire."

"You may sit."

She crossed the room and clasped her hands together. "Today we'll discuss the next five *sefirot* and how they may present themselves to you."

Leah leaned forward in her seat. She looked around the room and saw that a few others had done the same. Constance commanded the room, and almost everyone in it hung on her every word. All except Paige, who rested her head in her hand.

"I'd like someone to give a recap of what we've already gone over," Constance said. "Something quick and concise to catch our new students up to speed."

Several hands raised up in the air, and Constance nodded at an attractive Black girl with long hair who towered over the rest, even in her chair. "Pawn Finn, will you do the honor?"

The girl stood up and cleared her throat. "We've been studying creatures and beings that Mystics encounter while on missions. Last time you were here, we discussed the migration of the shifters, spreading around South America. Demons were part of the discussion before then, a continued threat, even though their numbers have decreased since the Demon War. Before that, we covered witch cults and spirits."

Constance smiled. "Very concise indeed. Well done, Pawn Finn. You may sit." Finn obeyed, and Constance continued. "Mystics deal with many threats, and we must know our enemy well if we want to eliminate or capture them. Who can tell me more about the shifters?"

Only a few hands raised this time, but Constance pointed toward Deepak Sarkar, a muscular guy with a strong jawline.

"Shifters were once human, but they do some kind of ritual that bonds their soul with an animal. After that, they can transform into that animal. The largest pack of shifters has been expanding in numbers in Venezuela, despite efforts from Mystics to stop them."

"Thank you, Pawn Sarkar." Constance rubbed her hands together. "One last bit for our new students, then I think we can continue with lessons. We classify demons as levels in the Infinity Board. A level one demon can possess and control a human's body. A level two demon can morph the host's body. Level three can possess a human that has a strong connection to the Trees, like Mystics or Druids. A level four demon is the most dangerous, having their own special abilities that manifest, regardless of whom they possess. We also have records of level four demons commanding lower-level demons. Can anyone give me an example of a level four demon?"

"Asmodeus." Leah blurted out.

The entire class turned, and Leah realized she had spoken up without raising her hand. She had blurted the name out, not even thinking about her actions.

"Sorry," Leah said, her face growing hot.

Constance winced and said, "No need to apologize, Pawn Ackerman. Asmodeus was in fact a level four demon. One of the strongest reported in the Infinity Board's records until his defeat nearly twenty years ago. Thankfully, his return was short-lived."

Memories flooded Leah's mind, dragging her back to the abandoned house and into the moment he drowned her in darkness. *Was that his ability?*

Constance gave Leah a warm smile before peering out to the rest of the class. "Well, on to our discussion for today. *Sefirot*. Every Mystic connects to the Tree of Life differently. Some connections are balanced, and they can connect to the proceeding five *sefirot*, while others have more of an affinity with one or two and have limited access to the others. Whether you have access to all five or only one, you are all Mystics.

"With *Yesod* opened and prepared for bonding, your connection to the Tree of Life has expanded. Have any of you noticed a difference in your energy?"

Leah noticed a difference, recalling Miranda flying up into the air from just a tiny sliver of *Malchut*. She wondered what would have happened if she'd unleashed more on her. Would she still be here at the academy? Would they even let her leave the grounds if she had killed another student?

Constance's voice pulled her out of her spiral. "Yes, Pawn O'Connor?"

Isaac dropped his hand and stared down at his desk. He cleared his throat and spoke in a whisper. "Well, I was at the library and—"

Constance cut him off. "Louder, please. Don't be shy."

Someone snickered behind Leah. She turned and saw Brandon covering his mouth to hold in another laugh. Worst of all, Leah also saw Paige staring at Brandon and playing with her hair. Brandon gave Paige a wink, and Leah turned back in her seat. *Out of all the dudes in this academy, she has the hots for the bully. Of course.*

Isaac ignored the laugh and spoke louder. "Well, it was late. I was in the library, and I bumped into a stack of books. The top one slipped off. It was one of those big tomes, wrapped in metal. I was worried about the sound, thinking it would wake someone up. Then, it just . . . stopped. In midair."

Constance nodded. "*Hod*, the Submissive."

That seemed to make Brandon, Kevin, and Brody laugh harder.

Constance locked eyes with Brandon and cleared her throat. Brandon looked down at the top of his desk, and Constance continued. "*Hod* transforms the kinetic into potential, stopping objects or people in motion."

She walked over to the desk and pulled a small dagger from one drawer before walking to Isaac's desk. "Here, stand and take this."

Isaac accepted the dagger, turning it in his hand and studying it. It was a small, double-edged dagger that could be easily mistaken as a letter opener. At Constance's request, he then stepped to the front of the room, standing fifteen feet away from Constance.

"Throw it at me," Constance said.

Several of the students gasped.

Isaac paused. "I—"

"That was an order, Pawn O'Conner."

Sweat collecting on his brow, Isaac waited for his hand to stop shaking before he threw the knife with precise aim, the tip aimed right at Constance's neck.

Leah couldn't watch; she turned her head and closed her eyes.

CHAPTER II
THE FIVE WELLS

Constance clapped her hands together, and a wave of energy rippled through the air.

The knife, aimed for her neck, froze in midair, stopping only inches away from her throat.

Cold sweat poured over Leah, and the memory of being in Eric's car, inches from colliding with another, surfaced in her mind. She fought against the invisible barrier, fear bubbling as her body didn't listen to her command. Her eyes could still move, and she focused on Isaac, spotting him in her peripheral vision, frozen with arm outstretched, his eyes locked on the blade.

Constance stepped out from behind the blade, her hands still together. "I can direct *Hod* to a single target, like this blade, or expand like a bubble around me and stop everything. It absorbs kinetic energy. The longer you hold it, the more energy it takes to maintain. Be warned, this *sefira* will feed off the energy of your other wells to maintain, and if you spend all your energy, you heart could stop beating."

She separated her hands, and the blade fell to the floor, accompanied by a loud gasp from every student as their lungs worked again. Leah spotted tears flowing down Serena's face, which she quickly wiped away, while others shivered or shifted awkwardly in their seats.

Constance waited for everyone to settle before continuing the lesson. "I won't speak much on the Tree of Death but to tell you enough to recognize the signs. The opposite to *Hod* is *Samael*. Where *Hod* converts kinetic to potential, *Samael* appears to do the same at first, but it decays all energy in a space. Had I used that instead of *Hod*, this blade would look rusted or pocked as if I had dissolved it with acid."

She turned to the board and drew the symbol for *Malchut*, drawing a line up to *Yesod*, and then a line slanting up and left to *Hod*.

Constance stepped forward and picked up the dagger from the ground, twirling it in her hands. "Each well comes with a weakness—a blind spot for the Mystic. Can anyone tell me what the weaknesses are with *Malchut*?"

Ricardo Lopez, a boy with dark brown eyes and broad shoulders, raised his hand. Constance nodded, and he spoke in a deep baritone voice, "It leaves you exhausted, and it's the easiest to fall to corruption."

"Excellent, Pawn Lopez. The Tree of Life and the Tree of Death connect between *Malchut* and the opposing *Nehemoth*. That corruption offers more power as it bleeds in and clouds your mind if you let it. We can only protect you with knowledge, but students have walked down that path before, only to perish from it." Constance paused, staring that the floor for a moment before looking back up. "So, I've already mentioned that *Hod* absorbs the energy from other *sefira* to fuel it. That leaves the Mystic with a jittery feeling, like they'd had too much caffeine. Overuse has caused some long-term sleep disorders, such as insomnia. What about *Yesod*? Can anyone tell me its function?"

Gabe raised his hand. "It bonds students to a master, so the student can access the different wells of the Tree of Life quicker."

Constance considered his answer for a moment, then tilted her head from side to side. "Yes, and no. Mystics can use *Yesod* to bond to the Tree of Life directly, but the process takes years, and many have failed. Long ago, the Infinity Board discovered a ritual that shortens the process by connecting Mystics to Mystics. Community was the faster way to enlightenment, so we create chains of successors back to the Tree. If the weakness before was time and personal commitment with a low level of success, could anyone guess what the weakness is today?"

Joanna shot up an arm and waited for Constance to give her a nod. "Death of a student or master?"

Constance nodded. "Death is painful. If a bond is severed, the grief that follows is thousands of times worse than any other loss. Once your bond settles, it connects your heart and soul to each other. Over time, you can feel the person you're connected with. You can sense their emotions, and some can even send messages through the bonds. The trials are in place to ensure compatibility and strong bonds. If a student or master dies, or there is a forceful severing, the result can be fatal. Not only that, but the connection to the wells beyond *Yesod* will be affected. For a Master to lose a student, their connection to the Tree may weaken and they suffer unimaginable grief. If a student loses a master, they could lose the access to the other *sefirot* forever."

Leah thought of Eric, knowing he'd lost his last Pawn, Jade. She reflected on everything Constance had just said, then it clicked. *That's why he drinks so much. Losing that bond must have broken him.*

Constance looked away from Joanna and tossed the

blade in her hands. "Moving on. Next to the Pacifist, we have the Invulnerable. I doubt any of you have noticed if you've used this yet."

Constance held up the dagger, gripping it in one hand. She took in a sharp breath and swung her arm down, the tip of the dagger aimed at her stomach.

A chill shot through Leah as Constance stood hunched over, and she heard others jump in their seats. Murmurs of 'is she okay?' echoed behind Leah, and Emma covered her eyes while Harry wrapped an arm around her shoulder.

Constance gasped and stood, pulling the dagger away. It was bent, and there was a small hole in her dress where the blade had torn it, but Leah didn't see any blood.

Smiling, Constance inspected the dagger. "No matter how many years I do this, that never gets old." She turned to the board and drew another circle to the right of *Hod*, connecting *Hod* and *Yesod* into one upside-down triangle. "*Netzach*, the Invulnerable, does just that, making the body impervious to any physical damage. Now, this one is dangerous, since the energy slips away without warning. Many Mystics have died using *Netzach*, believing they were still invulnerable while the energy had already burned out. It's best to use this in short bursts, since *Netzach* is hard to predict when it will run out." Constance tossed the bent blade onto her desk. "The next has to do with vision. Anyone notice anything with your sight?"

Paige raised her hand, her eyes darting back to Brandon for a second. "I think I've seen something like a color or haze around people. Sort of like I can see their energy or something. Knights and Bishops are way brighter."

Constance smiled and drew another circle higher than *Hod* and *Netzach* between the two. She connected *Hod* and *Netzach* to form a right-side-up triangle, then drew a line straight down to *Yesod*. "*Tiferet*, the Seer. With this, you can see beyond the physical plane. Some may only see the energy around a person, which varies from Mystics to non-Mystics. Others may spot signs of corruption forming, and even more rare, some may peer into the Astral, giving sight to demons or bonds. And even more rare, some can see glimpses of the future."

Leah's arm tingled, and the memory of her dream in the tiled basement came back to her. If he marked her, wouldn't they have seen it? They would have said something the moment she got off the bus.

Constance kept her eyes on Paige. "So, Pawn Jones, any weaknesses you suspect have come from using *Tiferet*?"

Paige looked around the room, noting all the eyes on her. She sat up and shook her head, smiling back at Constance. "No weaknesses that I've noticed."

Constance flicked her eyes at Brandon and pursed her lips. "I see. Well, the weakness that comes with *Tiferet* is with your vision. At your level, your vision might have a slight blur, but as you progress, you may lose sight for several minutes. And if you push yourself too far, you may end up blind."

Paige dropped her jaw. "Permanently? I . . . I can't go blind."

Constance smirked. "Then it's a good thing you're here, so we can hone your ability and teach you not to overextend yourself."

She turned and drew two more circles on the board, one above *Hod* and the other above *Netzach*. She drew lines down and across, forming a box around *Tiferet*, and then a line from *Tiferet* to each of the new circles. Buck's hand was in the air as she turned.

"Yes?"

"When do we learn how to use these wells?"

"With *Yesod* open, our focus is to find any natural affinities you might have and let you explore them. Without a completed bond, you cannot harness these wells to their full potential, and forcing them to come will only hinder the process." Constance looked around the room, smiled, and proceeded. "We have two wells left for today's discussion. As we proceed up the Tree, the *sefira* become harder, so I don't expect any of you to have experienced them."

She brought her palms together in front of her, then separated them slowly. Sparks formed in the space between her hands before a small ball of fire burst to life between her hands.

"*Gevurah*, the Elemental. With this, you have the potential to control the four classical elements: earth, air, fire, and water. Fire is the most common, while a manifestation of earth and water are rare. No one in recent history has even attempted to control air, but we know, in theory, that it is possible. Each element reflects internally as it does externally, causing severe health risks the longer you use it. Fire, for example, can dehydrate me until my organs fail." She closed her palms and snuffed out the flame. Writing *Gevurah* above *Hod*.

"*Chesed*, the Lover, is next. Underestimated by many, this *sefira* can heal wounds and bring someone back from the brink of death." She locked eyes with Leah. "Pawn Ackerman, please come to the front of the class?"

Leah stood and crossed the room, following Constance's instruction to stand next to her.

"I see Miranda landed quite the hit on your jaw. Looks like the swelling might last a few days, and a bruise will be there longer. Unless I were to intervene with *Chesed*."

Leah winced at the mention of her jaw, reminding her of the ever-present pain. What did Constance mean by intervening with *Chesed*? Could she make the pain vanish altogether?

Constance looked at the class. "The first rule is that you cannot just heal anyone you want. It must be someone you truly care about. This is the weakness of *Chesed*; any selfishness or hatred, and the well will become as corrupt as *Malchut,* transforming into its counterpart, *Agshekeloh*. Even prolonged use of *Chesed* can lure you into the Tree of Death, putting everyone around you in danger of imminent death."

Constance placed a hand on Leah's cheek. Warmth emanated off her palm and permeated into Leah's jaw. The throbbing vanished in an instant, and Leah could feel the swelling recede.

Constance pulled her hand away, and Leah worked her jaw, shocked by how the pain had vanished altogether.

"You may return to your seat." Constance interlaced her fingers and paced the front of the room. "I care very much about the well-being of all my students, plus a minor injury like that does not require much energy, especially with experience. More severe injuries require more energy and greater risk."

A girl, one of Miranda's friends with wavy blonde hair, spoke behind Leah. "What about healing yourself?"

Constance nodded. "To use the energy of *Chesed*, you need a clear head. It's difficult for many to achieve this with physical trauma, but it *is* possible." Constance turned to the board. "These are the seven *sefirot* that you might access in the coming months. There are three more, two mastered by Queens, and the third for a King to claim." She pointed to the board. "Each also has strong ties to the Tree of Death, to a corrupted form of that power. It may tempt you to use, but I shouldn't need to remind you of the danger."

"Why is it dangerous?" Joanna blurted out. "I mean, can't you use *Malchut* with *Nehemoth* to have an upper hand in a fight?"

Constance glanced her way and pursed her lips, but she answered. "The Tree of Death tempts you with power and infects your mind. The more you use it, the more susceptible you are to forces beyond what you see. It may strengthen you in the short term, but it will destroy your mind, body, and soul in the long run."

Joanna leaned forward in her seat, ready to ask more questions when the bell sounded above them.

Constance clasped her hands together. "My, how time flies. There are resources for you in the library that will help you as you learn more about the *sefirot* and your potential affinities. Atop that, you may come to me with any further questions. Be careful while training, and be cognizant of the weaknesses. Class dismissed."

CHAPTER 12

SMILES FROM THE PAST

Sarah feigned a punch in the air, and a light gust of wind blew Leah's hair. "I just don't get why it's so hard for you. Really, how different can it be to have a bond?"

Leah pulled the lever of the mop bucket and squeezed the gray water from the mop. Everyone else had the rest of the evening to relax in the common rooms while they were stuck in detention. "It's too strong. Back at the outpost, it felt like I was using all I had to make those dummies move. Now, even using the tiniest sliver feels like I'm detonating a bomb. I don't know what will happen if I use it again, but I don't want to end up in front of the dean again and lose more points." She clutched at her side, her ribs still sore from that day's sparring.

Isaac ran an eraser over the chalkboard, wiping away the notes from an old war tactic, Hammer and Anvil, and notes from the Battle of Zama. "Right, but you've got to practice. Sarah gave me some great tips today. I bet if you practiced before bed, then you'd figure it out."

"If I practice before bed, then I might end up blowing a hole through the third floor." A memory of her house flashed in her mind, and a pain shot through her chest. She shoved it down, pushing the mop hard against the floor. "Then what? They'd sever my bond. And Eric and I suffer whatever consequences come from that."

Sarah sighed. "But if you don't try at all?"

"When?" Leah said, looking up from the floor. "Between classes, homework, and now detention, how do any of us have time to do anything but sleep?"

"We don't. But if you practicing means dropping the roof on Paige and her annoying friends, then I say we practice before bed." A smirk grew on Sarah's face.

"Geez, Sarah, what is wrong with you?" Isaac said.

Sarah punched his arm. "I'm joking. Besides, I was just saying I'm not opposed to it. But what if we just blow off detention, instead? For like a half hour each night?"

"And what happens if we get caught?" Isaac said.

"No one has come and checked in on us all night. I bet if we find the right spot, no one will know. You two need the practice, right?"

Leah chewed on her lip. "Do you think we can really clean and have time for practice?"

Sarah pushed her mop along the floor. "If we put in a little more effort, yeah, I think so."

Isaac eyed the door of the classroom and nodded. "Yeah, I'm in. If I can get *Malchut* down, maybe then Brandon and his goons won't be able to pick on me."

The three of them picked up the pace, polishing off the classroom and moving into the hallway. Sarah and Leah silently raced the hall with their mops while Isaac dusted the frames and décor.

Leah stared down the clean hallway with her hands on her hips.

"Damn, we're fast," Sarah said. "Let's put this junk away and get out to the practice fields."

They started toward the janitor's closet, and Isaac whispered, "Hey, check this out."

Leah turned to find him studying something on the wall.

"What is it?" Sarah asked as they both joined Isaac.

He pointed at one of the class photos. "She looks a lot like you, Leah."

The photo was slightly yellowed, with lettering at the bottom of the frame stating, *"Class of 1985."* It depicted students in black uniforms standing out in front of the academy with stern looks on their faces. One of them had brown hair pulled back in a ponytail and eyes that matched Leah's.

"Wow, she looks just like you." Sarah said.

"I . . . I think that's my mom." Leah's stomach twisted in knots, and the last images of Elizabeth Ackerman flitted through her mind. The night she'd found her dead in the living room, when only hours before she'd seen her smiling face.

"Wait, is that Helen?" Isaac asked, his finger pointing at the woman next to Elizabeth.

Leah focused on the girl next to her mother. With pale yellow hair and piercing blue eyes, the girl in the photo looked exactly how Leah pictured Helen as a teenager, although not as happy as the smiling image staring back at her.

"Do you think they were friends?" Sarah asked.

"I don't know. Helen never mentioned it," Leah muttered.

"I bet they were," Isaac added.

"Well, when I become a Queen, I will let everyone know you two helped me get there. Well, maybe not Isaac." Sarah grinned.

Isaac elbowed Sarah's ribs. "Hey! You better mention

me, or I'll tell everyone that I let you cheat off my homework."

Leah wiped away a tear and laughed. "I'm glad I'm stuck here with you two. Really."

Sarah wrapped her arms around Leah and Isaac. "Okay, okay. Stop being sappy, and let's get some practice in."

CHAPTER 13
DUELS

Thursday morning, Leah sat down at their usual table with her tray of scrambled eggs with chives and toast with strawberry basil jam.

Sarah hopped in the seat next to her and rubbed her hands together. "Why on earth would you skip out on the French Toast? What kind of monster are you?" She smiled and dug into her food without waiting for an answer.

Leah shrugged and bit into her toast, the tangy sourdough and sweet jam hitting her just right.

Isaac showed up several minutes later, barely holding on to his tray, his face pale with dark bags under his eyes.

Leah raised an eyebrow. "Everything alright?"

"Couldn't sleep." He nudged a smoked breakfast sausage across his plate before putting down his fork.

Sarah dropped her half-eaten third slice of French toast and glanced around the room. "Brandon again? What'd they do?"

"Nothing. Just leave it alone, okay?" He bit off a corner of toast and held his head with his hand.

Leah hated seeing her friend like this, hated that he

didn't want her to do anything. "Isaac, if there is anything we can—"

"No. Drop it." He picked up his tray and left, dumping it as the bell rang.

Sarah shoved the last bit of food into her mouth and said, "We're going to help him, right? Even if he doesn't want any?"

Leah nodded. "We've got to do something." She spotted Ian talking with a sleepy-eyed Sid. As if Ian knew she looked at him, he turned, meeting her eyes. "We need to think of something they won't catch, and Isaac won't know about."

They dumped their trays and headed out of the cafeteria. In the foyer, Leah couldn't help but look at the large scoreboard, with the added Black Hills Outpost scrawled at the bottom. She found her name and traced her eyes across the board, seeing a minus three as her current score. Her stomach twisted in knots, and she pulled her gaze away, rushing to the fields.

They stepped onto the sand fields and saw a crowd around an octagonal platform in the center of the pitch.

White Pawns propped up stands around the platform, and Leah looked around to see other Knights, Bishops, and White Pawns coming out from the buildings and gathering around the sand field.

"The trial isn't today, is it?" Sarah asked, her voice trembling.

Leah's stomach lurched, and she did everything to keep her breakfast down. "I hope not."

Nykima hopped onto the platform and turned to the gathered crowd of Black Pawns. "Attention!"

Leah and her classmates all stood up straight.

"This morning will be a taste of what the trials will be like, audience and all. One-on-one combat, and you may use the Tree of Life. Winners will gain three points, while their opponents will lose three." Nykima spotted Leah in the crowd. "Note that you may only use the Tree of Life to incapacitate your opponent. Any attempt to cause serious physical injury, and we will deduct five points from your trial, depending on the injury. By leaving the octagon or tapping out, you have conceded the fight. Each battle will be five minutes. If neither has won in that time, it will be a draw and we will move on."

Leah peered through the crowd piling into the stands. She knew her uncle wouldn't be there. Something in her gut told her she couldn't sense him, yet she wished Eric were here to watch. Instead, she found Ian, the dean, and the administration all piling in with others whom she hadn't met.

Nykima grabbed a clipboard from a White Pawn standing just off the stage. "Pawns O'Connor and Roe, you're up first."

Leah spotted Brandon beside Paige, stepping forward with a grin on his face.

"This won't end well." Leah muttered to Sarah.

Sarah cracked her knuckles and turned to look at the platform. "It's not fair. They know it's not a fair fight."

Leah turned toward the dean. "They're doing this on purpose."

Isaac stepped out from the crowd a few feet from Sarah and Leah. He looked even paler than he had in the cafeteria, blinking as he stumbled forward.

He stood on the platform opposite Brandon. Isaac hunched over, staring at the ground as Brandon grinned at the Knights and Bishops who came to observe them.

Nykima stepped between them and looked out upon the crowd. "Everyone else may sit. Black Pawns, I advise you to pay attention, as White Bishop Johnson will use this opportunity to pick apart strategy in her next class."

Nykima stepped back to the edge of the platform and locked eyes with Isaac and then Brandon. "I want a fair fight. Ready?"

They nodded, Brandon stretching his arms and shaking them loose while Isaac placed one foot forward, his arms pulled in close to his chest, readying himself for defense.

Nykima blew a whistle, and the fight was underway.

Brandon hopped on the balls of his feet and lifted his fists. "Ready to get your ass handed to you again? Or are you gonna wuss out?"

Isaac took in a slow breath, his gaze locked on Brandon. Still a few feet back, he lunged a kick in the air, sending a wave of *Malchut* forward.

Brandon swung his arm forward, as if swatting a fly away from his face. The energy from *Malchut* diverted, flinging up sand from the field off to Brandon's side.

"Are you serious? That's it? Geez, you're worthless. They should call it now before I have to waste any more energy on you, Black Hills Square." Brandon glanced over to the stands once more and grinned. He lunged forward, then at the last minute, he threw himself backward, landing on his right hand and using the momentum to swing his left leg into a sweeping overhead kick that collided with Isaac's guarded arms.

The force lifted Isaac off his feet and sent him flying off the platform and onto his back in the sand field.

Nykima blew her whistle and stepped onto the platform. "Winner of the first fight with an excellent execution of his Capoeira technique: Brandon Roe."

Sarah leaned into Leah. "Well, at least it was fast."

Leah nodded, her eyes locked onto Isaac as he rolled over and tried standing, coughing hard as he did. Sid walked over to his side, kneeling down and checking his chest. He waved over a White Pawn, who helped him up and wrapped Isaac's arm around his neck, leading him off the field and to the building.

Leah gritted her teeth. "He didn't have to kick him that hard."

Sid stood up and stifled a yawn, nodding to Nykima.

Sarah clenched her fists. "Someone needs to teach him a lesson."

As they watched Brandon, his smile turned, and he raised a middle finger to the admins in the stands. Leah watched as their faces reddened and lips pursed.

"Happy I played your little game? Glad to see you all here instead of looking for my brother. Or did you forget about him?"

Silence echoed through the stands, and Black Rook Reginald Platt spoke calmly. "This is not the place for this discussion. Speak out of line again, and you'll lose all the points you just earned."

Brandon raised his finger higher. "Not the place? It's never the place for you, or anyone else. Why are you all so—"

A ripple of energy washed over Leah, and Brandon's word froze in his mouth as he stood as still as a statue. Frozen by *Hod*.

Reginald kept his hands interlaced in his lap as he spoke, his voice cutting through the crowd's silence like a knife. "We have already spoken on the subject, and my patience with your insolence grows thin. Black Pawn O'Conner will be declared the winner of this match. And you, Pawn Roe, will have four points taken from your score." Brandon's eyes locked onto Reginald, full of piercing rage as veins bulged in his temples and his face turned red.

"If you wish to be insolent, then you have no place at

this academy. And no chance of finding your brother then. Is that what you want?" Reginald said.

Brandon glowered for a moment longer before his eyes softened and his veins receded.

"Good." Reginald said with a smile.

Movement returned to Brandon, and he collapsed to the ground gasping for air, color draining from his face.

"You'll be spending a week in detention, in my office. Now, sit down."

Brandon crawled to the bench and sat next to Paige without another word.

Reginald waved a hand at Nykima as he sat. "Let's continue, shall we?"

Nykima nodded and turned to her clipboard. "Next, Ladmin and Spallino, you're up."

Leah stared down at Brandon as he shrugged off Paige's hand. "Well, I guess we got our wish."

Sarah groaned and whispered, "I guess. But do you really think being embarrassed like that is going to stop him?"

"No," Leah said. "I don't."

The fights spanned through the morning. After four fights, Isaac returned with the White Pawn, more color in his face but still with dark circles around his eyes.

From what Leah had seen so far, it was clear Isaac wasn't the only one lagging. Some fights ended quickly, with one swift blow of *Malchut* knocking the opposing student off the platform before the whistle even finished blowing.

Partway through the morning, Nykima read off the clip-board, "Tate and Lopez."

Gabe leaped up from the stands, followed by Ricardo. Leah hadn't realized how short Ricardo was until now, but what he lacked in height he made up for in muscle mass. She clutched at the bottom of her shirt, bunching it up in her sweaty hands as she waited for the match to begin.

As soon as Nykima blew her whistle, Ricardo rushed at Gabe, his fists moving at breakneck speed, aiming at Gabe's ribs and face.

Each punch from Ricardo slipped right off Gabe without even a flinch. Ricardo punched faster, using more *Malchut* to launch his arms like cannons at Gabe, but everything he tried failed. He gasped for breath as his punches slowed.

With ease, Gabe pushed Ricardo off him. He stumbled back outside the platform.

Nykima blew her whistle and raised Gabe's hand.

Leah wiped her palms on her pants and let out a long breath. "Was that *Netzach?* When did he learn that?"

Sarah clapped as Gabe hopped back up into the stands. "Who knows, but that was awesome!"

The sun stretched up the sky, and more battles ensued, most in quick succession. One notable moment came when Brody, Brandon's crony, used the Tree of Death, forming a thin ice layer across the platform while he absorbed energy before Nykima stopped him with *Hod*. He lost, and other fights continued.

Buck also knocked himself out of the ring before his opponent could even get a hit on him, but Nykima gave him a second chance. He screwed that up too.

With each name called, a weight in Leah's stomach grew heavier. Only six students had yet to battle.

Her eyes fell on Miranda. Would she have to fight her

again? She recoiled at the thought of tossing her back up in the air again, this time with free rein to use the Tree of Life. Could she win without hurting her like she did before?

Nykima's voice cut through her thoughts. "Fogle and Morales."

Leah let out a breath. At least she wouldn't be fighting Miranda again.

Sarah elbowed Leah. "Guess we don't need to worry about those two. You don't think they'd pair me with Paige, do you? I could use an excuse to yank out some of that pretty blond hair."

Nykima blew the whistle, and Miranda and Joanna met in the center of the platform.

Miranda stuck to the forms, focusing on each kick and punch, mimicking the movements perfectly from how they'd learned them.

Joanna dodged every blow, moving in close and jabbing elbows into Miranda's sides and knocking her off balance.

It became obvious that Joanna was playing with Miranda, fighting dirty and off the book to knock her off guard, only hitting her with enough *Malchut* to keep her barely standing.

This back and forth went on for minutes, and then Miranda dropped her form and clocked Joanna on the head with a *Malchut* blow that sent her straight to the ground.

"Win goes to Miranda." Nykima said before pointing to two White Pawns. "You two carry Joanna off to the infirmary. Next, we have . . ."

Sarah rubbed her hands together. "Please be me and Paige."

"Jones and Novak."

The stone in Leah's stomach settled as she looked at Sarah, her future opponent.

CHAPTER 14
FRIENDLY FIGHT

Leah couldn't stop her knees from shaking as Paige hopped onto the platform and rocked on the balls of her feet. Leah was up against Sarah next. Her friend. She couldn't—

Kevin Novak, Brandon's other goon, hopped off the stands and onto the platform.

"Don't go easy on me, okay? I can handle myself." Paige held up her fists and locked eyes on him.

Leah glanced over at Sarah, who had that same pale look on her face.

"Whatever you say," Kevin said, his eyes flicking back to Brandon as he raised his fists.

Nykima blew her whistle, and Paige rammed her fist into Kevin's jaw before hopping back.

"I warned you not to go easy on me."

Kevin rubbed his jaw, peeling his eyes away from Brandon and locking onto Paige's. "Be careful what you wish for, sweetheart."

Leah clenched her fist. She'd have to do that to Sarah. She'd have to go in fast and take her out before Sarah could land a punch against her. Leah shook her head. *No, stop.*

Paige smiled and leaped forward. She took another swing at his face, but he ducked out of the way, leaving an opening at his side that connected with Paige's knee.

He stumbled back, but Paige kept on him, her eyes glowing a soft yellow in the sunlight as she feigned moves or redirected his blows while getting in jabs of her own.

She moved seconds before him, as if she could predict every move he was about to make.

Leah noted all the admins leaning forward, intrigued by what they were seeing. Would her fight draw their attention?

Kevin's face turned red, and his attacks became wilder. It didn't matter, though. He continued to punch air, while Paige used every opportunity to knock him closer and closer to the edge of the platform.

One last knee to the gut, and Kevin stumbled off the platform. He glared at Paige and huffed, turning and stomping off the field, past the benches, and back to the academy.

Nykima blew her whistle. "Black Pawn Jones, winner."

Paige grinned from ear to ear and hopped off the stage, sliding in next to Brandon and nudging his shoulder.

Nykima flipped the page on the clipboard and cleared her throat. "Last battle, Ackerman and Turner."

Leah stood, looking down at her friend.

"I guess we're doing this," Leah said.

Sarah shrugged and smirked. "Don't forget what I taught you. I'll give you a free shot before I flatten your ass."

"Gee, thanks for the vote of confidence."

As they left the stands together, they passed in front of Paige as she was saying something to Brandon. She was gesturing at Leah and Sarah, and it was obvious she was talking about them, scowling and shaking her head.

"Fuck off, Paige." Sarah spat, turning and hopping onto the platform.

Leah walked to the other end of the platform and faced Sarah. Her blood throbbed in her ears. She didn't want this. She didn't want to face off against her friend.

Sarah, on the other hand, already had her hands up. Something in her eyes told Leah that she would not go easy on Leah.

Leah lifted her hands to match Sarah's. If she wanted a fight, Leah would give her a fight.

Nykima stepped back. "Ready?"

Both Leah and Sarah nodded, followed by the shrill of the whistle.

Leah stepped toward Sarah, her hand at the ready.

Sarah ran forward, dropping to the ground and sweeping a low kick to Leah's shin, carrying a blast of *Malchut* that knocked Leah off balance. Sarah took advantage and grabbed onto Leah's arm, pulling her close and readying to flip Leah over.

As Sarah squeezed Leah's arm, Leah came to her senses, grabbing tight onto Sarah's arm, and dropped low while yanking Sarah forward, countering Sarah's planned arm drag with her own.

Sarah rolled and was on her feet in an instant, jabbing Leah's defenses with sharp punches wrapped in *Malchut*.

Leah stepped back, closer and closer to the edge of the octagon platform with each punch. Her arms ached already, the punches rattling her bones. She watched Sarah and found the pattern, waiting for the right opening. *Malchut* unraveled within her, an old friend waking and filling every corner of her being. She focused it down into a point no bigger than a marble at the edge of her fist.

The opening came as Leah felt the back of her heel crest

the edge of the platform. She punched, landing on Sarah's shoulder, unleashing the energy.

Sarah flew backward, spinning twice before crossing the platform and landing facedown.

Leah had used more energy in *Malchut* than she'd intended, and a cold sweat formed on her brow. She eyed Nykima, nervous that she might have gone overboard, but the Knight stood still. For a second, she thought she had won. Then Sarah lifted her head, clamoring back to her feet, rage in her eyes as a streak of blood oozed out of her arm.

From across the platform, Leah formed a thin layer of *Malchut* inside her as she thrust her palm forward, throwing a wave of energy at Sarah.

Sarah's eyes glowed, and she dodged the wave. She propelled herself forward with a leap powered by *Malchut*, spinning and sending a kick right into the side of Leah's head.

Leah dropped onto all fours, the world spinning and the taste of blood in her mouth. Another kick from Sarah landed on her stomach, and she fell onto the edge of the platform.

Sarah came in for another kick, but Leah forced a wave of *Malchut*, knocking Sarah back enough for Leah to rise back to her feet.

Her arm ached, a pain under the surface of the skin that burned so badly that Leah lost her focus on her opponent.

Sarah saw the opening and delivered another kick.

Leah's feet lifted off the platform, and she felt her body flying back outside the boundary. The only thought that came to mind was that she had lost. That she'd faced off against her best friend and failed. Then the thought of Eric entered her mind.

She had failed him. Failed their bond. If she couldn't win one fight, how was she going to keep her bond?

The pain in her arm spread up and through her body, pins and needles coursing through her as she continued to fly backward.

Her arms moved against her own accord, extending behind her as if to brace for impact.

No, if I do that, I'll break my—

Power coursed through her, *Malchut* racing to her palms, energy surging through her body and pulsing out like jet-fuel.

Leah's descent stopped altogether, and she flung herself back, away from the sand field, and landed firmly back onto the platform.

She glimpsed Nykima's shocked face and heard gasps from the crowd.

Sarah's eyes widened, and she looked at Nykima, who nodded in return. Sarah clenched her fists, and her face contorted into a sneer as she threw wave after wave of *Malchut*.

Something else awoke inside Leah. A different serpent, resting somewhere deeper within. It rose out from somewhere dark and filled every corner of Leah, spreading the sense that she could take anything Sarah flung at her.

Malchut rammed into her body. But this new serpent shrugged it off. Blasts of energy collided with Leah, each stronger than the next, but the power wrapped around her, shielded her.

Sarah screamed, swinging her arm forward, cutting through the air.

A blade of *Malchut* collided against Leah's chest. She grinned, knowing a cut like that should have seriously injured her. Instead, the energy sent sparks up in the air as Leah stood like a statue on the other end of the platform.

As quickly as the serpent came, it vanished, but a fresh

wave of confidence filled her. She could beat Sarah and end this.

Leah raced forward, focusing on a thin layer of energy on her fist as she swung it at Sarah.

Their fists met, *Malchut* unleashed on both sides, and a concussive pulse burst between them.

They both fell backward, Leah to her knees, catching her breath.

She looked at Sarah, who was in worse shape than she was. "You won't win. Just concede."

Sarah stopped gasping for air and glared at Leah, wiping blood from her lip. She propelled herself forward again, like a leopard pouncing on its prey. She collided with Leah and jabbed her over and over with *Malchut*.

Pain blossomed in Leah. She wouldn't win if she let Sarah keep doing this. Worse, one of them could end up getting seriously injured. How long had this been going on? Hadn't they reached the time limit already? Leah had to earn back some points. She needed to even the score on her trial for her bond's sake.

A cool energy surged into her when she took in a breath, and she let the serpent inside her build over every corner of her being. She squeezed her eyes shut and let out the tiniest pulse of *Malchut* that tore Sarah off her back and sent her flying into the air.

Leah heard the thud, opening her eyes to see Sarah lying on her back outside the perimeter of the platform. Leah fell to one knee, relief washing over her as she tried catching her breath. The serpent inside her receded, the pins and needles trailing back to her arm. She had done it, she had won.

Sarah rolled off her back and stood. She glared at Leah, hatred burning in her eyes before she lunged forward once more.

Leah lifted her arms, trying to pull on the energy inside her.

The match was over. What was Sarah doing?

Leah stood, but before she could react, Sarah was inches from her face. She took a swing, clocking Leah on the side of the head.

Everything went dark.

CHAPTER 15

CORRUPTION

Leah stood in the darkness. Water lapped against her ankles, a vast, shallow ocean spanning into eternity around her.

"Hello?" Her voice didn't echo, the sound consumed in the dark.

A pinprick of yellowed light flickered far in the distance.

"Is someone there?"

She waded through the lukewarm water, moving closer to the flicker.

The point of light formed into a light bulb, dangling from a cord that vanished into the dark. Below the light was the silhouette of a person, crouched over and kneeling in the water.

She paused several feet from them. "Are you okay?"

The silhouette shuddered at the sound of Leah's voice. It breathed slow, haggard breaths, and a small whimper came from their lips.

Leah moved closer, reaching out a hand. "Are you okay? Where are—"

A man looked up; a smile stretched across his face.

"Finally. I'd hoped you wouldn't leave me down here forever."

His hand shot out, wrapping around Leah's arm, burning beneath her skin. Pain ebbed into her vision, searing white, and she screamed, clawing against his grip.

Sunlight beat down on Leah as her eyes cracked open. She came back to her senses, and the aches and pains of the battle ebbed back into her body.

She groaned, feeling the hard mat of the octagon platform beneath her. Leah tried rolling to her side when a hand stopped her, connected to a man with dark skin and a short black mohawk and beard.

Sid let her go. "She should be fine. Maybe a slight concussion."

"Good. Thank you, Black Bishop Gunn." Nykima stepped forward onto the platform.

"Pawns Turner and Ackerman, I blew my whistle, and yet you both continued fighting." Nykima wrote something down on her clipboard. "A week of detention for you both for refusing to listen." Nykima gestured to Sarah, who stood near Leah, blood still oozing out of her arm. "Help your opponent up to the stands so we can close this out."

Sarah glared at Leah and stomped over, offering her hand and helping Leah to her feet.

Leah couldn't take her eyes off Sarah, anger bubbling up inside her. Why did she come after her and knock her out?

Sarah averted her gaze, pulling on Leah to walk with her back to the stands.

Nykima took the center of the platform. "That's all for

the one-on-one sessions today. To the Bishops and Knights looking for a Pawn to bond with, I hope this gives you an idea of what this term's students are capable of. Now, Pawns, back to the academy and clean up before lunch. You're dismissed."

Sarah leaped off the stands, leaving Leah behind as she headed back to the academy. Leah watched as she left, another pain in her chest building the farther Sarah went.

In the girls' bathroom, Leah stared at herself in the mirror. She could barely recognize herself, with a blackened eye and swelling across half her jaw. She ran a finger along it, expecting a sharp pain. Instead, it was numb. Was that normal? She washed her face and waited for the next available shower.

A stall opened and Sarah stepped out, her tightly curled black hair still dripping against her brown skin. Her eyes were red, like she'd been crying in the shower. She crossed in front of Leah, her head bowed, ignoring Leah's gaze.

"Hey, Sarah, I—"

"Fuck off," Sarah said without looking up.

Heat rose in Leah's face. Everyone in the bathroom went silent, their attention turned to the two friends. An anger bubbled up in Leah. "Are you being serious right now? You attacked me after Nykima called the fight!"

Clenching her fists, Sarah finally looked up at Leah. "This is bullshit."

Leah furrowed her brow. "What's bullshit?"

Sarah jabbed a finger into Leah's shoulder. "You! Everything about you is bullshit! You already have a bond. Why are you getting paired up with us? It just makes whoever fights you look like a loser."

Sarah was right. Leah could see it in everyone else's eyes. Even Paige, who nodded along with what Sarah said. Leah didn't belong with them, and a fight against her wasn't a fair fight at all. Still, Leah couldn't stop herself. "It's not like I got to choose."

Sarah rolled her eyes. "I helped you. And for what? For you to kick my ass in front of everyone? The only reason you won is because of that stupid bond."

Leah wanted to back down, to agree with Sarah. She had a point, but why did she have to do it here? "What do you want me to do? Just let everyone beat me so I get my bond severed? I've got something to lose."

Sarah spread her arms, scanning the other girls in the bathroom. "I can't be the only one. Everyone here thinks it's bullshit too. We get it; you've got your problems. But what about us? What happens if we don't pass the trials? Anyone teamed up against you will fail. And that could mean becoming bondless."

A weight formed in Leah's throat. It was her. She was the reason all the students from the outpost had been given a hard time by the others since their arrival. That had to be the reason all this was happening. But Sarah was supposed to be her friend. She pushed the thought aside. The others didn't deserve to see her cry. "I beat you. I don't see anyone else being such a whiney bitch about getting their ass handed to them."

Sarah's eyes widened. "What did you just say?"

"I don't make the rules. They paired us together, and I won. I beat you fair and square, and you can't handle that."

A rattle emanated from the bathroom stalls, an invisible force shaking the doors on their hinges. It grew louder as the rattle spread, reaching the mirrors and paper towel dispensers. Frost formed on the mirrors, and cooled steam settled into low a fog. She eyed Sarah, ready for another attack.

Sarah frowned and stared at the mirrors forming ice around her. "That's not me."

A voice shouted from behind the stall. "Stop it! Please, stop! I can't take it."

Leah took a step forward and looked at the closed stall. "Um, hello? Everything okay in there?"

The voice shouted again. "No! They're in the walls. Slithering. Why are there so many?"

A familiar voice grumbled in Leah's ear. *Do you feel that? The Tree of Death is near.*

Leah jumped and turned around, looking at the confused stares from the girls behind her. No one had been close enough to whisper in her ear. How was it possible? He was dead, eaten by that dark creature with chains.

The girl shouted once more. "I said stop!" The door to the last stall burst off its hinges and flew into the sink. Water sprayed out from crushed porcelain, and many of the girls took that as their cue to leave, some still dripping from their shower.

A girl with dark hair stepped out, clutching her hands to her head, hyperventilating as she stumbled forward. Joanna.

Leah stepped away from Sarah and toward Joanna. "Are you okay?"

Joanna peeled her hands away from her face and stared off at something that wasn't there. "They're everywhere, slithering in the walls, crawling on me. I can't take it; I don't want to. Please, not me."

Sarah turned to the girls near the door. "Go get help."

A girl nodded and grabbed onto the door.

"No. No. No." Joanna shook back and forth before a

burst of energy flew out of her, throwing the girl up against the door. Joanna fell to her knees and whispered, "It's so cold. So dead."

Joanna's lips turned blue as the temperature in the bathroom continued to drop. Shards of frozen water shot out from cracked pipes, and icicles formed on the ends of Sarah's hair.

Whispers gathered in the air, foreign tongues shouting obscenities. Only one voice drilled into Leah's mind. *She'll kill you. Kill all of you. You must eliminate her. Don't wait. End her now!*

Waves of *Malchut* sent the room into turmoil. They tore out of Joanna as she screamed and writhed on the floor, energy slamming into stalls, breaking mirrors, and tossing everyone in the room around like rag dolls.

Leah's elbow slammed into the tile floor, a jolt of pain shooting up her arm. "Joanna! Stop!"

That familiar voice whispered again in her ear, clear as day. Asmodeus. He sounded amused, and she could picture him smiling. *You need to end this. Now. Else the corruption will spread to everyone in the room.*

Leah took a step back. "No. You're not there. Get out of my head!"

A sigh sounded from beside her, and she could feel hot breath on her ear. *If you don't listen to me and stop her, your friend here will tear this entire building down.*

Leah looked over at Sarah and some of the other girls crouching next to the sinks, trying to avoid the attacks. A wave of *Malchut* knocked Leah down, and she had to hold on to the sink to keep from launching back into the doors.

The energy inside Leah woke, uncoiling and pressing up against her arms. She launched repeated blows of *Malchut*, matching Joanna's and deflecting the energy from the others. "Just tell me what to do!"

Joanna's face paled, and she drew in another deep breath. The temperature in the room continued to plummet, and the tips of Leah's fingers turned blue. The waves of *Malchut* seemed to wash over Joanna, as if she were absorbing everything Leah flung at her. Leah could barely keep up, focusing on sending out as little as possible to deflect waves, cracking mirrors and tiles instead of bones.

Asmodeus spoke again, rushing his words. *Something is infecting her thoughts. You need to find the source and kill it.*

Joanna threw another wave of energy straight for Leah's head. She dropped but was too slow and caught the tail end of her energy. She went flying, landing on her back under the sinks.

Leah shook her head. She was losing it. This voice, certainly a byproduct of the Tree of Death, wasn't real. It wasn't him. But it was right, at least she guessed. "I can't hold on much longer! I need to get closer to her!"

Asmodeus let out a low growl. *I have an idea.*

Pain throbbed out from under Leah's left arm, and a cold gel spread across her entire body. The black mark blossomed into her vision, a stain on her otherwise pale skin.

The light in the bathroom dimmed all at once to a familiar sickly yellow she had seen before. Voices behind her, of girls shouting and scrambling to get out of the bathroom, sounded distant, like Leah had stuck her head underwater. She stood up from under the sinks and peered into the mirror, but no reflection looked back.

She stared at her hands and back at the mirror. "What the—"

Joanna screamed, looking at where she had last seen Leah. "See? They killed her! coiled around her and consumed her. I'm next."

Get behind her, Asmodeus whispered.

Leah tiptoed forward, avoiding the broken glass on the floor.

As she moved closer, she noticed a blackened miasma floating around Joanna's head. She slipped by her, pressing up against the sinks before positioning herself behind Joanna.

Then she saw the large, blackened leech-like creature latched onto the back of Joanna's neck, wrapping its body partway around her torso.

Asmodeus let out a faint laugh. *I wonder how this got here? These little monsters rarely venture this close to life. Be careful, they'll rot your brain.*

The creature undulated, and a cloud of black mist burst out, wafting into Leah's face. It filled her senses, an acrid metal that burned her nostrils.

Thoughts crept in. Was she safe? What happened if Joanna knew she stood behind her? Was this his voice? Was this a trap? She was all alone again.

Asmodeus snapped her out of her trance. *Don't breathe in, or the madness will get to you as well. Aim for the base of the neck and cut it off at the root.*

Leah held her breath, wondering if the madness had already gotten to her since she was talking to an enemy that should be dead. She raised her hand as if it were a blade and locked her eyes onto the base of the leech. She sent a small slither of *Malchut* to her hand, hoping it would be enough.

A shining white slash of energy cut through the leech, spewing black liquid into the air.

The creature tore away from Joanna and writhed in the air behind her, black liquid and smoke encompassing it. Then it vanished, black smoke and all.

A throb pounded in Leah's arm, and Asmodeus spoke,

as if he were far away. *Well done. It would have been a shame to see you die do soon. I have so many more plans for us.*

Sound flooded her ears again, and the color returned to her vision, the sickly yellow replaced with vibrant white tile.

Joanna slumped in front of Leah, and Leah rushed to catch her before she hit her head on the ground.

She looked Leah in the eyes and whispered, "I can't take this anymore." Her body went rigid, and her eyes rolled to the back of her head.

Leah put her hand on Joanna's face. "Stay with me, Joanna." She convulsed in Leah's arms. Leah looked around the room. "Someone, help!"

Without warning, Joanna turned her head and vomited on the floor.

"Help! Please!" Leah screamed.

Nykima rushed into the bathroom, followed by William and Constance. They pushed through the crowd and arrived at Leah and Joanna on the ground.

As Constance secured Joanna's head, Nykima pulled Leah away. "Out of the way, Ackerman. We've got it from here."

Leah stood up and pointed at Joanna. "There was a demon or something latched onto her."

William eyed Joanna and raised an eyebrow. "Thank you for what you've done. We'll take it from here."

"Is she going to be okay?"

Nykima narrowed her eyes. "Ackerman! Return to your room at once! We will handle this."

Leah nodded and backed away. She left the bathroom without another word, ignoring the gazes of the other students as she retreated to anywhere she could be alone.

CHAPTER 16

DETENTION

Rumors spread like wildfire, and Leah struggled to rein it all in. Stories of what had happened with Joanna changed every second, turning into the idea of Joanna doing it all for attention. No one wanted to ask Leah either, so by the time she heard the latest news, it was already far contorted from the truth.

Leah sat down for evening lessons with Grace, listening in as people argued over a theory that Joanna was another trial from the academy. Grace cleared her throat, and after that didn't quell the students, she clapped her hands together.

"Pawn Morales was a prime example of the corruption the Tree of Death is capable of. These things can happen, especially as you first learn how to use its power. We can only teach you what is right, but the Tree of Death will perpetually tempt you, and you must have the willpower to stand up against it. We push you to your limits, and for some who want a shortcut, the Tree of Death is the answer. Let this be a warning about what can happen if you let it corrupt you."

Leah nodded and looked down at her desk as Grace

started her lecture. As Grace broke down the highlights from the fights that day, Leah brought her thoughts back to the thing that had been attached to Joanna's neck. It wasn't corruption; whatever that thing was doing to her had caused the outburst, and Asmodeus hadn't liked it.

His voice echoed in her mind, and she shivered. He was back—and inside her head.

She blinked, forcing the thought out of her mind. He was dead. Gone. That voice was just part of the corruption, dredging up her fears.

But then how did I know how to go invisible?

Leah chewed on her lip, uncertain what to think. Was it worth talking to someone else about it? Someone she could trust?

Well past sunset, Leah headed to the offices to start her first night of detention with Sarah.

Sarah stood outside the offices, and by the time Leah arrived at her side, the door swung open and Ian stepped out, grinning.

"The dean will see you now." He shouldered past them and bounded out of the offices.

They stepped inside, standing at attention at the end of William's desk.

"Pawns Ackerman and Turner reporting for duty," Leah said.

"At ease, both of you." William stood and walked around his desk, leaning against it and crossing his arms. "You two have turned into quite the handful."

Leah frowned. "We're sorry, sir. We were just—"

He raised a hand and began counting. "Bullying a

student, injuring another, disobeying the rules of the one-on-ones, and ending up fending off a corrupted student. Either you two look for trouble, or trouble finds you."

He waited for another reply from Leah or Sarah, but both remained silent. Then he curled his fingers and looked at his nails. "Although, I can say that you, Pawn Turner, show a fierce determination, even when facing off against someone bonded. And you, Pawn Ackerman, showed bravery while containing Pawn Morales. While Pawn Turner's actions are one to look out for during the trials, Pawn Ackerman, your actions today have earned you two points. You stopped the situation from escalating to something more life threatening."

Leah tilted her head to the side. "Dean Wright, I—"

"You managed restraint in handling a corrupted Pawn." William smiled slightly. "And you did it single-handedly. That shouldn't go unnoticed. Keep it up, and don't make me regret rewarding you."

He stood up from the edge of the desk and returned to his leather chair.

Leah saw Sarah clenching her jaw out of the corner of her eye. No doubt the added points only made her further frustrated.

"Now, on to your assignment. I want the hallways, offices, and the upper lobby floors clean enough to eat off. Understand?"

Leah and Sarah spoke in unison. "Sir, yes, sir!"

"Good. Better get started. You're dismissed."

They left the office together and headed down the stairs to the first-floor janitor's closet without a word.

Sarah uncapped the cleaning solution and poured it into the bucket. "So, Leah gets rewarded again for no good reason, other than she's stronger than the rest of us. Congratulations."

Leah set the hose in the bucket and turned on the hot water. "What's your deal? It's not like I asked for this."

Sarah pulled the bucket forward, splashing some of the liquid onto the floor at Leah's feet. "Tell me I'm wrong."

Leah grabbed a broom off the wall. "You're wrong. I don't get why you want to fight over it. It's not my fault."

"Nothing is ever your fault," Sarah said. "And you can just cheat your way back into the ring and win."

"That's what this is about? I didn't cheat."

"Keep telling yourself that," Sarah said, dragging the bucket out of the room.

"You know what? Fine. When you can grow up and have an actual conversation, you can find me sweeping the first floor. Have fun mopping by yourself."

Leah walked out of the closet toward the classroom. Her steps bounced off the stone walls of the dimly lit hallway, the moon's silver light shining in through the windows. She reached the foyer and started down the stairs when a sound caught her attention.

A voice echoed from the hallway, thick and accented. "I'll be back in the morning to check on her."

Dr. Toppen stepped into the light of the lobby and turned to face Sid. "Keep the restraints on her until we can get one of your seers to confirm her condition has improved."

"Thank you, doctor."

She nodded and smiled. "You should get some sleep. Her treatments tomorrow will not be pleasant."

Dr. Toppen turned on her heel and left while Sid looked up the steps at Leah. "What are you doing out of bed?"

She lifted her broom. "Uh, detention, sir."

"Ah, right. Well, steer clear of the infirmary. You can clean it later."

"Sir, yes, sir."

Sid shook his head and headed out the back entrance, toward the sleeping quarters of the Knights and Bishops.

Leah started down the hallway. The dull light played tricks on her eyes. The hallway looked different at night, more daunting as the shadows in the corners of the room seemed to transform into leering creatures, spreading long tendrils, waiting to pounce.

She headed to the classroom, stretching her hand into the dark and grabbing hold of the light switch while shutting the door behind her.

"Much better," she whispered as the light pooled into the classroom, and anything beyond the door was now out of sight.

As Leah swept, her mind wandered back to what had happened in the bathroom. She knew two things about the incident, for sure. One, she had been invisible, or at least Joanna hadn't been able to see her. That was nothing like any ability she knew. Maybe if *Tiferet* had to do with sight, then this was something from that?

Second, and a thought she'd rather not have, was that Asmodeus had spoken to her. She was certain it had been his voice whispering to her, as if his leering face had been inches from her ear. But she had watched him die, twice. Once by Alma's hands, and a second time when he had been devoured in Leah's dreams. How was this possible?

Her arm let out a single throb, and the memory returned of Asmodeus reaching out, of her feeling a slight moment of sympathy as he grabbed her arm. Was he there inside her?

And Asmodeus aside, things had only gotten worse since arriving at the academy. Leah had never felt so alone in her life; she had already lost her parents, and now her best friend hated her. She didn't even have Eric to lean on, as they had instructed her and her uncle to keep a distance from each other.

The sound of shattered glass tore Leah out of her thoughts. She froze, holding tight onto the broom. She strained her ears and listened. Something inside her untangled and stretched her senses. The room brightened, her eyes warmed, and the sounds grew sharp and clear.

Leah tiptoed to the door, turning the knob before peeking into the hallway.

It was the same silent dark hall as it had been before, the shadows still lurking in the corners, watching.

Another sound of glass cracking sounded just beyond the infirmary doors.

She slipped out and walked across the hall to the infirmary, pressing her ear against the door. Then she twisted the doorknob and cracked the door open enough to peer through.

It was darker than the hall, but she could see the curtains in the far corner shifting from the night breeze. She pushed the door open more and felt the cold blowing into the room. It would have made the room too chilly to sleep in. She leaned in, her heart pounding in her chest. "Anyone in here?"

Silence.

She reached for the wall beside the door and flipped the switch.

A row of beds, divided by curtains, lined the wall to her left. She could see enough to know most were empty. All but the last one near the shifting curtains.

Leah could feel that something wasn't right, like a looming shadow waiting to grab her. She pooled the small bit of *Malchut* that had replenished inside her into her fist and stepped forward.

Leah passed the beds, her eyes locked on the curtain.

With outstretched hands, she grasped the edges and flung it open.

The night air blew in from a broken window, shards of glass landing on the floor below. Darkness engulfed the training fields behind the house outside, but her eyes settled on tufts of strange orange fur and blood lining the edges of glass on the window.

Blood covered the bed, and two leather cuffs lay on either side of the bed, torn in half. Leah took a step back, realizing that had to be Joanna's bed.

CHAPTER 17
IN THE SHADOWS

Leah raced out of the infirmary and down the hall to the stairs, her mind reeling. Before she made it to the stairs, a voice boomed behind her.

"Where are you going?"

Energy burned in Leah's hand as she spun on her heel. She peered at the front door and saw Sid stepping in and closing it behind him.

"You gonna tell me what that noise was?" he asked.

Leah frowned. "You heard it too? But you went to bed."

Sid held up the remains of a cigarette. "I was having a smoke out front. Thought I heard a crash. Was it you?"

Leah shook her head. "Joanna's missing. Her bed . . . there's blood. And the straps were shredded."

Sid put out the remains of the cigarette and tossed the butt into the trash, his chest puffing out and his gaze peering over Leah's shoulder. "Black Pawn, with me. Stick close."

He led her through the hallway, and Leah noticed he was limping as they rushed to the infirmary. At the foot of the door, Sid scanned the room up and down with glowing eyes before rushing to the last bed. At the window, he picked a tuft of fur from the glass and inspected it.

Then he stood at the foot of the bed for a long time, staring at the bloodied blankets.

After what felt like forever, Leah opened her mouth. "What—"

"We thought she was stable after what you'd done. She showed signs she was a flight risk, consistent with those corrupted by the Tree of Death."

Leah raised an eyebrow. "What about all the blood? Why would she escape?"

He sighed. "When that animal part of you needs to escape, you'll stop at nothing to get out." He held up one cuff. "Why else would these be torn like this when there is just a buckle you or I could use?"

Leah stared at the window. "But the glass?"

He turned and eyed her. "I'll need to wake up a team to investigate this. In the meantime, your chores are over for the night. You're dismissed. Return to your room until morning."

"But—"

He held up a hand. "That's an order, Pawn."

Leah looked up at the ceiling and said, "Sarah is cleaning too. On the second floor, I think."

Sid faced the window and spoke from the corner of his mouth. "Gather her on your way back to your room and let her know I dismissed her for the evening. Now, go along, Pawn Ackerman."

A flash of lightning lit up the bunk bed above her as Leah lay awake.

The crack of thunder followed six seconds later. Leah hated this. Hated that Sarah didn't want to speak to her. Hated that she knew Joanna was missing and was told to go straight to bed. Hated that Bishop Gunn seemed to think Joanna had broken free when something obviously broke in.

Another flash of lightning. Leah held up her hand, seeing the outline in the dark. Thunder boomed. *Five seconds.*

She had been invisible, sneaking right around Joanna so she could get to that thing around her neck.

Another flash came, and the light burned the image of her hand in Leah's mind. She blinked a few times until it faded away.

She sat up in bed. *That's it. If I just turn invisible again, I could listen in on what they say about Joanna.*

Wind rattled the window as the storm outside rolled in. She focused her memory on what had happened when she vanished. That voice, *his voice*, had whispered in Leah's ear. Then her left arm had throbbed before something wrapped around it, bringing a cold, electric feeling.

Leah closed her eyes, knots forming in her stomach at the thought of Asmodeus, while she ignored the flashes from the storm outside. She took in a deep breath and imagined that feeling again, the cool energy washing over her. Leah didn't know what well it came from, but if she could imagine the sensations again, she was sure it would come to her.

Her left arm throbbed once, a single, weak twinge, before cool air wrapped around her. Pins and needles tingled through her body as a thick and invisible gel washed over her. The storm outside grew muffled, the rattling of the window sounding as if it were underwater.

Leah studied her hands, but she still saw the outline of

them in the dark. She stepped out of bed and tiptoed near Paige's bunk, hoping her compact mirror was open. It wasn't.

She stepped out into the common area, looking for any reflective surface until her eyes fell on the entrance to the bathroom.

Someone had taped it off with blue tape and a sign that read, "*Bathroom closed until further notice. Please use the first floor.*"

Leah slid under the tape and slipped into the bathroom, closing the door before flipping the light switch.

On the other side of the room, she spotted the wisps of smoke from the noxious gas the creature had left behind. Next, she turned to the only mirror still intact. Nothing. She looked closer into the mirror but only saw the stalls behind her. She was invisible again.

Flipping the light switch off, Leah slipped back out of the bathroom. She cracked open the door to the common room and tiptoed out without a sound.

Light flashed in from the stained-glass windows, illuminating her way down the stairs to the first-floor lobby. She crept down the hall and to the infirmary entrance.

A voice whispered behind her. "So alone."

Leah's heart leaped into her throat. She turned around, back pressed up against the door, her eyes darting into the dark. She peered left, toward the end of the hall, to a corner shrouded in darkness next to the library entrance. Something sat there with a faint pale face, staring back at her. It hovered in the air, no body attached, studying her with hollowed-out eyes.

Another flash of lightning, and the face vanished. "I see you both. You two are never alone." The voice sounded as if it were coming from right next to her.

Leah jumped, her back ramming into the door with a loud bang. She looked to her right, but nothing was there.

Footsteps sounded from the main entry, and a beam of light shone on Leah.

"The damn power's out. Do you see anything?" a voice whispered from the lobby.

Leah covered her eyes and backed away. The beam from the flashlight didn't follow her.

Another voice said, "No, but I swear I heard something."

The first voice spoke again. "Well, nothing's here now. Come on, the dean is gonna be pissed if we don't go straight to him."

The light stayed on the door for a few more seconds before flicking away, followed by footsteps on marble that faded.

Leah glanced back at the corner. "Hello?" she whispered. Nothing. Whatever had been there had vanished.

She wiped cold sweat off her forehead and breathed, calming her quickened heart.

A raspy voice then whispered again, cold air blowing against her ear. "Help me." The voice shifted, high and low tones screeching in her ear as if multiple voices were vying for her to hear as they screamed, ". . . or I'll tear your flesh from bone and devour your soul!"

A cold, clammy hand wrapped around Leah's neck and pulled her toward the ground. She clawed at her neck, breaking free and lunging forward, racing down the hall and away from the voice.

She looked back, expecting to see the pale face pursuing her. Instead, Leah saw nothing. She kept her eyes behind her while she raced forward, and she slammed against something solid, recoiling back and landing on her backside.

Sound blossomed back in her ears, and the slight glow of the hallway dimmed into complete darkness.

The solid thing she'd run into recoiled as well. It was a person, caught off balance, and falling backward with a familiar shout. They turned on their flashlight and waved it about. "Who's there?"

Leah propped herself up on her elbows. "Isaac?"

The beam of light settled on her. "Leah? Where did you come from?"

"There was something in the hall. Like a . . ." Leah frowned. "Wait, Isaac, you can see me?"

Isaac reached a hand down and helped pull her up, a confused look on his face. "Yeah, I can see you. Why?"

Leah turned back down the hall. "Never mind, sorry. Just . . . what about you? What are you doing out of bed?"

Isaac stared at the ground and shook his head. "Couldn't sleep."

She saw through his lie and placed a hand on her hip. "Isaac, come on. It's just me here."

Isaac let in a slow breath and sighed. "It's Brandon. Him and his two jerks kicked me out of the room."

"Kicked you out? Why?"

Isaac lifted his shirt, showing off several bruises to his side. "They didn't like when I asked why. They never do."

Blood drained from Leah's face, a cold sweat forming on her palms. "Isaac, you can't keep this a secret. How many times has this happened? We have to tell someone."

Isaac straightened up, sticking his finger out. "No. It'll make things worse. Don't tell anyone, Leah."

A weight settled on Leah's chest. From her own experience at the academy, she couldn't say Isaac was wrong. It was backwards from any school she'd been to, almost encouraging students to fight their own battles. "So, where have you been sleeping?"

"In the common room. The couches aren't too bad."

Leah clenched her fists. "Are you sure there is nothing I can do? I want to help."

"Thanks, Leah. But the dean made it pretty clear I need to fight my own battles. Besides, no one's keeping tabs on me at night, so this place is all mine." He paused and rubbed his neck. "But uh, since you're down here. This thing between you and Sarah . . ."

Leah crossed her arms. "Nice segue. What about it?"

He looked down at the ground. "I don't want to pick between you two. I'm not going to. So, what's it going to take to get over it?"

"Get over it? She started it! She can come to me when she's ready to talk."

Leah heard a creak of the floorboards ahead. She lifted her finger to her lips as Isaac flipped off the flashlight.

The creak sounded again, and a shadow passed under the library doors.

Leah pulled Isaac to the wall and whispered, "Someone's in there."

"No way. I just came from there. I was alone."

"So, no floating pale faces in the shadows? It could be the thing that took Joanna back for round two."

Isaac raised an eyebrow, his mouth open, ready to ask a question before heavy steps echoed from inside the library. Leah grabbed Isaac's hand and pulled him to the entrance. He shook his head. "I don't like this."

"It could be whoever took Joanna. Bishop Gunn made it sound like she was a runaway, like Theodore, but I'm not buying it. This could be our only chance."

A thud sounded, far off inside the library.

Leah crept forward, despite Isaac's objections, and opened the door, slipping inside. Isaac took a deep breath and followed.

A scent filled her nostrils right away, pungent and musky. Leah covered her nose and tiptoed to the shelves. She slipped deeper into the library, past several aisles, peering down each before moving on to the next.

The thing inside the library moved again, casting a shadow at the end of the aisle as Leah peered down. She pressed her back up against the shelf, taking in shallow sips of air. Isaac crouched next to her, his face pale and eyes darting around.

Leah peeked her head out, down the aisle of books, and saw a figure standing at the opposite end, its silhouette cast by the windows behind it.

Lightning flashed, and before Leah could move, she spotted two massive eyes staring in her direction. She whipped her head back, hoping the entity hadn't seen her.

The floorboards creaked again, followed by a rustling and a clatter of books. Thunder rumbled outside, and its cracking boom deafened the sounds in the library.

Leah turned to Isaac and shook her head, mouthing. "I don't think it saw us."

Isaac wasn't looking at her, though, his eyes trained on something past her.

Leah turned around slowly, sweat forming on her brow.

Through the shelf, on the other side of the aisle, two shining eyes stared back at her. A low growl sounded, and a mouth full of teeth glistened in the next flash of lightning.

Isaac pulled on Leah's hand. "Run!"

A roar came as Leah whirled around. She didn't see it, but she felt an icy hand press against her forehead. The world around her melted away, and the sound of thunder echoed into silence.

CHAPTER 18

JADED PAST

Leah blinked a few times, the sound of rain hitting a metal roof stirring her out of her thoughts. She sat in a parked car on the road of a neighborhood of tall, looming homes. The taste of alcohol and cigarettes lingered on her breath. Something was off. Her gaze trained on the entrance to a home, a green door lit by a single light above the door frame.

How did I get here? Leah reached into the glove compartment and pulled out another cigarette. That's when she noticed the hand.

It wasn't hers.

It belonged to a man.

What the hell?

A car pulled up and stopped at a home across the street, and Leah watched a man and woman step out of the green door, dressed in fine clothes, while another man held an umbrella above them.

Who are these people? Where am I?

The rain fell harder, and the man and woman picked up their pace, descending the concrete stairs to the car. The moment the streetlight hit their faces, pain rippled through her body, emanating from a black hole torn from her chest.

Words involuntarily fell from her mouth. "Jade, I'm sorry."

A voice echoed in her mind, scoffing at her plea. *You let me die. You let me die, and they don't even know what happened to their daughter. Do they even remember me? Or did you take that from them too?*

Leah rammed the heel of her palm to her head, jostling the voice from her mind as she pulled the flask from her pocket. She took a long drink, the burning taste of cheap whiskey coating her throat and warming her insides, quieting the voice.

The man and woman stopped at the door of the car, frozen for a second before both of them looked directly at her. Something in them knew she was there. Leah saw the emptiness in them. A hole missing that they couldn't quite understand.

The man started toward her, his eyes wide as he stepped out from under the umbrella. He waved wildly at Leah, flagging her down.

Leah fumbled for the keys, tears forming in her eyes. She couldn't face them. She'd never be able to face them. She was a coward.

Leah jammed the keys in and started the ignition, slamming on the gas and racing out onto the street, the man still waving her down in her rearview mirror.

A cool breeze brushed against her face. She woke to Eric's brown eyes looking back at her. His face brightened, and he squeezed her hand briefly before standing. "How are you feeling?"

Her head throbbed, and the light from the morning sun pooled into the room, forcing her to wince. "Headache," she whispered before covering her eyes.

Eric let go of her and closed the curtain, blocking the sun. "Better?"

Leah peered out from under her hands and nodded. Her eyes tried to focus, but they couldn't. "Where am I?"

Eric sat back down, reaching for her hand once more before pausing and leaning back into his seat. "The infirmary. I raced right here after I . . . I couldn't feel you."

Memories strained to come to the surface. She remembered being in bed, then she was downstairs, running. The more she focused on them, the more they seemed to fall apart.

"What happened?" Eric asked.

"Last night? I dreamt I was in a parking lot. There was a green door?" She winced at the sharp pain that rattled inside her head, strengthening every time she focused on last night.

Eric's face grew white. "Do you remember anything before that? In the library."

She remembered running in the dark, afraid of something. Then colliding with someone. She looked up at Eric. "Where is Isaac?"

A voice, even weaker than her own, spoke from her left. "I'm here." She turned and saw Isaac smiling back. "It's all jumbled for me too."

Eric leaned back and eyed both of them. "Well, what were you two doing out of bed in the first place?"

Leah paused, shutting her eyes tight and ignoring the pain, her memory stitching together. "I . . . I wanted to see if I could find out more about what happened to Joanna."

Eric frowned. "Why? The report said she cut through her restraints, climbed through the window, and broke it from the outside to look like a kidnapping. It's an open and shut case from what I've seen. Once you get corrupted, you don't really think straight. It's hard to . . ." Eric looked down at the ground, rubbing his thumb into his palm.

Pain washed over her. Not a physical pain, but the same pain she'd felt the night she lost her mother, a weight that sank into the depths of her soul. The feeling wasn't her own, but all she wanted to do was cry. "I saw people too. Coming out from the house with the green door. And a voice from a girl, blaming me for—"

Eric shook his head. "Stop."

"But you know what I'm talking about, don't you?" Leah asked.

He nodded. "Whatever happened must have sent your mind through the bond. What you saw . . . it was personal."

Leah stared at him, wanting to push for more.

Eric eyed the ground. "Jade, the first pawn I bonded to . . . she died. We were in trouble, and she let the Tree corrupt her. She saved me, but it consumed her. Consumed everything."

A wave of pain poured out from him. The guilt and sorrow reverberated in the bond, and all Leah could muster was, "I'm sorry."

He took in a breath, looking at Isaac who sat in silence. "That's why we warn you all so much about it. If you let it in, it will do everything it can to consume you and take over. Jade still held on until the end, but many others flee, becoming a danger to anyone that comes across them."

Leah shook her head, which sent the room spinning. She fixed her eyes on a point on the ceiling and ignored the nausea. "No, that's not it. Not with Joanna. Just hear us out."

Eric crossed his arms. "There's more than what was in the report, wasn't there?"

Leah nodded. She told him everything she remembered while he and Isaac took it all in. Eric remained still the entire time, without a single ping of emotion within the bond. Leah looked toward the broken window, now covered up with a plastic sheet. "I don't think Black Bishop Gunn is telling everyone the truth. That orange fur I saw . . . he pocketed it. Did he report that?"

"Not that I recall," Eric said. "But Sid? Concealing evidence? That's hard to believe. Could be classified, especially if he's working a case around it." He ran his hand through his hair and let out a sigh. "Look, I get Joanna is your friend, but we have protocols and procedures for this kind of stuff. You can't be out running around playing detective, not when we've got to get you through the trials."

Leah felt the pit in her stomach grow, a feeling that wasn't her own, a worry that ate at her core. It was a lost battle to argue with him. If she wanted to sort this out, she'd have to do it without him. "I understand. I'll try to stay out of trouble."

Eric smiled. "That's all I ask."

CHAPTER 19

THE DOCTOR VISIT

Dr. Toppen opened the door to the infirmary and walked over to Leah and Isaac. Leah noted the tight black lab coat cinched around her waist, making her look more like a woman from the Victorian era than a medical doctor. She grabbed a clipboard off a table with her leather-gloved hands and looked over the paper before smiling at Leah. "Glad to see you two are awake."

"How are they looking, doctor?" Eric blurted out.

The doctor approached Leah's side and checked her vitals. "She appears to be in stable condition. Would you mind notifying William? The administration wanted a word with the both of them when they woke."

"Sure thing, doc." Eric stood, grabbing his brown leather jacket from the back of his chair, and exited.

Dr. Toppen moved in one fluid motion, checking Isaac's vitals before claiming Eric's chair beside Leah. She took notes on the clipboard for a few moments before peering at Leah. "How are you feeling this morning, Miss Ackerman?"

Leah winced, another shot of pain boring through her head. "My head hurts. It's like everything is scrambled in there."

The doctor took notes and looked at Isaac. "And you?"

"Same. When I try to think about what happened, my head gets all fuzzy and aches."

Dr. Toppen wrote a few more notes, her lips pursed. As she wrote, she shifted in her seat, and Leah frowned. The movement was slight, but it seemed like her cinched waist made her top half move in a strange, abnormal way.

The doctor rested her warm hand on Leah's arm, grabbing her attention. "Miss Ackerman, what else? Dizziness? Problems with vision? Sensitivity to light? Numbness?"

Leah blinked a few times, looking at the doctor's face. "All the above? It gets worse when trying to remember what happened."

Dr. Toppen shifted her eyes between Leah and Isaac. "Interesting. I need to check for a concussion, if you don't mind." She pulled a small flashlight from her pocket. "Look straight ahead, please."

She leaned in close to Leah's face and held her thumb against the lower part of the eyelid to ensure she kept it open. She waved the flashlight by a few times, then switched eyes. The light intensified her headache each time it passed by. Leah covered her eyes right after that as the doctor went to Isaac's bed to test him.

Dr. Toppen grabbed the clipboard from the chair and jotted down some more notes. "You have a bond, Miss Ackerman, yes?"

Leah nodded.

"I thought so. You were in worse shape when they brought you in. Now you seem better than your friend here."

The infirmary doors opened, and six people entered the room. The dean, Nykima, and Eric followed the administrators, Reginald, Grace, and Constance in as they made a semi-circle around the two beds.

Constance looked as if she had barely slept. "What's the status, doctor?"

Dr. Toppen flipped through the chart. "Based on the symptoms, they each suffered a moderate concussion. They're experiencing memory loss and both have migraines. The medication is mitigating some of the pain. Miss Ackerman is healing rapidly, thanks to her bond. Both may need a couple more days of recovery and some more *Chesed* treatments before I'd recommend discharging them."

Dean Wright nodded. "Thank you, Dr. Toppen, for coming on such short notice."

She glanced at the clock. "You should be able to take it from here. I have other patients back at the hospital I need to tend to. I've left some medication for these two to take if the headaches get any worse. If you need anything, I'll be at St. Brendan's."

Dr. Toppen left without looking back.

Dean Wright stepped forward and paced between the two beds. His eyes locked on Leah. "Would either of you be able to tell me what you were doing out of bed last night?"

Leah peered past the administrators, grasping for any memories she could reconstruct from the night before. A pale face staring at her from the shadows, Isaac and her standing in a hallway, leaning against a stack in the library. Pain blossomed, and she winced, her mind revolting against her, searching for answers. "I couldn't sleep. Not after what happened with Joanna. I wanted to get some air. I remember leaving my bed and going for a walk."

Nykima crossed her arms. "Quite the number your little 'walk' did in the library. You knocked half the stacks down. Luckily, none of the books were damaged beyond repair."

Eric glared at Nykima. "We still don't know what

happened. Stop making them feel worse when we know weirder things have happened in that library."

William shot Nykima and Eric a glare before turning back to Leah. "Pawn O'Connor was awake when we came in earlier. He told us he was out for a late-night walk. Strange that the both of you met."

Reginald cleared his throat and shrugged. "We've all been there, honestly. What do you expect from two young teenagers who might be looking for some privacy in the library stacks?"

Leah's face flushed. She looked at Isaac, who had the same doe-eyed expression, and glanced away. "What?"

William opened his mouth to speak, but Reginald spoke first. "The details don't matter. It isn't the administrator's duty to punish this type of conduct. Clearly, neither remember what happened, and for that, unless there is concrete evidence that these two intentionally vandalized the library, then the administrators' course of action will be to increase security to ensure that there isn't anything that could pose a threat to the safety of the students. William, you ultimately decide on student affairs, but that is my recommendation."

Reginald stepped back in line, Constance and Grace nodding in agreement.

William inhaled and looked over at Leah and Isaac. "Thank you, Black Rook Platt. Regardless of the involvement in the library, you two were out of bed after the incident involving Pawn Morales. While Pawn O'Conner may not have been aware, the punishment for the two of you will be the same. Four points for insubordination. Consider yourselves lucky it wasn't worse." He paused and stared at his fingernails. "If I hear of either of you out past curfew again, the repercussions will be much worse. Do I make myself clear?"

"Sir, yes sir," Leah and Isaac said in unison.

William smiled. "Very well. That will do for now. Stay here and rest."

Constance approached the beds, passing by William before saying, "You two will receive *Chesed* treatments every five hours for the next few days until the headaches have subsided. If you remember anything else, please let us know."

William eyed Eric. "Now that you see she is well, you are excused. Please resume keeping your distance from Pawn Ackerman."

"Yes, White Knight," Eric said.

A pain formed in Leah's chest. She wanted to leap out of bed and hug Eric and tell him not to go. Every fiber of her being trusted him, and she wanted him to know that things weren't as safe here as everyone wanted her to believe.

Eric closed the space between them and hugged her. Warmth bloomed inside her, and she squeezed him back. "I'm sorry," she whispered in his ear.

"Just keep going. Prove to them why you deserve this bond." He pulled away and brushed past the administration to the door.

CHAPTER 20
AN EMPIRE IN PERIL

The Kyjak pinched the bridge of his obsidian nose and rubbed his eyes, trying to regain focus after sitting upon his throne for what felt like an eternity.

He gazed out the window, taking in the barren red sand dunes of a once vast ocean that trailed off into the horizon. Only a small garden surrounding his castle held trees that clutched onto life among the fallen relics of a once glorious empire. Crumbled canals that once supplied his people, the veins of life that were filled to the brim with vibrant turquoise energy, flowing freely from the Great Sea, now dried up and empty. His Kyem and his land lived off what little energy was left inside them, shedding it for others and for their lands.

He looked at the map strewn out across the table at the center of the throne room. The scarcity of energy had severed nearly all his alliances, and the figurines on his map surrounded his land in all directions as the endless bloodshed continued to spread ruin onto the lands.

He, the Kyjak, ruler of the lands, knew he only had a few days left to fend them off before they overtook the palace.

Fear crept in, something he'd refused to let happen since he'd taken the throne. He shook his head. "No, I am Asmodeus, Kyjak of the Rasha Empire. I will not let fear be my last thought. I—"

"My Kyjak," a voice called from the other end of the room.

Phenex, a thin female with grayish stone skin, fiery red hair, and eyes to match, bowed her head in deference. The only marquis he could trust to find what he needed to change the tide of war.

Asmodeus sat up in his chair. "You better have good news."

Phenex smiled. "We request your presence in the Seeker's Hall."

"Very well. Go on ahead, and I'll be there in a moment."

Phenex bowed once more and left the room.

Asmodeus drew in a breath and struggled out of his chair, his glassy obsidian skin cracking even more. No servant to the Kyjak should see their leader in this weak state, yet he knew every drop of energy was precious.

He grabbed onto the cane he'd leaned against the throne and hobbled to the back of the throne room to a simple wooden table.

Glass bottles filled the table, most of them empty but some containing dim glowing lights of reds and greens. He even had a blue, albeit stored in a box, far from his tempted eyes, until he absolutely needed it. He pulled a red off the table and uncorked it, letting the glowing crimson mist intermingle with the air for a moment before taking in a deep breath. The mist streamed up his nostrils and vanished within him.

Energy coursed through his veins. What was once frail had a new life. The cracks on his stone skin joined back together, his back straightened once more, the proper ruler they meant him to be. Kyjak of Rasha, ruler of the largest border to the Great Sea.

He walked out of the throne room, leaving the cane behind.

Phenex waited for him in the Seeker's Hall, along with one of seven wards. The ward kneeled, his eyes trained on the stone floor.

"What news do you bring?" Asmodeus asked.

Phenex looked at her ward and smiled. "One turn around Iya and ten around Kyet. That is how long ago you ordered my wards to seek the light. I thought they had all died until this one returned."

The ward, a muscular, squat male with dark brown marbled skin bowed, flicking his emerald eyes to Asmodeus before locking them back onto Phenex.

Phenex drew an enormous smile across her face, and the look of hope was infectious. "I didn't think you'd be right."

Asmodeus smirked, trying his best to remain calm. "The ancient legends mentioned it too much for it to only be a story. What did he find? Another red? Or was it a green?"

Phenex gestured to the ward, and he pulled a bottle out from the pack at his side. A bright violet hue, almost white, illuminated the entire room.

Had he not been a Kyjak, he would have let his jaw drop to the floor. Energy that he had not imagined he would see again, mere feet from his hands. His body felt more alive just by its presence.

Asmodeus eyed the ward. "Can you remember the way?"

The ward nodded, and Phenex grinned.

Asmodeus let a grin stretch across his face, and his eyes teared with hope. "Then we can save our lands. We can save the Kyem."

Leah opened and closed her hands, relieved to see the pink fleshy skin instead of black obsidian. *What was that? A memory from Asmodeus?*

Out the window, the deep blue sky gave way to a faint pink. Sarah, Emma, and Paige were all still fast asleep as she rubbed her face and stepped out of bed.

Several days had passed since the incident in the library, and Leah still couldn't remember any of it. She and Sarah still weren't talking, making things awkward, especially for Isaac.

As she headed to the restroom, a faint whisper caught her ear. She froze, standing in the middle of the common room. The whispers drew her attention to the entrance as the voices muffled into recognition.

"We found you. Come here."

Leah tiptoed toward the voice and the door, grabbing the handle. She pressed her ear against the door, straining to hear anything.

The whispers filled her ears, talking on top of each other in a strange indiscernible language. Her arm twinged, but she ignored the warning, taking a deep breath and opening the door.

The pale and sickly face of Joanna stared back at her, covered in small circular bruises and wrapped in a white sheet, her blue lips moving in small twitches as she muttered to herself, "Help. Please, help me."

CHAPTER 21

BREADCRUMBS

"I don't get why they won't let us see her," Leah said, looking up from her plate of eggs at Gabe and Isaac.

Gabe rested his arms on the table and looked out at the exit. "It's been over a week. They keep saying she's a flight risk."

Leah pushed her food around with her fork. "So, they still refuse to believe someone took her? Great."

Isaac cleared his throat. "Have you talked with Eric yet? Maybe they'd listen if they heard it from him."

"No," Lead said, "I haven't seen him since we were in the infirmary. I bet they have him running back-to-back missions to keep him away."

Suddenly, the cafeteria went quiet, and Gabe's face paled. He stumbled to stand, his eyes locked on the doors behind Leah.

She turned and spotted Joanna, with dark bags underneath her eyes and cheeks sunken in.

Joanna crossed the room, and everyone's eyes followed her. She reached Leah's table and turned around. "Yep, I'm alive. Sorry to disappoint all of you."

She found a spot next to Leah and sat, her back facing the rest of the cafeteria. "Hey assholes, thanks for visiting me."

Gabe reached out a hand. Joanna hesitated, but then reluctantly slipped her hand into his.

"They wouldn't let us see you," Isaac said. "We wanted to."

"How are you feeling?" Leah asked. Joanna shrugged. "Honestly, I look like trash, but I feel fine.

Leah laughed and nudged Joanna's shoulder. "You really do look terrible."

"What, emaciated isn't a good look on me?" Joanna asked as she grabbed a piece of toast off Leah's plate.

Gabe rubbed his thumb across Joanna's hand and said, "What happened?"

Joanna finished her toast and looked up at the ceiling. "It's all hazy. They said I ran away. I remember being scared that night. Like, terrified. Something here was wrong. There was a big room, I think. I remember hiding out there, but I don't know for how long. Then I was on a road, and it was like I woke up from a dream. I was only a mile away from the academy, so I hopped over the wall. Then things got blurry again until I saw Leah opening the doors to the common room."

Isaac leaned back in his seat. "So, did you? Run away?"

"I don't know. I mean, I made a mess of things. They said the girl's bathroom is still being repaired."

"Yeah, but no one blames you for that," Leah said.

Isaac shook his head. "Something still doesn't add up. You were pretty far gone with the Tree of Death when Leah stopped you. Were you using it before?"

Joanna shook her head. "Not intentionally. They told me you don't always know, but I think I would know."

"Did they say anything else?" Gabe asked.

"Just that once I was gone, they had to wait it out. I was either going to come back or not."

Leah frowned. "And what happens if you didn't?"

"Then I'd become another case for the Knights to close," Joanna said, grabbing toast from Gabe's plate and taking a bite.

Nykima's voice broke over the speakers. "Black Pawns, report to the classroom in fifteen minutes."

CHAPTER 22
A TOUGH OPPONENT

Nykima stepped into the room full of students. "Attention!"

They all snapped their feet together in one swift move.

She smiled and said, "You may sit."

The three administrators stepped into the room. Reginald wore a sleek, tailored black suit, Constance wore a woolen white dress, and Grace wore a pearlescent white pant suit and tall white heels.

Grace stepped forward from the three and addressed the class. "Pawns, consider today the official start of the trials. We have all watched you grow and learn these past few weeks, and now it's time to put that knowledge to the ultimate test. Tomorrow you will have your first trial. Some of you have a head start with the points you've accumulated, while others begin at a disadvantage. For those of you who are lagging, this is your chance to prove yourself and show us what you're made of." She rubbed her hands together and paced the room. "The first trial will test your combat skills. There's no better way to display your connection to the Tree of Life. We handpicked these matches, and you can find them in the foyer, hanging next to the scoreboard. The rules are simple: no weapons, five-minute time limit, win by subduing your opponent or knocking them out of the ring."

A murmur filled the room. But Nykima quickly silenced it, clearing her throat to gather everyone's attention. "Trials begin nine a.m. tomorrow. You have today off from class and training so you can prepare."

"Best of luck to you all," Grace said. "And remember that together we show our greatest strength."

Grace stepped back in line with the other administrators, and Nykima put her hands behind her back. "Attention!"

Everyone stood from their desks as the administration left the room.

"At ease," Nykima said. "And you are dismissed and free to go check the board for your matches."

Knights and Bishops crowded around the bulletin board, trying to catch a glimpse of the Pawn's ratings. As the Black Pawns stepped forward, their superiors cleared a path to the mobile board that stood next to the scoreboard. Others shouldered past Leah to get a better view of their names, but it didn't matter. Leah's name was above the sea of heads, listed first against an opponent she hadn't seen or heard of before: Barton Reed.

Leah stepped back and scanned the other Black Pawns in front of her, ticking off the names of the people she knew. The crowd in front of her grew as more students pooled in, and the Knights and Bishops lined the walls, noting the reactions from the Pawns.

She backed up and bumped against Gabe, turning around to see him squinting at the bulletin above her, his face pale. "They. They put me up against Joanna."

A lump formed in Leah's throat. She reached out and grabbed his arm. "I'm sorry."

He shook his head, looking away from the bulletin board. "What about you? Who are you against?"

"Barton Reed. Any clue who that is?"

Gabe blinked a few times and frowned. "That's Reginald's White Pawn. We met him when we got off the bus."

Leah stepped back and looked around. "A White Pawn? That doesn't make sense. I'm not skilled enough to fight a White Pawn."

Without another word, Leah turned from Gabe. He tried to call her back, but Leah raced up the stairs without turning back.

It had to be a mistake. Someone had typed a name wrong or something. She arrived at the dean's office and raised her hand to knock when a voice called from down the hall.

"Pawn Ackerman, is there a problem?"

Leah turned and spotted Grace walking toward her. Leah dropped her hand and took in a breath. "I think so. I want to ask about the Trial assignments."

Grace stopped in front of her and tilted her head. "And why is that?"

"Well, I'm paired with a White Pawn."

Grace raised an eyebrow. "And?"

Cold sweat formed on the back of Leah's neck. "And it has to be a mistake. I'm not ready to fight a White Pawn."

Grace paused for a moment, her eyes locked onto Leah's. "You have a bond, making you a White Pawn in everything but title. I paired you with Barton to ensure that you'd have an equal opponent. While Pawn Turner held her own against you, we realized we shouldn't pit you against your classmates in the trials."

"But White Pawns have established bonds. You all have forbidden me to even have contact with my uncle, Eric. How can I—"

Grace put up a hand. "We have already taken your concerns into account. Mystics gain points on their fighting skills, not on if they win or lose. Put up a good fight, and you'll be rewarded with a good score. While you won't have the full strength of your bond, we have granted proximity rights to Eric during your fight. It won't give you the full strength of the bond, but you will be stronger than you would otherwise. That should answer all your questions. Now, I suggest you go on to the fields for some practice before tomorrow. I have some preparations of my own to do."

Grace moved past Leah and headed down the hall into her own office, leaving Leah alone in front of the dean's office. Leah rushed back to the girl's dormitory, ignoring the blue tape as she entered the restroom. Inside, the broken sink hung, partially attached to the wall. However, someone had already replaced the cracked mirror.

Leah crossed the bathroom and locked herself in the first stall, finally alone.

How am I supposed to defeat a White Pawn? They've had months or even years with their bond, and mine is so weak.

The bathroom door creaked open, and Leah jumped, wiping at the tears in her eyes. She had gone there thinking she'd be alone.

Leah peered through the crack in the stall and immediately recognized Paige's long blond hair as she bent over the sink, her hands covering her face.

"Paige?" Leah said in a low voice, opening her stall.

Paige jumped and turned, her blue eyes swollen and red. "What? Why are you here?"

Leah stepped out of her stall. "I didn't think anyone else would be stupid enough to come in here," she said, turning to see Paige's red eyes again. "Are you okay?"

Paige wiped at her tears and glared. "Does it matter? Not like anyone cares."

Leah frowned, all desire to leave suddenly vanishing. "Well, I was hoping to have a cry session alone, and you showed up. Black Hills Outposters should stick together, right?"

Paige's frown cracked a slight smile and her gaze shifted to the sink. "They paired me against Sarah, okay? That's why I'm in here."

Leah let out a laugh. "And you're worried? You're one of the top Pawns. Why are you worried about Sarah?"

"Did you forget what she did to you? You have a bond, and she still knocked you out. If I don't win this, what are the others going to say? What will my parents say? I've given Sarah so much shit, and she's about to beat me sense-less." Paige's breathing sped up, and tears filled her eyes.

Leah put her hand on Paige's shoulder. "Slow and deep breaths. In through your nose, out through your mouth. Like that, okay?"

Paige complied, and her breathing slowed.

"Who cares what others think, anyway?" Leah asked. "You're Paige Jones, top bitch of the academy, right? I'm confident you'll put up a good fight and, win or lose, convince everyone you definitely belong here."

Paige scoffed. "You're probably just as glad as she is that she gets to fight me. Hell, you're probably jealous of her."

Leah shook her head. "Maybe a few weeks ago, but not anymore. We're all just trying to make it to the next phase, right? And I think we'd be better off encouraging each other than bringing one another down."

Paige turned on the sink and splashed water on her face before staring at her reflection. "I look like a mess."

Leah grabbed a handful of paper towels and laughed. "What do you mean? Your makeup is pretty hot now. What would you call that look? Melted chic?"

Paige rolled her eyes and cleaned herself up. "You never told me what you're doing in here."

Leah shifted her weight and looked away. "Same reason as you, I guess."

"Who are you up against?"

"Barton Reed."

Paige stopped cleaning her makeup and gaped at Leah. "Shut up! The White Pawn?!"

Leah nodded. "I don't know how I'm going to even get a hit in."

Paige shrugged. "Well, if you do what you did with Sarah, I don't see why they wouldn't give you enough points to pass you."

"But what if it's not enough? I'm already at a minus ten."

"No," Paige said. "You don't get to give me a pep talk and then put yourself down. You're making it through these trials. I need you around so I can complain about someone. Besides, you took on a demon, right? What's this little White Pawn compared to that?"

"Thanks," Leah said as she let out a laugh.

"Now get out of here. I need to reapply makeup before anyone sees. Oh, and if you tell anyone about this, you're dead."

CHAPTER 23

STUDY SESSION

After working up a sweat practicing outside with the dummies and grabbing something to eat, Leah joined Isaac in the library, which was packed with students sitting in groups with old texts open. She collapsed into the seat next to him and mumbled, "I'm so tired."

Isaac pushed a book toward her. "I'll kick your shins if you fall asleep."

She eyed the massive tome Isaac was burying his face into, filled with ancient diagrams and photocopied texts about *Hod*. Since his last battle, he had done everything he could to learn about it, the only *sefira* that seemed to work for him.

Leah flipped open the book in front of her, *Advanced Martial Arts*, and flipped through diagrams of footwork in Muay Thai, Judo, Silat, and Capoeira. Propping the book up against the pile of books Isaac had on the table, Leah pushed herself out of her seat and flowed from one form to the next. If she was going to battle a White Pawn, she needed to practice every counterattack she'd learned.

"Practicing for the ballet?" Joanna asked, slipping in behind Leah and sitting down at the table. She picked a book from Isaac's stack and started flipping through it, her eyes looking back at the entrance to the library every few minutes.

"Is everything okay?" Isaac asked after the third sigh came from Joanna's mouth.

"Yeah," she said, stretching her arms overhead. "It's these damn trials getting to my head."

"Same here," Leah said, lifting her knee up and kicking in one fluid motion.

Joanna closed her book and looked at Leah. "Do you think he's a good fighter?"

"Who?" Leah asked.

"Gabe. I mean, he's good, right?"

Isaac looked up from his book. "Is that what you're so worried about?"

"Worried? No. I just want to know what I'm up against," Joanna said.

Leah shrugged. "He was pretty strong back at the outpost. And he kicked Ricardo's ass at the duels a couple of weeks ago. But you should know better than either of us. You two are practically inseparable."

"That's what I'm worried about," Joanna said.

Isaac scoffed and buried his nose back in his book. "I don't think a little fight is going to make you two break up."

Joanna playfully punched his arm. "It's not that, dork. I'm worried he's been holding out on me. He never wants to spar, and now I think he's going to throw the whole thing."

Leah stopped practicing her moves and stared at Joanna. Between the two of them, she'd want to see Gabe win, but she couldn't say that. And Joanna was right. Gabe had been falling head over heels for Joanna. A part of Leah wondered if he would throw the trials for Joanna, and what that would mean.

"Then don't let him," Leah said.

Joanna frowned. "Don't let him? He won't listen to me if I tell him."

Leah crossed her arms. "You're smart enough in the ring to not knock him out in one blow. Sure, you'd probably pass, but where is the fun and skill in that? If he wants to blow his chances, then make him work for it."

Joanna nodded. "I like what you're thinking. If I get him riled up enough, maybe he won't hold back."

"Okay, I think I've got it." Isaac said, pushing his chair back. He pulled off one of his shoes and held it up. "If my form is just right, I should be able to do this." He threw the shoe up into the air. It arched and descended, aiming for the center of the table. Before it could hit, Isaac clapped his hands together. The shoe hung midair, hovering inches from the table. Then it wobbled and fell. Isaac dropped his hands and looked down. "Dang it. I almost had it."

"Nice one!" Leah said. "I still can't get a handle on that well. How did you do that?"

Isaac grinned, waving his hands around in different gestures. "So, you know how it feels when you do *Malchut*? Well, instead of projecting it out, I've been focusing it on my hands. When I clap, it's like the energy inverts before projecting out, if that makes sense. It's supposed to be easier if you focus on one thing and envision the inverted energy pinning it down."

Leah frowned and stared at her hands. "That almost makes sense. I think. You'd think being bonded would make figuring all this out easier."

Isaac smiled, grabbed the shoe, and tried it again with a little too much enthusiasm this time, hitting the light panel above them. The bell sounded at ten, and everyone cleared out of the library.

Joanna slammed the tome shut and pushed herself up out of the chair. "I guess we'll see if all this practice was worth it."

Leah joined her, looking back at the table one last time before starting toward the exit. "I guess so."

CHAPTER 24
THE FIRST TRIAL

The morning of the trials arrived, and Leah forced herself out of bed and stood in an empty room. Her body felt like she hadn't slept at all, but she dragged herself to get dressed and head to the cafeteria.

Everyone else seemed to be in the same mood as her, except Buck, who tried his best to entertain his crowd of melancholic friends by pretending to be a confused zombie who was intent on eating all the toast, bagels, and cereal he could find.

Leah joined her friends. Isaac had his nose in a book, and Joanna and Gabe were there, awkwardly trying not to look at each other.

Joanna punched him on the shoulder, one of her knuckles sticking out to give that extra bit of pain. "Don't go easy on me. If you do, I'm going to beat your ass, got it?"

He jumped and rubbed his shoulder. "Okay, okay. But don't come whining to me when you're knocked out of the ring."

"Good! That's what I wanna see. I want a challenge." She gave him a kiss on the cheek, and he blushed.

Leah took a bite of her omelet filled with Swiss cheese,

seared mushrooms, and peppers on top of a toasted bagel. Her gaze trailed across the cafeteria, finding Sarah laughing at something Miranda had said. At the same table, Emma and Serena rested their heads in their hands while their legs bounced underneath the table. But Paige looked the worst of them all. Her usual glow and bright blond hair seemed dim, and the bags under her eyes didn't help.

The bell rang, and nearly everyone jumped, forming a procession out to the fields. Leah sighed when the brisk air hit her, sending some clarity to her mind. Fog had rolled in overnight and stayed around, keeping the early winter sun from offering any heat.

More Bishops, Knights, and White Pawns packed the ring around the octagon this time, all dressed in crisp, thick uniforms of either all black or white, depending on their titles. Cold pins and needles shot through her body as she found a seat among the Black Pawns, her stomach now regretting what she'd had for breakfast. She wasn't ready. She couldn't do this.

Warmth washed over her, burning away the pins and needles and replacing them with a sense of peace. She felt something inside her shift, and she knew it was the *Yesod* bond. She scanned the stands and spotted Eric.

He had large bags under his eyes and his uniform was not as crisp or clean as the others. He smiled down at Leah, and offered an awkward thumbs up. Whatever sense he'd sent to her was soothing, easing the doubting voices from her mind and replacing them with a sense of serenity.

Nykima, also in a crisp white military outfit, took the center of the octagon. "Today starts the first trial. Our judges will rate your strength, technique, and strategy. I want fair fights. If I see anyone in mortal peril, the fight will end. And if you are the one to cause the mayhem, you'll not only lose your points, but we will expel you from this academy. First up, we have Black Pawn Ackerman against White Pawn Reed."

Leah heard the loud thrum of her heart in her ears. She stood, passing through the other Pawns, many of them glaring at her, knowing her only as the cheater who already had a bond and didn't belong. When she saw Gabe, he nodded and wished her good luck by mouthing the words.

When she reached the edge of the octagon, Leah slipped off her shoes before stepping onto the cold platform. Her attention turned to Barton Reed, a guy who seemed like he could be a freshman in college, with curly brown hair and a firm jawline that Leah could have found attractive if she wasn't about to fight him.

She took a deep breath and pulled her hair back into a ponytail. "Mom, if you can hear me, please give me your strength," she whispered.

Nykima looked at Leah. "Ready?" Leah nodded, and Nykima stepped back. "Begin!"

Leah didn't have time to move before Barton crossed the octagon. His fist came down like a hammer, and Leah had only seconds to raise her arms and cover her head.

The blow sent a jolt of pain down both her arms, and she staggered back. She lost her form and left a wide opening. Barton seized the opportunity and took another swing.

Time slowed, Barton's fist aiming for the side of her head.

Get it together, Leah, she thought.

The anxiety within her loosened, and she slipped her head out of the way of his fist. Leah lifted her hands quick, grabbing onto his wrist and using his own momentum to pull through his punch and launch him over her shoulder.

He landed on his back but recovered, smiling at her as he rolled to his feet.

Now, with her head in the game, she uncoiled the

energy pent up in her chest. Barton came in for a low tackle, his eyes blazing. Leah swung her leg to meet his shoulder and knock him off course, sending with it a wave of *Malchut*. He seemed to expect it, ramming his shoulder into her leg.

Energy billowed out from his shoulder, and the two energies met in a loud clash, and they were both flung back. Barton recovered quickly, making it back to his feet while Leah stumbled.

As soon as she stood, Barton leaped at her like an animal and began raining punches on her left and right. Leah dodged as many as she could, until one landed square on her left arm, sending a jolt of burning pain up into her shoulder.

A voice, *his* voice, sounded in her head. *Create some distance from him.*

Desperate, Leah listened. She built up pressure underneath her skin, unleashing an explosion of *Malchut* that slammed into Barton and sent him across the platform, knocking him down.

She gasped, knowing it was stupid to use that much *Malchut* in a fight. Knowing that she couldn't gauge how much energy Barton had left.

Barton got up. Lifting his head, he smiled and kicked the air.

Move! Asmodeus shouted.

Leah jumped out of the way as a thin wave of energy passed by her ear. Before she could think, a wave of energy collided with her shoulder, cutting through her skin.

She grabbed her now bleeding arm and shouted, "Fuck!" She glared at Barton, who pointed his right hand at the floor after sending a second cut through the air after his first.

Her left arm throbbed, and Asmodeus spoke again. *He is not holding back. Why are you?*

Barton launched at her again, closing the space in seconds as he threw a jab at her shoulder.

Leah blocked the attack. Barton then followed up with an upper kick to her ribs. The blow landed, and the air left her. With Leah doubled over, Barton aimed a kick at her head.

Leah heard a low, guttural growl come out of her. Her arm throbbed and moved on its own accord. Before Barton could land the blow, her left hand had wrapped around Barton's ankle and yanked him off his feet with surprising ease.

An energy moved through her, slower and thicker than *Malchut*. As it filled every corner of her being, all her pain vanished.

Her focus dropped to Barton, and before he could recover, she kicked him in the abdomen, sending out a sliver of *Malchut* to harden the blow.

Barton stumbled to his feet, clutching at his ribs.

Leah didn't give him a chance to recover, instead sending out slashes of energy. They left her one by one, like throwing knives.

He tried to block them, his eyes burning with the light of *Tiferet*, but they cut into his arms and tore at his white shirt, leaving behind gashes that were deeper than the cut on Leah's shoulder.

Heat built behind her eyes, and then the arena glowed with a soft light. Had it been any other time, she'd marvel at the sight. Instead, her focus remained on Barton.

He blurred in Leah's vision, and a projection of him streamed off toward her, raising his arms to send another wave of *Malchut*.

She didn't lunge out of the way, sending her own

Malchut at him, assuming the tail end of the *Malchut* would hit her as she rolled away.

Instead, as the heat behind her eyes left, the two waves of *Malchut* clashed close to Barton, pushing him back a few steps.

Leah raised an eyebrow. Had she predicted Barton's move with *Tiferet* just then?

She grinned and raised her fists. Maybe she could do this.

Barton recovered, his self-assurance replaced with wild, burning eyes. He ripped off his tattered shirt, showing off his toned muscles, covered in sweat and blood.

He ran at her like a bull, head down, ready to trample her. She sent out several slashes to keep him away, but he pushed past each one. The slashes that landed slid across his body, never piercing through the skin as he closed the distance.

Netzach, Leah thought. But the realization came too late. He pulled back his fist and thrust it right into Leah's face.

It was all over, she thought as she shut her eyes and braced herself for the pain. A part of her hoped she'd black out before any of the actual pain started.

Instead, she felt a cold, rippled breeze on her face. She opened her eyes and saw his fist sliding across her skin, and she couldn't feel a thing.

Adrenaline coursed through her veins, and she laughed. As he pulled back his fist, she sent her own, backed with *Malchut.*

As her fist collided, he didn't move, as if they were two granite statues. Both sent fists and kicks flying into each other, but neither seemed phased. Anger overtook over Leah. She was invincible, but so was he. Leah wanted to win; she had more to lose. Energy built up inside her, but she kept it at the edge of her skin, holding it back until she couldn't anymore.

She let the wave of *Malchut* loose, and Barton flew back. Shock flashed across his face—she'd moved him while he'd been using *Netzach*.

Leah didn't let him think long. She launched herself on top of him and landed blow after blow while he blocked and covered his face.

She didn't let up, letting the power fuel her. Barton dropped one of his hands and slammed it to the floor, launching them both into the air, spinning with *Malchut*.

He threw himself far enough away from Leah that he could get to his feet. He clutched at his ribs, doubled over, but was not quite ready to give up.

Leah could do this; she was sure of it. As she stepped forward, her knees buckled underneath her. Leah looked down, seeing her uniform was torn and bloodied. But more than that, pain blossomed all throughout her body. She had spent too much energy too fast, and *Netzach* had emptied. As her face collided with the platform, the world around her faded away.

CHAPTER 25

HERETIC

Red sand scratched against Asmodeus's skin as a gust of wind blew across the gardens. Plants lay withered at his feet, holding on to the last remaining drops of energy that his groundskeeper could sacrifice.

Phenex stood at the palace gates holding the vial of purple energy in her hand. "My Kyjak, are you sure this is wise?"

Asmodeus ran a hand across a flowering pod plant, the crystalline petals polishing his glass fingertips. He heard the muffled sounds outside his gate and knew the Kyjak of Baalan had finally arrived.

The Kyjak of the southern border of the barren sea was slow to respond to the call, likely demanding sacrifice from his people to prepare him from facing off with another Kyjak.

Asmodeus nodded. "We won't survive another turn without their help. They must know."

Phenex handed Asmodeus the bottle before reaching for the gate. "Please be careful. I can't imagine living long under his rule."

Asmodeus peered into the purple vial before placing his arms behind his back. "Trust me. With this, there is no challenge."

Phenex cracked open the gates. On the other side stood a massive marble statue with biceps larger than Asmodeus's body and deep cracks forming jagged edges along his arms. Asmodeus clenched his fist, his obsidian glass skin etching into his palm as he stepped through the gates.

The marbled Kyjak turned, massive white eyes locking onto Asmodeus, eyeing him up and down before letting out a boisterous laugh. "So, this is the great Kyjak of Rasha?"

A collection of small stone warriors stood behind him, joining in his laughter. Each one looked weaker than each of Asmodeus's people, likely from sacrificing their reserves to strengthen their Kyjak.

Asmodeus nodded. "That I am. And you are Bezel, Kyjak of Baalan, yes?"

Bezel stared at the crumbling palace towers and sneered. "Your Kyem are dying."

Asmodeus eyed the stone men and women behind Bezel, all withered and weak. "As are yours."

"Why have you summoned me? Have you given up on your Kyem? Are they ready to see how a true Kyjak can lead?"

Asmodeus squeezed the violet bottle behind his back. "A ward of mine has returned with news of another land. Another place filled with energy."

"Heretic," Bezel spat. "You dare make your last words filled with lies?"

"It is our salvation," Asmodeus said. "With more of us working together, we can craft a bridge to this world. We can give life back to the Kyem."

Bezel shook his head. "Your lies killed your Kyem. I won't let you kill mine too."

"We can break tradition now. We can be two Kyjak, working together for a greater good."

"Only the weak seek a truce. Your lands are mine."

Asmodeus sighed. "I'm afraid you won't win this fight."

Bezel laughed and held out his hand.

A thin, metallic child stepped forward, handing Bezel a small vial that glowed a dull green.

They stood in front of Bezel, rearing their head back and letting out a loud chittering call to the sky.

Phenex stepped forward, in front of Asmodeus, and did the same. They performed the call, signifying a battle between Kyjak, then circled the two. Both this child and Phenex kept their eyes locked as their feet swept across the sand, drawing a ring around the Kyjak.

Once the circle was complete, Asmodeus said, "Baalan rules? One round. Winner gains the lands as their rightful Kyjak."

Bezel cracked his knuckles. "You've been studying, I see." He crossed his arms. "Accepted. I can't wait to taste every drop of Rasha." He uncorked his bottle and breathed in the green smoke.

The cracks in his flesh smoothed over, while brutish spikes jutted out from his biceps.

Asmodeus uncorked the purple bottle. "Ancestors, watch over me," he muttered as he breathed it in.

An energy unlike anything he'd tasted before surged through him. His obsidian flesh glowed a deep cherry red, and every crack smoothed over until he stood like molten glass.

Bezel stared wide-eyed at the transformation. "What is this? How?"

"The texts are true. The other world exists."

"Heretic!" Bezel shouted. He lunged forward, a massive fist aimed at Asmodeus's head.

Asmodeus lifted a hand, catching Bezel's fist. The force of the blow rippled through Asmodeus's body like water. The ripples grew bigger, energy feeding into the waves until a massive wave rolled up his arm and crushed Bezel's hand.

Bezel backed away, holding onto the stony stump remaining, his eyes wide in shock.

"Admit defeat now, or I will take more than your hand." Asmodeus said.

Bezel planted a knee on the ground, his head low. "I concede. You have my people, Kyjak of Rashabaalan."

CHAPTER 26
SCORES

Isaac's voice filled Leah's ears. "Wait, she's waking up."

"We've been here for over an hour; she's not waking up."

"There, she did it again. Her eyes. See? They're fluttering."

The voices were like soft echoes in her head, but they tugged on her, pulling her away from her empire. She couldn't leave her Kyem. They needed her; they needed energy to live, otherwise they would all—

"Leah? You there?" Isaac asked.

She felt his breath on her skin and sensed his hand on her arm.

Leah slipped back into her body. Her bones ached, and pain shot up her shoulder. Her eyes fluttered open, and she groaned. "Did a bus run me over?"

"Ah! See!" Isaac said. "Told you she was awake."

Leah's eyes adjusted to the whites and yellows of the infirmary. To her left, she saw the bag of saline hanging with a tube descending past her vision.

Sarah came into view, sliding up beside her, her eyes

wide. Her face had several bruises, along with a cut just beneath her eye.

Leah spotted Isaac's arm in a cast. "What happened to you two?"

She tried to prop herself up on her elbows, but Isaac rested a hand on her shoulder. "Take it easy."

Memories flooded back. The fight, the energy that coursed through her, how she was seconds from victory. Then, nothing.

She looked back at Sarah, anger bubbling up inside her from the weeks of silent treatment. "What are you doing here?"

Sarah moved her jaw, but nothing came out.

Isaac jumped in. "We've both been here since the trial ended."

Leah jolted up, wincing at the pain that blossomed in her ribs and lower back. "How long was I out?"

Isaac and Sarah stared at each other, then Sarah spoke. "A couple of hours. It's almost time for dinner."

Isaac tried pushing Leah back down, but after the news, she shook him off, sitting up and ignoring the pain in her ribs.

"But what about the fight? Did they hand out the scores? What's going to—"

"No, they haven't said anything yet," Isaac said. "When the duels ended, the administration said they would analyze the results and left. You should have seen Sarah. She was furious."

Leah felt a pain in her stomach, and for once she couldn't tell if it was her pain or someone else's she felt. "So, I lost then? My bond . . . what's gonna happen if they sever my bond?"

Sarah cleared her throat. "You did great. Your fight was amazing. You lost, but you're still gonna get points. I'm sure of it. When that doctor checked you out on the platform, she said you pushed yourself too far, but the administration seemed pleased."

Leah stared at Sarah. She hadn't said a single word in weeks. And now, this? "Thanks, I guess. But why are you here? It's not like we're friends."

Tears formed in Sarah's eyes, and she looked toward the window. "I'm sorry. I was too focused on the wrong thing, and I didn't see what they were going to do. Putting you up against a White Pawn with no warning? It's not fair, but you still put up a hell of a fight!"

Leah let out a slight smile. "Glad I wasn't the only one who thought it wasn't fair."

Sarah met Leah's eyes. "So, can we be friends again? Please?"

Leah considered for only a second, the past few weeks dissolving away. She couldn't imagine it any other way. "Friends."

Isaac clapped his hands together and leaped up, racing to the other side of the bed and wrapping his arms around Sarah and Leah.

"It's about time!"

Sarah swatted at his arm. "Ugh, no. Stop!"

Leah laughed, and when Isaac pulled back, she said, "I almost had him, though. Almost."

Sarah smirked and gestured to Isaac. "You should have seen what this one did to poor Haru Ki."

"What happened?" Leah asked, picturing the quiet kid who was the only one who beat Miranda in sparring.

Isaac nodded and looked down. "It was nothing special, though."

"Nothing special?" Sarah punched his arm. "Ok, well, remind me never to piss you off if that was nothing."

Leah scooted up the bed and rested her back on the wall behind her. "Well, now I have to know."

Isaac took in a deep breath. "It started off rough. Haru is good at overwhelming you with punches, so he got the upper hand quick. I tried using *Hod,* but it wasn't working. He had me on the floor and was trying to pin me down when I tried it one more time. Next thing I know, Haru let me go and fell backward, holding his throat. His face turned beet-red."

Sarah leaned forward. "Had to get the White Pawns involved. This little devil used *Hod* on his lungs and wouldn't let him go. Nearly asphyxiated him. It took four of them to get Isaac to stop. The admins seemed pleased, though, once Haru could breathe again."

Leah swatted Isaac's arm. "Shut up!"

"I got carried away, I guess. I don't know. Still felt wrong to do it."

Sarah shrugged. "Yeah, but at least you know you're making it to the next round."

Leah caught the smirk on Isaac's face before turning to Sarah. "And you? How did you do?"

Sarah stretched her arms overhead, moving side to side while holding back a grin. "Well, I think I did all right."

Isaac scoffed and shook his head. "All right? You knocked Paige out in seconds."

"Oh," Leah said, a mix of emotions bubbling up.

Sarah rested her hands behind her head. "Well, I had to practice like they'd put me up against you again. But it was Paige, and she wasn't prepared. Felt good to give her a taste of her own medicine."

Leah shifted, ignoring the pain as the memory of Paige sobbing in the bathroom surfaced in her mind. It was then that she caught a glimpse past her curtain dividers and saw the others in the infirmary, realizing it was packed with students in beds.

Omer Sediki sat next to a sleeping Gabe, whose head was wrapped in a bloody bandage. There were other Pawns whom Leah had only seen in passing, but she recognized Brody, fast asleep, in the bed next to the window.

"Leah?" Sarah asked.

Leah shook her head. "Sorry, still a bit out of it. That's awesome, Sarah. I'm thrilled for you." She peered back out toward the others in the infirmary and added, "This trial really took a toll, didn't it?"

Isaac nodded. "Yeah, they said I might have cracked my wrist, but they wrapped it and told me to go on my way. They only admitted those with serious injuries."

"How were the rest of the trials?"

Sarah gazed at the ceiling. "Well, Emma won her match against Olivia."

"Olivia? Who?"

"Olivia Smith. She's the quiet dark blond girl with pimples. She hangs out with Miranda sometimes."

Leah strained to remember but failed to put a face to the name.

Sarah said, "Doesn't matter. Emma won. Serena and Ricardo both did well. Their fight was the only one that lasted the entire time limit, so they tied. Oh, and . . ." She nodded to the bed opposite them and whispered, "Buck lost his fight against Miranda. He didn't go down without a fight, though."

Leah spotted Buck, barely able to recognize him. His face was swollen and bruised, and he had a cast on his leg. Serena sat next to him, her head down as she held his hand.

"Oh, wow," Leah said.

"Serena's been in here as long as we have, watching over him," Isaac whispered. "It was a rough fight."

"Yeah, Harry was here too, with Serena, before you woke up," Sarah said. "His fight didn't go so well either, but at least he didn't end up in a bed."

Leah remembered he was up against Deepak, the short, muscular guy with a slight Indian accent and glasses. He was definitely a threat, nearly winning all his sparring matches. "I take it Deepak won?"

Sarah nodded. "Oh yeah! Blew him out of the octagon with three *Malchut* pushes. He was a little banged up, but I think he was more worried about what that meant for his score."

Leah jumped when she realized she hadn't even asked about her other friends. "What about Gabe and Joanna? What happened there?"

Sarah half smiled. "Gabe didn't stand a chance. Joanna must have been holding back in sparring, because that girl was practically invincible in the fight. Gabe tried, but she took him down fairly quickly."

Leah gasped. "No way! Is he okay?"

"He used *Netzach* for most of the fight," Isaac said. "Seemed good at it too. I bet if anyone else was against her, they'd have ended up here."

The infirmary door swung open, and Dr. Toppen stepped into the room. She looked right at Leah, and her eyes widened. She crossed the room in an instant and stooped at the foot of Leah's bed, eyeing her chart.

"We meet again. How are the headaches? Any new symptoms?"

"No more headaches. My ribs hurt, though."

Dr. Toppen squeezed past Isaac, pressing up against him. Isaac flushed red, and he stepped away to the foot of the bed.

Sarah stifled a laugh, focusing on the floor at her feet.

Dr. Toppen pressed a hand on Leah's side. Leah winced

but kept her mouth shut. Dr. Toppen adjusted her long black coat and said, "Cracked ribs, but they are healing nicely. You Mystics are fine specimens of health. You always bounce back. Good thing, too. With your recent head trauma, we were just discussing transporting you to my hospital this evening if we didn't see any improvement, but now I'd say you should be ready for discharge before dinner."

"Yeah, good thing, I guess," Leah said, eyeing her friends.

CHAPTER 27

NIGHTMARE

Leah blinked a few times, the window in her dorm room coming into focus. Her pain and soreness from the first trial washed away, and she had sat up on her bed, staring out at the dark, starry night.

She looked around and saw the empty beds. *Where had everyone else gone?* She racked her brain to remember, but no recent memories came to mind.

Then she felt it—a massive vibration in the ground followed by a faint shrill at the edge of her hearing. She stood up and pressed her ear to the door. The scream came again, louder this time, and Leah's heart thumped in her chest.

She opened the door and peered out into the common room. Moonlight poured in, bouncing off the old furniture. All the other doors to the dorm rooms were closed, and the room was empty.

Leah stepped out into the common room, and the light behind her shifted, darkening with every step. Flashes of brilliant white light illuminated the room, followed by loud booms of thunder that shook the ground. Rain sounded overhead, but the scream tore through it all, piercing Leah's eardrums.

She raced to the common room door and out to the lobby, peering down the steps. Her eyes locked on to a pair of legs halfway out the enormous front doors, flailing as something dragged them out.

Her heart pounded in her chest as she raced down the stairs. A pale face caught the corner of her eye, staring out at her as she passed by the hallway to the library, watching her as she raced out the door. She kept running, passing through the doors and out into the rain, across the gravel road and near the tree line. A massive figure, shrouded in shadows, dragged someone through the muddy grass while they screamed and kicked. Leah raced to them, feeling the mud on her bare feet and the rain against her face.

No matter how fast she ran, she couldn't reach them. It was as if the space between them stretched and contorted, and she was always too far away. She glimpsed the perfect blond hair wrapped around in the fist of her captor. The shadowed figure pulled again, and Leah saw Paige's terrified face.

Paige screamed again, her voice sounding more and more hoarse as she clawed at something wrapped around her neck. Leah made out a thick tendril, almost like the one that had wrapped around Joanna's neck, wrapped tightly around Paige's neck.

Leah shouted and screamed back, but neither seemed to notice her.

She raced forward, only to have the space between them stretch and grow. Her eyes tried focusing on the person dragging Paige, but it was as if her eyes slipped off their face and as if the shadowed cloud obscured whoever was behind it.

A bright white light came out of her fist as she thrust *Malchut* forward. The energy connected with the shadowy figure, and they stumbled forward. The tendril around Paige's neck loosened, and Leah spotted a set of strange suction cups marking circular bruises around Paige's neck. Leah looked down at her hand, faded now as if it were vanishing into the dark. The energy behind that push should have been enough to throw them like a rag doll.

The figure paused, looking around into the dark. Paige's eyes glowed and locked on Leah.

"Help! Help me!" Paige shrieked.

The tendril squeezed Paige's throat, and the shadow figure gripped her hair, dragging her again toward the tree line.

Leah reached forward, stumbling to get a grip on Paige, but she grabbed at the air as they vanished into the shadows of the thick forest.

She got to her feet and raced after them, the branches scratching against her face as Leah ran through the dark.

Leah froze, peering out into the dark woods. Eyes were on her, somewhere in the dark. Paige continued screaming ahead of her, but the fear inside Leah grew stronger as she looked left and right, searching.

Eyes shone in the dark, the same set of eyes that picked at the edge of her memory. A cluster of hazy memories stitched together.

Those eyes, staring back at her in the library.

A flash of light from the storm above shone through the treetops and onto a coat of orange fur, a creature that stood on two legs, taller than her, eyes locked onto hers.

Her feet took command, and she ran, racing after Paige and away from that thing that stood in the dark.

She slipped on mud, her feet stumbling and cutting into broken branches while her arms pushed her away from trees. She pushed through the pain, her mind focused on saving Paige.

The padding of feet sounded behind her, but she didn't look back. If that thing was going to get her, she suspected it would have done it already.

Leah broke free from the trees, and her knees landed on solid pavement. She looked down at her legs, shocked that there wasn't any pain.

She glanced up, and the world shifted and melted in front of her. The forest behind her vanished, replaced with large, old buildings. In front of her, a massive sign stating: Portside Warehouses.

The smell of the ocean filled her nostrils, and when she blinked, her surroundings changed again to an entrance with the number 27 plated above the massive open door.

Paige's scream echoed from the shadows within. Leah squinted and glimpsed Paige's blond hair before large tendrils, like massive serpents, wrapped tight around her.

Leah let out a gasp, torn from her sleep by some unknown force. Tears streamed from the corners of her eyes as the morning light beamed in from under the door.

She rubbed away the sleep, wincing as her hands rubbed at the raw skin on her cheeks. She pulled her covers off and stepped out of bed, stumbling from the shock of pain. Fresh, tiny cuts covered her feet, splitting open and dribbling blood onto the wooden floorboards.

Her face paled, and cold sweat formed on her brow. She turned, finding both Sarah and Emma still asleep in their beds. Paige's bed, however, was empty, and her covers were neatly folded.

She raced over to Paige's bed. There was nothing. No blood or hint that someone had taken her. A glint out the window caught her eye, and when she leaned forward and peered out, she saw a red pickup pulling up the driveway.

A tall figure in an oversized black coat with a hood stepped out, scraping mud off his boots before limping toward the academy. As if some strange sense overcame them, the figure paused and looked up at the academy, right toward Leah.

She jumped back before she could see their face, ramming her elbow into Paige's bedpost.

"Leah?" Emma called, her eyes half-open as she yawned. "Is something wrong?"

Leah caught her breath, rubbing at her elbow as her heart slowed down. "It's Paige; she's not in her bed."

Sarah turned over and wrapped a pillow around her head. "She probably went to get breakfast. Why don't you go see?"

Leah shook her head. "No. Something's wrong. She's gone. I—"

Sarah flopped over on her bed, a glare on her face turning into concern when her eyes met Leah's.

Leah stood and pulled on a jacket over her pajamas. "Someone just came into the academy. I need to see who it is." She turned and left without another word.

Her hopes faded as she walked down the stairs and arrived at an almost empty foyer, except for a group of five students gathered in front of the scoreboard.

Leah scanned the floor, trying to find a hint of the muddy footprints or anything that could lead her to the cloaked figure.

"They cut that many already?" one of the five students said.

"Yeah, they came in and just dragged him out last night while we were asleep."

"That's fucked up."

Leah turned on her heel, joining the others and looked at the scoreboard. A chill ran down her back when she saw that almost half of the nearly fifty names had been crossed out.

CHAPTER 28
TRIAL RESULTS

One girl huddled around the scoreboard glared at Leah, her lip piercing glinting in the light as she spoke. "Why do you get to stay here? You lost."

A lanky boy with a sad attempt at a beard turned and crossed his arms. "She's got her bond already. She's just here to knock everyone else out of the running."

The other Pawns joined in, nodding and glaring.

Leah stepped back, clenching her jaw, her hands curling into fists. "I'm just looking for Paige. Have any of you seen her?"

"Brittany would still be here if it wasn't for you," the girl with the lip piercing said. "You and the rest of your Black Hills Squares shouldn't even be here."

The serpent in her chest wriggled free, building pressure against her skin as anger boiled up inside her. She didn't come down here to be belittled. She came to look for Paige.

A voice spoke behind her, cutting Leah off from what she was about to say. "Drop it, Karen. She belongs here just as much as you do, so stop being a bitch."

Karen's face turned red. "No one asked for your opinion."

Leah looked over her shoulder and saw Miranda coming down the stairs. Her hands were in her pockets, and she stood tall as she came to a stop at Leah's side.

Miranda shrugged. "No, but you're getting it anyway. If they crossed someone off, then they weren't good enough. Plain and simple. Some of your friends should have tried harder. And if you can't keep up, maybe you should join them."

Karen's eyebrow twitched. "Seriously? And you don't care that one of us is cheating?"

"Leah was up against a White Pawn. She fought well and you know it. You got paired with Brody, who has the IQ of a turtle. You had the easiest fight of anyone."

Other Pawns headed down the stairs, crowding in to get a look at the scoreboard.

Sarah pushed past others on the stairs and stepped up beside Leah. "Is there a problem?" She asked.

"No," Leah said. "I'm just looking for Paige."

Karen rolled her eyes. "Whatever. Paige is gone with the rest of them." She turned and headed into the cafeteria, followed by the other four who'd been around the scoreboard.

Leah turned and faced Miranda. "Thanks."

"She's just wants someone to blame," Miranda shrugged, then turned to look over at Sarah, giving her a slight smile before heading toward the cafeteria.

"What was that about?" Sarah asked.

Leah stepped up to the scoreboard, a crowd of Pawns closing in on her. "They took some of us last night, when we were sleeping."

"Oh, shit."

Leah found the Black Hills Outpost members at the bottom of the list and scanned the names.

Leah Ackerman - 71
~~Buck Bacchus~~ - 67
Serena Bacchus - 82
~~Harry Douglas~~ - 42
Paige Jones - 75
Emma Mitchell - 81
Isaac O'Connor - 79
Gabe Tate - 81
Sarah Turner - 85

Leah's stomach twisted at the sight of both Harry's and Buck's names crossed off. They were gone. Removed from the academy, just like that. She fought back tears as she realized she wouldn't hear their jokes again or laugh at Harry trying to make his moves on Emma. *Where are they now?*

She frowned at the list of names, noting that Paige's name was still intact. "Paige's name isn't crossed off, but she's gone."

Isaac approached Sarah and Leah with a newfound spring in his step. "What's everyone looking at?" he asked before his eyes traced over the board. "Oh. Wow!"

"Buck and Harry? Really?" Sarah said, her shoulders drooping. "They're both just gone?"

"No!" someone shrieked behind them.

They turned and found Emma holding Serena, who had tears streaming down her face. "Where did they take him?"

The collective voices grew louder, and White Pawns and Knights poured out from the halls and cafeteria.

A loud whistle tore through the chants, and Nykima, flanked by Grace and Reginald, stood at the top of the stairs. She waited for their voices to die down, then said, "We told you this would happen. So why are you acting like a bunch of children?"

Nearly all the Pawns dropped their gaze, eyes trained on the floor, except Serena. With tears still flowing down her face, she shouted, "You took my brother! I didn't even get to say goodbye. Where is he? Where's Buck?"

Before the other Pawns could chime in with their grievances, Nykima spoke as she descended the stairs. "Whoever does not meet the standards of the Maimonides Academy will be removed immediately and their name crossed out. That was clear to all of you on day one. Their journey with the Infinity Board leads down a different path from yours, and we will not impede either process."

"But what about Paige?" Leah asked. "Her name isn't crossed out."

Nykima frowned and looked at the scoreboard for a second before straightening her stance and looking back out at the Pawns. "You have today and tomorrow off from lessons to recover. There will be no more uproar over this, understood? The next person to raise their voice at me will be one step closer to following the others who we removed last night."

Her eyes fell on Leah, then Serena who looked like she was about to say something, shout something at Nykima, but then she lowered her head, her shoulders slumping.

"Very well. I think that's enough review of the scores this morning. How about you all head into the cafeteria and get some food in you before you try to start another revolt?" Nykima said.

Leah prodded at her apple cinnamon oatmeal from a corner table. Everyone remained quiet, whispering to each other at the tables and casting glances over at Nykima and the Administration.

"Are those scratches?" Isaac asked, looking at Leah's face.

Sarah squinted. "Yeah, did you get into a fight with a hedgehog?"

Leah felt at her face, the memory of running through that forest surfacing in her mind. "I had a dream last night."

As she told them, recounting the events through the woods and to the warehouse, both Sarah and Isaac stared at her, wide-eyed.

"So, this was like one of those dreams you had back in the outpost?" Sarah asked.

Leah nodded. "Felt exactly the same."

Isaac frowned. "What about the driver? Did you see who it was?"

"I didn't get a good look. They looked up toward me in the window, but I hid. They had a limp, though, and something tells me they're connected to the dreams, especially with the mud."

Sarah rubbed her eyes. "But what about the students they took last night? I mean, you heard Nykima. It's all part of the rules, right? Are you sure someone kidnapped Paige? She lost."

"They didn't cross her name off the list. She had enough points to make it, so I think whoever took her used the ousted being taken as cover."

"We should tell the administration," Isaac said. "They need to know about your dreams."

Leah shook her head. "They'll just call it another escape. You know how they treated Joanna's disappearance. Even now, they act like it was nothing. If I say anything now, then the person who took Paige will be one step ahead of us. Do you want one of us to be next?"

Sarah popped the last bit of her bagel, caked with an onion cream cheese, into her mouth before speaking. "She's got a point. If we don't know who it is, then we'd be at risk of them taking one of us."

They dumped their trays, and Leah whispered as they left the cafeteria, "The admins have to know about Paige by now. We need to find out who was in that truck."

Leah froze as they stepped into the main lobby.

Sarah stopped and turned. "What is it?"

Leah stared out the front doors, through the crack in the door letting in the cool early winter air. In her field of view was the red truck, and inside, in an oversized black coat, sat Black Bishop Sid Gunn.

CHAPTER 29

AN UNEXPECTED ALLY

"And you're sure that was the same truck?" Isaac asked as he sat on the sofa in the girls' common room.

Leah peeled back a banana and took a bite. "Yeah, I'm positive."

"What if he borrowed it? I mean, are you sure it's his truck?" Sarah asked.

Leah paused. "Fine. Maybe it isn't his truck, but it was the same coat. And he was outside when Joanna went missing. For all I know, Joanna was in Sid's truck when he came running back in. Everything just points to Sid."

"You said someone dragged Paige into the woods. When was she in the truck?" Isaac asked.

"I thought that too. But the dream sort of jumped ahead. Like there was a piece missing between the woods and the warehouse. It's miles to the ocean. No way they made that on foot."

Isaac nodded. "But you never saw the red truck in your dream?"

"I saw it when I woke up. No one else drove in or—"

"Yet, it wasn't in the dream," Isaac interrupted.

Leah threw up her hands. "Why are you being so critical? It fits together. We need to do something. We're wasting time."

Sarah leaned in and waved her hands. "Okay, okay, time out. No need to end up in another fight over this. If we had more evidence, then maybe the admins would listen to us. But they won't believe a bunch of Pawns over a Bishop, especially if we just come to them with a dream and a hunch." Sarah caught Leah's glare. "However, I'm not saying that I don't believe you. If you believe it, then we just need to find more evidence."

"Same here. I believe you," Isaac added.

Sarah leaned back in her chair and crossed her arms. "We just need something to show the admins it's true. If we're going to find out who is responsible for Paige's disappearance, we need to—"

A voice sounded behind Sarah. "And who is that? Who do you think did it?"

All three of them turned, spotting Emma Mitchell coming out of the bathroom. Her eyes were red and puffy, like she had been in there crying for hours.

Isaac shook his head. "It's nothing."

Emma looked down at the floor. "No one will talk to me. Serena has said nothing since this morning. And Paige? Her name isn't crossed off, you know? When I told Nykima, she just told me she 'was aware' and sent me on my way. If you know something, please tell me."

Sarah let out a small laugh. "Why would we tell you anything?"

Emma glared at Sarah. "Because I'm her friend. What would you do if one of your friends here went missing and I knew something? They aren't looking for her. And I bet they'll say the same thing they did with Joanna, that she couldn't take it and escaped. But I know she didn't run. That's not Paige."

Leah sighed. "You're right. Take a seat. We've got to get you up to speed before the others come back."

Emma sat down next to Isaac. "What others? Joanna and Gabe?"

Sarah laughed. "They're off making out in some dark corner somewhere. No, we came up here to talk before everyone else comes up."

Isaac looked at Leah. "Are you sure you want to do this? No offense, Emma, but the more people that know, the more likely the person we're after is going to find out."

"She should know," Leah said. "Like she said, if one of you were missing, I wouldn't stop until she told me everything."

The dream spilled from Leah, followed by the truck, and Emma took in everything. Her face was unreadable, even as Leah revealed whom she thought did it.

When Leah finished, Emma sat for a long moment before speaking. "After what happened at the outpost, I'm willing to believe you. So, if your lead is Bishop Gunn, then we start there. How can I help?"

Sarah rubbed her hands together. "Alright, Isaac, you're the one saying we need hard evidence. How do we get that?"

His face flushed, and he looked to the ground, shifting his eyes back and forth. "If we got into his room, we could look for something in there."

Emma chewed on her lip. "The Knights' and Bishops' sleeping quarters are off limits, so any suggestions on how to get in?"

"We could break the door," Sarah said.

Leah shook her head. "You'd be too loud. Besides, we don't even know which room is his."

Emma perked up. "2C."

Everyone stared at her.

She shrugged. "I was in the library, and he had a big stack of books he was trying to check out. I offered to help."

Sarah scoffed. "That's oddly nice of you."

Emma rolled her eyes. "We're supposed to bond with one of them, you know? Paige said we need to step up if we were going to get selected."

Isaac shook his head. "Focus. How do we ensure he won't be in his room?"

After a few seconds of silence, Leah took in a breath. "We sneak in during the day."

Sarah took her eyes off Emma. "Yeah, most of them will be out on some mission anyway, but the ones still here seem to always be outside in the fields."

"If one of us monitors him, one of us can be a lookout, and then we can get into the room," Isaac said.

Emma nodded. "I'm all for it, but breaking the door down is a terrible plan. What are you going to do if he locked the door?"

Isaac dropped his head and smiled. "Well, there isn't a door I've met that I can't pick."

All three girls looked at him, their eyes wide.

"What?" Isaac spoke. "I picked up a few things before life at the outpost."

Sarah continued to eye Isaac with wide eyes as she said, "Ok, so that puts Isaac inside the building. We need one of us with Sid, another on the outside to keep the ones inside posted if anyone comes, one in the hall, and then one in the room."

"Tomorrow is the last day without training," Leah said. "So, we should do it then, or else we'll be back on schedule and have no time. Emma, you helped with his books . . . any chance you remember some titles? You could use that to distract him while the three of us go to his room."

Emma nodded. "I think I can do that."

"Good," Leah said, looking at Sarah. "Then you keep watch outside his door while Isaac and I go in.

"You should let me go in with Isaac," Sarah said.

"No," Leah said. "If things go wrong, I'll take the blame. Okay?"

Sarah drew in a breath, ready to protest, but Leah shot her a glance. She let out a breath. "Okay."

Leah heard the footsteps of the others coming back from lunch. She turned to her friends. "Tomorrow we'll have something concrete enough to show the admins. Something that will help get Paige back."

CHAPTER 30
BISHOP'S QUARTERS

During lunch the next day, Leah barely touched her food. They had run through the plan three times now. Despite that, she couldn't shake the feeling that something would go wrong.

Leah eyed Sid, who had limped into the cafeteria and sat with a handful of others who Leah had seen working around the grounds. He stood and headed to the trash can alone, clearing his tray and stacking it with the other dirty ones.

Emma shot a glance Leah's way, sitting at her usual table to keep appearances.

Leah caught her eye and nodded.

It was time.

Leah stood, followed by Sarah and Isaac.

"Where are you headed off to?" Joanna asked.

"Physical therapy," Leah said, clutching at her side. "These two agreed to help me with a couple of things the doctor wanted me to do."

"Need us to come with?" Gabe asked, moving closer to Joanna.

Leah shook her head. "No, we'll catch up with you two later."

Without another word, the three turned, clearing their trays.

Leah turned and saw Emma speeding up to catch Sid as he left the cafeteria. "Bishop Gunn! I noticed the other day that you had a book on the medical applications of *Hod*, and I had some questions if you were free."

Sid paused, looking down at Emma and smiling. "I could talk your ear off, but yeah, I have some time. How about we go to the library, and I grab a few books? I'm sure you'd be . . ." Sid led her out of the cafeteria and beyond earshot of the other three.

"So, are we ready to do this, or what?" Sarah asked.

The three of them stepped outside, crossing the grounds and reaching the building that housed the Knights and Bishops. The same stonework and columns as the rest of the campus supported this building, but they were muted compared to the main academy building, no stained glass or fancy stairs leading up to a main entrance. Instead, the path from the academy led to a small set of glass doors.

Sarah paused in front of the doors and said, "I'll find a spot somewhere around here. If Sid comes back, I'll race up and grab you."

"Sounds good," Leah said. She gestured to Isaac, and they entered the lobby.

It was simple, showcasing white walls and white and black tiled floors with black couches and a small elevator. They found a side door to the stairs and listened for any sign of someone coming down.

After a few moments of silence, they crept up the stairs to the second floor and down the hall until they came to the room with the brass number 2C screwed to the door.

Isaac pulled the paper clips from his pocket, fashioned

into what he called a rake pick and a tension wrench. Leah didn't have a clue what he was talking about, but he seemed certain that they'd do the job.

As he wriggled the lock, Leah looked up and down the hall, her heart beating faster the longer this took.

The door to Sid's room clicked, and Isaac opened the door slowly.

A creak sounded at the end of the hall, and Leah shoved Isaac into the room. He turned and hissed, "Hey, what the—"

Leah pressed a finger to her lips and closed the door behind her. She waited a second, and footsteps sounded past the door, followed by the click of the stairwell door closing. Leah dropped her shoulders. "Let's do this quick."

Her focus shifted to the room, a space larger than her dorm, with both a kitchenette and a private bathroom.

Almost everything was tidy, with crisp, folded towels stacked on shelves and clean covers pressed smoothly over the bed. Sid had even lined his pillows perfectly atop his bed and organized his shoes by formality.

Leah and Isaac set their eyes on the desk, made of a rich, dark wood. It was the only place in the entire room that lacked any sense of order, with books and papers in haphazard stacks on and around the desk.

Leah pointed toward his bed. "You check his closets and cupboards for anything. I'll start here."

She flipped through a handful of papers, including sketches of bats with oversized ears and one that seemed like a terrible comic version of a vampire. Underneath those was a book, old and tattered. She took her time, carefully opening the cover and finding the title page. She read it out loud. *"Vampiric Resurgence of the 17th Century: The Return of Chimeric Tradition."*

She looked at Isaac. "So, vampires now?"

Isaac shrugged. "Supposedly, they're all dead. Hunted to extinction."

Leah set the book down and picked up another, *The Chimeric Tradition: Notes, Journals, Essays Collected from Chimera Practitioners*. As she flipped through the pages, she realized this book contained the actual notes and essays, the different pages all bound by glue or sewn in.

She paused on a sketch, a diagram that resembled dissection images in her biology books back in high school. This thing was different, though. A bulky outline of a man, drawn with fur, sharp teeth, pointed ears, and a reshaped nose into something that resembled a canine. The artist had left the eyes of this creature open, a bright yellow that peered into Leah's, sparking a memory locked away.

Everything in Leah's vision faded to black. The memory unfurled around her, flashes of lightning among tall book-shelves. The memory shifted, and she saw Isaac crouching a few stacks away, waving for her to come along. His eyes traced behind Leah's, widening. She turned, and the eyes that were once peering through the books were now towering above her, the heaving orange-furred creature looking down at her, its sharp teeth bared as it let out a low growl.

Leah jumped back, shielding herself from the monster, and the memory shattered, transporting her back into the sun lit room.

She looked down at the diagram, the memory of the creature staring back at her. "I know what attacked us that night we can't remember. It's here, a chimera."

"No. That's not possible. They're extinct. It would have to be a shifter if it was anything."

"Unless shifters can look like nine-foot-tall wolf men, then it was a chimera."

Leah flipped through the pages, diagrams with flecks of brown stains strewn across them. Diagrams that showed bodies torn apart, how to stitch together flesh, tentacled creatures, rituals and symbols that meld souls and bodies together. The more pages she turned, the more stained and darker they became.

She shut the book; her stomach couldn't take in any more diagrams of viscera.

Isaac banged his head on the cupboard under the sink, groaning as he held something up for Leah to see. "This is weird. Check it out."

Orange fur lined the plastic bag he held in his hand. He walked over to Leah, and she inspected it closer. They were bristly and long.

"What do you think it's from?" Isaac asked, holding the bag close to his face. "A horse maybe?"

"I've seen these before, on the broken window in the infirmary, the night Joanna disappeared. I bet it's one of these. A chimera."

"But it can't—"

A loud crack sounded from outside the window, cutting Isaac off. They rushed over to see Sarah in front of the remains of a practice dummy.

"What the hell? She's supposed to be guarding the door. What if Sid . . ."

Isaac shook his head and pointed. "No, look."

Sid was walking along the sidewalk, back toward the dorms. Sarah shot a glance up at the windows, catching Leah's eye and nodding toward Sid.

Isaac turned from the window and raced back to the sink. "We need to go."

Leah returned to the desk, lifting papers and books. "No, there has to be more. Something we can use."

"We don't have time." Isaac opened the cupboard and reached back inside with the bag.

"No, wait, what are you doing? We could use that."

"Hair that you claim was on a window, but no one else saw. It won't work, trust me. And it'll tip Sid off that someone was in his room."

Dammit, she thought. Leah slammed the book on the table and followed Isaac to the door, locking it behind them. They pushed open the door to the stairwell as the door to the first floor opened.

Sid's voice carried up the stairs. "You're not listening. I need to get back there."

Leah faced Isaac and pressed him up against the wall. They didn't have anywhere else to go, nowhere they could hide down the hall on the second floor.

Sid's footsteps echoed on the stairs as he continued talking. "I'm doing this with or without your help."

They needed to hide. Needed for Sid to walk right past them as if they weren't there. Instinct kicked in, and Leah wrapped her arms around Isaac's. "Just stay still," she whispered in his ear. Cold spread across her skin, like submerging herself inside an icy lake. Sounds muffled, and the dark of the stairwell brightened to a sickly yellow. Sweat formed on her brow as she focused on holding Isaac and imagining the cold water washing over him as well.

Sid reached the top of the stairs, his muffled voice saying, "I'll get her myself if I have to," before he walked right past them, as they weren't even there.

Isaac pushed away from Leah, looking back and forth from Leah to the door. He then locked onto Leah's neck and frowned. "What's that?"

She lifted her hand, touching a slimy tendril latched on to the back of her neck. She wrapped her hand around it and pulled, yanking off the leech-like creature, much smaller than the one that had latched onto Joanna.

Asmodeus spoke from inside her head. *Damn things, always trying to infect the mind. Good thing the boy spotted it before it was too late.*

She squeezed her hand, crushing it as it dissolved into black smoke.

CHAPTER 31
PLANS IN MOTION

Leah and Isaac raced out of the building, running straight into Sarah.

Before she could speak, Isaac turned to Leah. "How did you do that? What . . . what was that?"

Sarah tilted her head. "What are you talking about? Did you guys get caught?"

Leah doubled over, her hands on her knees, trying to catch her breath. "No, we didn't get caught." She glanced up at Isaac. "I don't know how to explain it."

"What did you do?" Sarah asked.

Isaac looked up at the dorms they'd come from and shook his head. "Sid came up the stairs, and we had nowhere to go. Leah did something. It felt like I was under water, and Sid just walked right past us."

"What? How?" Sarah asked.

"I don't know," Leah said. "It just happened."

"Oh," Isaac started. "And she had a weird slug thing on her."

Sarah grimaced. "Well, that's gross. But the other part is pretty badass."

Leah smirked. "Yeah, it was."

Isaac rubbed the back of his neck. "But there isn't a *sefira* I know of that can make you invisible."

Sarah laughed. "And do you think it would be smart to teach that to an academy full of teenagers? I bet it's a specialty, like slicing with *Malchut* or something."

"I don't know," Isaac said. "It was too different. And what the hell was that slug thing?"

Leah shrugged. "I think it was some kind of parasite. There was one on Joanna when she lost it in the girl's bathroom. That one was bigger, though. And I think it was causing her to lose it."

Isaac took a step back. "Well, are you okay? Do we need to get someone?"

"No," Leah said. "I think I pulled it off before it could do anything. If it had been there any longer, maybe it would have done something."

Sarah put a hand on her hip. "Hold on. This is what you did in the girl's bathroom too. How many times have you ghosted?"

Leah scratched her head. "First was with Joanna. It just sort of happened, and I was able to restrain her. Then I tried doing it again, the night I bumped into Isaac."

Isaac started toward the academy. "I still don't like it. It could be from the Tree of Death for all we know."

Sarah rolled her eyes. "Oh, come on. Don't you think you'd know that by now? She's done it three times now, and she still seems the same. Did you hear any voices or feel your mind slipping when she did it?"

Isaac shook his head. "But not all wells from the Tree of Death do that."

Leah scoffed. "So now what, you're the expert on the Tree of Death?"

"No, but I've had plenty of time to read in the library at night, and from what little that has been written on the subject, only *Nehemoth*, the opposite of *Malchut*, brings voices. The others do other stuff, like corrupt flesh, or taint the ground like radiation."

Leah's left arm twinged. Asmodeus was the one who had brought it up. He'd guided her through using it when Joanna had lost control, and Leah let him. She rubbed her arm and shook off the thought, not ready to tell her friends. "I don't know. Either way, it worked. We got out of there and I feel fine."

Isaac sighed. "You should have told someone. It's a new ability, and you don't even know where it's coming from."

Sarah clapped Isaac's shoulder and squeezed. "Dude, we've got a secret weapon. I think we should keep it that way, especially while we're looking for Paige. I say we do our own research. Me and Leah can scour the books in the library with you. Maybe we'll find out where it comes from."

Leah caught up with Isaac and said, "I'll only use it if I absolutely have to, okay? At least, until you learn more about it."

Isaac bit his lip. He looked between Leah and Sarah before dropping his head. "Fine, but I still think it's dangerous."

They entered the academy building and stopped talking as they saw Nykima standing with Emma.

Emma stared down at the ground, her shoulders slumped as Nykima left her. The administrator marched past the three of them, her lips pursed as she looked over the tops of their heads.

They caught Emma's eye, who gestured to the stairs. They followed in silence as they made their way to the third floor.

Leah ushered Isaac into their dorm room after one quick look around the common room and shut the door.

"What was all that about?" Sarah asked Emma.

"She wanted to know why I was bothering Sid. She came into the library and asked him to grab something from his room. I tried to keep him there, but she wasn't having it. She clarified that I'm to leave him alone."

Leah smirked. "She thinks you want to bond with him."

Emma's face flushed, and she frowned. "Why does she care?"

Isaac peered out the window. "He's Grace's bond. She probably has orders to push him to pick certain students."

"I'm just as good as anyone else if she'd just give me a chance," Emma huffed.

Sarah tilted her head. "Wait. You'd wanted to bond with someone who abducts people?"

"Well, no. I just . . . I think I'm worth bonding to, that's all." She looked at Leah. "Find anything?"

Leah and Isaac filled the other two in on what they'd discovered. They argued over the importance of the orange fur, but both Sarah and Emma seemed interested in it.

"When I was flipping through one book, there was a diagram of a chimera in there. It triggered a memory from the night Isaac and I blacked out. I think whatever was there, in the library, looked a lot like the picture. I remember it was tall and covered in fur. Orange fur."

"So, if that were the case, and you saw this orange fur on the window in the infirmary, then we suspect that one of these chimeras kidnapped Joanna," Isaac said. "If that's true, then it's suspicious that Sid has books on the topic and the fur hidden away. I'll admit, that's off to me."

"It's weird though," Emma said. "I didn't get the vibe that he was a kidnapper. He's been nothing but helpful and nice."

Sarah laughed. "Yeah, Ted Bundy was nice too."

Emma rolled her eyes. "I mean, yeah, I'm not an idiot.

Still, what if he's trying to figure it out like we are? He could be on assignment for all we know."

Isaac leaned against the windowsill and crossed his arms. "But then why hide the fur under the sink? If he was working with the dean or the administrators, he'd have no reason to keep that tucked away."

Leah shifted in her seat after a long moment of silence. "What about my uncle? I could ask him. He dated Nykima apparently, so he probably knows Sid or Grace. Maybe if I lay it all on the table, he'll help us. He should be easier to convince than others that we're onto something."

Emma pinched the bridge of her nose. "I hate this. Why aren't any of the administrators taking this seriously? Why do we have to play detective while they act like it's normal for us to just run away? Paige is probably stuck somewhere being tortured for all we know."

The echo of Paige's screams sounded in Leah's head. "We don't have any better ideas. Not unless you think running away and being cut off from the books they have here will help, which it won't. Not until we know exactly what we're up against."

"I think talking to Eric is our best option," Sarah said. "Until then, we watch Sid's every move. Look for anything else we can use against him."

Tears fell from Emma's eyes, but she nodded at the rest of them.

Leah wrapped an arm around Emma's shoulder and said, "We'll get Paige back. She's part of Black Hills, so we'll do whatever it takes."

CHAPTER 32

WHITE MEMORY

A few nights later, Leah, Isaac, and Sarah hunkered down in the library, flipping through flashcards while cramming in all the different symbols that altered *Malchut*. Everyone's points had reset back to zero, and the quiz the following morning was Leah's first chance to earn marks for her next trial.

"Okay, what is the ideal blood when crafting sigils?" Leah asked, her face hidden behind a red leather booked called *Malchut Sigils: One Thousand Variations and Forms*.

Isaac frowned. "Doesn't it depend on the spell? Like one calls for sheep's blood, I know that, but another is cattle. So, wouldn't any blood work?"

Leah ran her finger along the text. "Well, yeah, but they all have something in common. Only blood from warm-blooded creatures. That matters enough for them to note it on nearly every blood sigil."

Isaac slumped in his chair. "Well, I'm failing tomorrow. I'm never going to memorize all this."

Sarah leaned forward and rested her head in her hands, gazing out past Leah and Isaac. "Relax, it's just another dumb quiz. Not like they matter all that—" She paused, and her eyes grew wide. "Holy shit, it's snowing!"

Leah and Isaac both turned toward the large window and spotted the flecks of white landing on the bottom of the windowsill.

Sarah sprang to her feet. "Fuck the quiz! We need to go outside!"

Isaac scratched his head. "But we need to study. I don't wanna fail this quiz."

"Oh, come on," Sarah said. "I rarely see snow back home. If we take a break, get some fresh air, then we can come back and study refreshed. What about you, Leah? You down?"

Leah watched the snow fall lazily past the window, and a memory surfaced in her mind. She was a little girl again, staring out the window, a row of candles lit in the reflection.

"Leah?" Sarah said.

She pulled herself out of the memory and shook her head. "You guys go ahead. I saw enough snow in Chicago to last a lifetime."

Sarah rolled her eyes and stood. "You two are so boring. Well, I'm going to enjoy the snow all by myself then."

Isaac raised his hand. "Wait, I'll go with you."

Leah faked a yawn and eyed the window. "You two have fun. I think I'm going to head to bed soon, anyway."

Sarah wrapped her arm around Isaac's and pulled him toward the door. "All right. You and I are building a snowman."

"Uh, I don't think there's enough snow for that."

Their voices trailed off as they left the library.

Leah stared out the window again, and the memory returned.

She felt her father's warm arms holding her still as her

mother lit the menorah. They sang Hanukkah prayers that Leah could still feel on her tongue. Snow seemed to fall every year when they lit the menorah.

Tears fell from her cheeks, the memory playing through her mind over and over for what felt like hours. She'd never have those moments again. At least, not with her parents.

A hand rested on her shoulder, and a whisper sounded in her ear. "Sorry for your loss."

Leah jumped, whirling out of her chair, her eyes scanning the empty library.

The door to the library slowly creaked open. Her hands balled into fists, and she readied herself for whatever was about to come through.

A woman with a streak of white hair peered through the doors. "Leah?"

Constance stepped through the door and paused.

Leah wiped away her tears and stood at attention, but Constance quickly raised her hand and dismissed it. "At ease. I'm just making the rounds and sending the last stragglers to bed. I already found Pawns Turner and O'Connor outside, and they told me you were still in here."

Leah stared at the ground. "Sorry. I didn't realize it was so late already."

"Is everything alright?"

"Yeah, I'm fine. Just studying for the quiz tomorrow."

Constance crossed the room and spoke in a soothing voice, "You don't need to always hold it in, you know. You can say what's on your mind."

Leah looked back toward the window, tears forming in her eyes again. She brushed them off and said, "I just . . . I realized Hanukkah starts soon. Or maybe I missed it already. I don't know. My mom was better with the lunar calendar stuff."

Constance peered out the window and nodded, a smile

forming on her face. "I see. Please, follow me." Without waiting for an answer, she turned and walked out the door.

Leah followed, unsure what to expect as they crossed through the corridor and up the stairs without speaking.

Constance guided her to her office and opened the door. It was smaller than William's, but cozier, with warm lights and a simple wooden desk that matched the large bookshelf on the left. Pinned on the right wall, world and regional maps overlapped each other, while a large window overtook the wall behind Constance's desk.

Constance shut the door and walked past Leah, disappearing behind her desk as she pilfered through the drawers.

"Ah, there it is," she said as she popped back up, holding a small silver menorah in her hands.

Leah's eyes widened. "Wait, you're Jewish?"

Constance smiled. "More agnostic, but my mother survived the holocaust before immigrating to America. We never practiced, but she still kept this silver menorah." She paused, handing it over to Leah. "Would you like to see it?"

Leah ran her fingers along the scratched silver. It was heavy in her hands, like generations of memories were carried inside, calling her to add to them. "It's beautiful," she said.

"We can light it, if you like."

Leah inhaled sharply and handed the Menorah back to Constance. "What? I don't think I can. I mean, are we even in Hanukkah?"

Constance took the menorah and placed it on the windowsill. She bent down and opened up the cabinets and peered in. "It can be something between us. Early, late, or on time, I'd say it's the act that matters."

She pulled out a pack of tall white candles and a box

with matches, placing the candles in the menorah one by one.

"Yeah. It would mean a lot," Leah said.

Constance smiled. "Well, I don't know all the prayers, but hopefully, we can bring some of those happy memories back. If not for just a moment. Will you do the honors?"

Leah rubbed her eyes and smiled back. She grabbed the matches and lit one candle. "Why are you doing this?"

Constance eyed the flame. "Like you, I've lost loved ones. And I know what tradition can mean to someone still holding onto that pain. Maybe tonight can be another step toward holding on to the good still left in the world."

Leah lifted the center candle and lit the rest, left to right, like her father had taught her. Each flame uncoiled a knot in her chest, loosening a pain she didn't know she still had. Memories came too, of her and her parents eating the sweet, jelly filled sufganiyots, her dad belting out tradi-tional songs as if he were an opera singer, and her mother wiping away tears from laughing so much.

She sang with him, her voice cracking as she followed along with the memory.

Once done, she placed the candle back in the center of the menorah and stared at the flames with Constance standing quietly next to her.

Leah turned and looked at Constance. "Who did you lose?"

Constance stayed silent for a long while, before running her fingers through her streaked hair. "Mystics lose many. It's part of the job we sign up for. I've lost family and Mystics. One of my first Pawns was the hardest."

"I'm sorry. I shouldn't have asked," Leah whispered.

"It's fine. You know so little about all of us, so it makes sense to ask. The day it happened, only William—my other Pawn at the time—and I survived."

"William? As in Dean Wright?"

Constance nodded. "It was a long time ago, but yes. He's grown into a respectable White Knight."

Silence fell between them, and Leah stared at the candle flames as they danced on the windowsill. "Does it get any better?"

Constance rested a hand on Leah's shoulder and said, "The losses remind me to see the beauty in everything and cherish the moments I still have left."

CHAPTER 33
A KNIGHT RETURNED

One morning, well into February, Leah and Sarah dragged themselves to the cafeteria after a long night of homework.

"I think I might die," Sarah said.

Leah smelled the sweet scent of blueberry and buttermilk pancakes, her stomach grumbling from hunger. "Not before me."

A voice boomed behind them, one that Leah hadn't heard in a long time. "Well, look who dragged themselves out of bed."

Sarah winced and croaked. "Ugh, no one should shout this early."

Leah turned, seeing her uncle enter the lobby and drop a massive duffel bag. A smile stretched across his face, his facial hair longer and scragglier than it had been the last time she'd seen him.

Emotion ran wild in her, a sense of joy that reverberated back and forth, compounding on itself until she couldn't hold it back. Newfound energy coursed through her, and she raced over to him, throwing her arms around him.

Eric laughed. "Woah, easy there."

Leah let go and backed away, her face turning red as she noticed his black eye. "Are you alright?"

He pointed at his black eye. "This? All part of the job. Looks worse than it is." He turned toward Sarah. "Good to see you, Pawn Turner. Have you been keeping Leah out of trouble?"

"Pretty sure you know that's impossible," Sarah said.

Leah glanced around the foyer, noting that no one was within earshot, and whispered, "Look, there's something we need to tell you in private."

"I wasn't even supposed to come in here, but I insisted after I felt something odd with our bond a few weeks back," Eric said, leaning back.

"Odd? What was odd?" Leah asked.

Eric's eyes grew distant. "It was like I couldn't feel you. Like you were gone. Not dead. Just gone." He blinked twice. "But you seem fine now, which means I need to keep my distance and report to my quarters."

"No. Wait. Please? It's urgent. Just give me two minutes."

He sighed, running a hand through his hair while he looked left and right. "Fine. But make it quick."

Sarah followed them into the empty classroom and closed the door behind them.

Eric rested his back against the chalkboard. "Okay, I'm all ears."

The events of the past few weeks spilled from Leah, from her encounter with what she thought was a chimera, to the dream with Paige, to everything they did, and why they suspected Sid. Eric crossed his arms and listened to every word in silence.

Once she finished, Eric let out a long sigh. "Black

Bishops research fringe topics all the time. His White is Grace; she probably set him on the task."

Sarah stepped forward. "But why do they keep telling us she ran away? Do you know if anyone is looking at Paige's disappearance as a kidnapping? Would Sid be a part of that group?"

"I wouldn't," Eric said. "That isn't how it works. The Infinity Board prefers us to work and complete our duties in secret. I can't tell you what Sid has been working on any more than I can tell you where I've been."

Leah frowned. "Why?"

"Secrets keep the Infinity Board alive. Else, if one of us gets captured, or a demon finds its way in, they'd know everything and put the entire organization in jeopardy."

Leah paused. She knew her uncle wanted to say more, feeling his resentment billowing off him. "And the fur he pocketed. What do you think about that?"

"I trust that his work and standing orders are being done in the best interest of the Board. It is not my place to question." The words sounded hollow leaving Eric's mouth.

Leah clenched her fists. "You can't be serious. I know you can't. What about the thing I saw in the library?" A wave of frustration hit her, emanating off him, followed by the sinking feeling of guilt.

Eric stepped away from the wall. "No matter how I feel, I must respect the rules of the Infinity Board. The evidence you think you have is all over the place, and it's more likely to get you in trouble than it is to do anything to Sid. Besides, suggesting you saw a chimera to the administration, or the dean, will be laughable to them."

"Why is that?" Sarah asked.

"Aside from the surveillance and protections in place to keep this academy safe, chimeras are extinct. We took all the books on rituals and burned most of them, and only kept what was relevant. The rituals were unstable, and too many people were dying. The last practitioner to show was in the early 1800s, and it didn't go well for them."

"What about shifters, then?" Sarah asked.

"There aren't any in the US, and the ones who do exist don't look like wolves. They shift fully into other animals."

Leah wanted to say more, wanted to get him on her side, but the overhead speaker crackled to life, and Reginald's voice drowned her thoughts out over the intercom.

"All Black Pawns, report to field three in fifteen minutes."

Eric frowned at the notice and eyed Leah. "I can't have you getting in any more trouble, okay? You've got to focus on the trials. You need to stop chasing after these conspiracies."

Anger overcame Leah, and she clenched her jaw. "You're not even going to help? And you expect me to trust the adults around here, even though they aren't willing to show us they are trying? Paige has been missing for over a month! And Theodore's been missing since before we even got here!"

Eric shook his head. "Leah, you've got to stop—"

"Save it. I shouldn't have even told you." She turned and stomped to the door.

Eric grabbed her arm, holding her in place. "Five Pawns ran away when I was in the academy. Five. And all of them ended up corrupted by the Tree of Death and trying to start different cults and sects that hurt people. One of them was even a friend. Something in them snapped, and they couldn't take it anymore. We all thought someone kidnapped them too, but no. Stop trying to blame Sid, and focus on your future. *Our* future."

Leah pulled her arm away and glared. "I bet Mom would have reacted differently. I bet she'd stand up against the Infinity Board if they tried to cow her. She'd actually do something useful."

A wave of grief and guilt hit Leah hard. She'd hit a nerve, and all she wanted was to drown out the pain. She turned to Sarah, trying to hold back tears that were not entirely her own. "Let's go."

CHAPTER 34
THE SECOND TRIAL

"Where were you two?" Isaac asked as he exited the cafeteria and found Sarah and Leah in the lobby. "You missed breakfast."

Leah's stomach growled as she looked past him and into the cafeteria. "I ran into my uncle. He's here."

Isaac's eyes widened, and he nodded. "And what did he say?"

Sarah shook her head. "No offense, Leah, but your uncle wasn't much help."

"It didn't go well," Leah said.

Isaac let out a groan. "No. We needed him."

"No, we don't," Sarah said, crossing her arms. "He's just like the rest of them."

"So, what now?" Isaac asked.

Leah grabbed her winter jacket, hanging on a row of hooks near the exit of the academy. "We move on without his help. I'm not willing to give up."

Isaac pulled on his coat. "Yeah, me neither."

They gathered with the others on the grassy field surrounding Nykima.

"Attention!" she called, and everyone stood up straight.

She paced the center circle, eyeing each of them in their stance before she spoke. "Today, your second trial begins."

Leah glanced at Sarah from the corner of her eye, seeing the same shock that Leah felt.

She wasn't the only one to lose composure. Half of the others did too as they fell out of formation and whispered to each other.

"Silence!" Nykima shouted. Silence washed over the crowd of Pawns, and she continued. "While this trial comes with no warning, you've been preparing for it for weeks. Form a double line. We're jogging the rest of the way."

The Pawns scrambled to form the lines, awaiting Nykima's next command.

"Double time! March!"

They jogged in the frosty morning air, reaching the edge of the forest in no time and passing right through onto a dirt trail. Leah recounted all the trails in the woods they'd jogged through, but as Nykima took them deeper into the woods, the path looked more and more unfamiliar.

They passed by deep stone canyons, a waterfall, and several wooden bridges. The place reminded Leah of Starved Rock, a park her parents had taken her camping at once—a magical place of stone, waterfalls, and happy memories.

The woods opened to a massive field filled with short concrete pillars. Over a hundred of the pillars lined the field, grouped together in threes. On the other side of the field, the Knights, Bishops, and White Pawns stood in bleachers, awaiting them.

They passed by empty stands onto the edge of the field, and Nykima raised her hand in the air. "Halt!"

They stopped jogging at the edge of the field. Nykima turned to them and spoke. "Form up, rows of five."

Reginald stepped away from the crowd of spectators,

his black and gold cane shining in the light as he stepped onto the field. His voice boomed as he spoke. "Welcome, Black Pawns, to the second trial. The pillars before you will test your control, precision, and strength of *Malchut*. The first will test control, when you push you pillar without it toppling over. Points will be earned by the distance the pillar moves. The second focuses on precision, as you slice it in half. A clean, vertical cut will grant you the most points, followed by diagonal and horizontal. But note, cleaving through the stone will result in more points than a partial cut, so know your limits. The last pillar tests your strength. Destroy the pillar with as much force as you can muster. The larger the pile of rubble you create from destruction, the more points you will be awarded. Each pillar can earn you thirty-three points, a total of ninety-nine points for a perfect score."

He nodded at Nykima, who pulled out a list and cleared her throat. "First up, we have Black Pawn Tate. The rest of you may find a seat in the stands behind you."

They gathered in the stands behind them, facing off toward the White Pawns, Knights, and Bishops.

Leah spotted Sid immediately, and anger bubbled up inside her. She didn't care what her uncle thought; Sid shouldn't be free to walk around. There was enough evidence for her to know about his involvement in Paige's disappearance.

A stiffness rose in her neck, a slight pain that forced her to clench her jaw. The sensation wasn't her own but brought on by something else. *Someone* else.

She felt his eyes on her before he found Eric staring straight at her, his lips pursed. The sensation she felt was annoyance, and Eric shook his head slowly, as if to tell her to stop worrying about Sid and keep her head in the game.

Leah stretched her neck and looked away, burying the feeling inside her while she focused on the field.

She eyed the three pillars off to the side, standing two feet taller and thicker than everyone else's. Her heart skipped a beat. Were those hers? It made sense that she'd be tested on a different scale than the others, but those pillars were enormous in comparison.

Sarah elbowed Leah and pointed at the pillars. "Are those yours? No way that's fair. Those are huge."

Leah sighed. "I don't know. I get that I have more strength, but I don't even know if I can move the smaller ones. I mean, they're solid concrete, right?"

Isaac leaned in from behind them. "You've got this. Don't let them get in your head. You've always been good with *Malchut*, even before the bond."

Leah half smiled. "Thanks."

"Just picture something you hate," Sarah said. "Like that demon, Asmodeus. Then that pillar wouldn't stand a chance."

The image of her father, his body beaten and bruised, ebbed from the memories she tried to bury. Cold sweat formed on her brow, her fingertips went numb, and a pain twinged her arm. The serpent inside her wriggled, and she drew in a deep breath.

Nykima lifted her arm, and Leah stuffed the memory away and leaned forward in her seat, ready to watch Gabe in action.

The whistle blew, and Gabe made quick work of the first pillar. He stretched his hands overhead, then positioned himself, hands forming a triangle behind his back while he stood grounded. He swung his hands out in front of him in one swift motion and pushed them forward. The pillar slid back a few feet before he dropped his hands.

He faced the second, holding one palm perpendicular to

his chest before bringing it up and chopping it down like an axe. Ten feet away, the stone wobbled as a paper-thin cut appeared partway down the stone column.

Last, he balled his hand into a fist, reeling it back before punching it forward. Two consecutive punches, and a torrent of energy flooded out of him, slamming into the stone, crumbling it to bits.

The people in the stands across the field clapped, the Black Pawns joining in with cheers while Gabe looked back at them and smirked. He'd set the bar for everyone else.

Reginald, Constance, and Grace stepped forward from the front row and inspected each stone, measuring the distance, quality, and depth of the cut and the size of the rubble made from the third stone.

One by one, the Pawns were called up to complete their trial. Few kept the column upright, let alone push theirs as far as Gabe had. For as cruel as Brandon was, he slid the stone column double the distance of Gabe's, his skill in sustaining *Malchut* clear.

Many sliced their second stone horizontally, certain that they'd at least make a clean cut through. For a long time, no one opted to make a vertical slice. Then Miranda took to the field and sliced it clean through, vertically splitting the column into two halves. At the end of her round, the administration admired her ambition but noted the cut was not as clean as it could have been. Surprising even herself, Emma sliced through the column vertically as well, her cut much cleaner than Miranda's.

Leah's chest tightened after each name was called. She took minor comfort when Karen Rodman, the girl with a lip piercing who'd tried to blame her after their first trial, toppled her pillar. Then she barely scratched her second pillar and finally broke her last one into big chunks, with half of the pillar still standing. Karen stomped back to the stands and shoved off Brian Buadhach's hand as he tried to comfort her.

Other Pawns went on, and the rubble began building up in the field, stones cast astray into other columns nearby. While Joanna failed to move the column, toppling it over on the first try, it did not surprise Leah that she made a clean diagonal cut through the stone, forming a nearly polished edge in the two halves. When she reached the third pillar, she rendered it to tiny pieces in two consecutive blows. The energy inside her was strong, even stronger now that she'd been back.

"Black Pawn Turner." Nykima shouted.

Sarah grinned. "My turn."

Where Joanna failed, Sarah exceeded all expectations. She was focused, well trained, and strong. She slid the first column back, one foot short of Gabe's, but gave up when it wobbled. The second was just as clean and controlled as Emma's, but her cut not only passed through the stone, but cut into the dirt below. When pulled apart by the admins, the two halves were glossy, clear that she'd cleaved it even better than Emma. She ran back up to the stands after rendering her third to rubble and fist bumped Isaac and Leah before sitting.

"You killed it!" Isaac said.

Nykima eyed the clipboard and shouted the next name, "Black Pawn O'Conner."

Isaac raced off into the field and waited for her whistle. Leah stared in awe at Isaac. With one position to the next, he moved like a dancer. With perfect form, he slid the stone back, meeting Brandon's distance before turning to the next pillar, opting for a clean diagonal cut. His downfall was the last pillar. No matter how hard he tried, or how precise his moves were, he only cracked the stone. He stopped and looked at Nykima, accepting his failed attempt before heading back to the stands.

"You did great," Leah said.

He shrugged. "Yeah, until that last one. Hopefully, the first two pillars are enough."

The trial continued, every name another inch closer to Leah being called and facing her trial.

It wasn't the trial that was the long part, but the inspection afterward. The three admins would double- and even triple-check the work before they gave Nykima the signal to continue.

As the sun drifted halfway across the sky, the groupings of intact pillars dwindled more and more. It didn't take Leah long to realize that they were saving her for last, and knowing that only made her more anxious.

Nykima called down Serena, and Leah realized this was the first time she'd really gotten a good look at her since Buck had left. Serena hid in her room most days, away from Emma and the others. Her cheeks were sunken in, and she had dark bags under her eyes. She barely moved her first pillar. Her cut on the second wasn't the cleanest, and she barely cracked her last. The silence that followed was deafening. Serena stared at the administrators for a long moment before turning and running off into the forest.

Emma stood and raced down the stands to follow, but Nykima raised her hand and gave her a warning glance.

"It's like she wanted to fail," Sarah whispered.

"Yeah, she can do better than that. I know it," Leah said.

Movement across the field caught Leah's eye as Sid left the stands, heading toward the woods.

This would be the perfect time to take someone. Don't you think? Asmodeus said.

Leah's heart pounded. He was right. With everyone out

here, the academy was empty. And if Serena went missing now, they'd call her a runaway.

An elbow jabbed Leah in the ribs, and she shook herself out of her trance. Both Sarah and Isaac were leaning in close, their eyes wide on her.

Leah shook her head again, regaining the sound in her ears. "What?"

Sarah flicked her eyes toward the field. "Uh, it's your turn."

Blood rushed to Leah's face as she peered onto the field, catching Nykima's glare from her clipboard and the three administrators looking up at her.

All the Pawns were looking at her, and her face grew hotter. She eyed the woods one more time, certain she'd have to make quick work of this if she had any chance of catching up with Sid.

Leah slipped down the stands and onto the field, arriving next to Nykima.

Nykima gestured to a mark in the field, noting a farther distance from her set of massive pillars than the others Pawns had. "Are you ready, Pawn Ackerman?"

Leah sized up the pillars. From this angle, they looked even taller and thicker than she'd thought they were in the stands. She took in a deep breath. "Yes, White Knight Amana."

She heard Nykima's whistle, but her mind was on Serena and Sid.

Leah took position in front of the first pillar, settling her hands behind her back and taking in slow deep breaths as she regained focus on the trial. She let *Malchut* uncoil and press against her chest and hands. She swung her hands out front, mimicking what Gabe had done, and let *Malchut* flow out from her. Instead of a burst of energy, she focused on it flowing from her like a breath of air.

It hit the pillar but slid it back with more strength than Leah had intended. Before she could stop it, it gouged into the ground and tumbled over with a loud thud.

The silence surrounded Leah. She refused to look back at the others, or even to Nykima. Instead, she faced the second pillar.

Alma's teachings back at the outpost surfaced in her mind. The day she'd stood in front of the class, the first to blow out the candle with a sliver of *Malchut*. She focused the energy to the edge of her hand, not a sliver, but imagining her hand transforming into a sword.

She took in a breath, ready to raise her hand when she lost focus again. Her mind wouldn't let go of Sid, and this trial stood in her way. She thrust her hand forward but released her energy too early. The cut was deep, but only went halfway through the pillar.

Leah drew in another deep breath, opening and closing her fists and trying her best to numb the jittery feeling underneath her skin. She turned to the third pillar, knowing everything banked on this one. She had to pass, for the sake of her bond. But her mind remained elsewhere. She could still hear Paige's screams, and she couldn't let it happen again. The memory of them still burned into her. What if Serena was next, and she failed to do anything once more? She had to get this done, had to finish this and find them.

Leah focused on the third pillar. She to obliterate it, making it crumble to a pile of dust. The mark on her arm quivered to life, and a small voice sounded in her head.

Let me help you, Asmodeus whispered in her ear.

She didn't hesitate. Instead, the energy in her moved, uncoiling from her chest and slipping down to her arm. It never pressed up against her skin, just vanished, more and more into the mark. She pulled on more energy, figuring she needed to feel something so she could use it against the stone. Despite that, nothing. No pressure formed against her skin, and she worried about where all that energy had gone.

She kept her eyes on the pillar and stopped pulling on the energy. Had she lost it? How would she do anything to the pillar without feeling *Malchut* at the edge of her hands?

The pillar in front of her cracked. She frowned and tilted her head. Then the stone exploded.

The sound of the explosion rocked through Leah, and she swung her arms to her face, expecting shards of rock to slice through her as she fell to the ground.

She heard shrieks from the crowd, but to her surprise, no pain came. No sound of falling rock met her ears.

She uncovered her eyes and stared at a floating ball of dust and tiny pebbles hovered in the air around where the pillar stood, more like a blown out holographic version of the pillar that stood there before.

Leah looked at the administrators and saw all three holding their hands together. They looked strained, like they were pushing back or holding on to something that fought to get free.

One by one, their faces calmed, and they lowered their hands. The pillar slowly lost shape as the dust and pebbles fell to the ground in a heap of sand.

Leah stood, spotting Reginald eyeing her, before taking a bow to the admins and racing off the field and toward the forest.

CHAPTER 35

HIDDEN IN PLAIN SIGHT

Their faces burned in Leah's mind. She'd messed up. Done something even the administrators weren't expecting. And now, as Leah ran through the woods, she could still see their faces, pale, staring back at her. Not with anger, but fear.

Malchut was a force that projected out of you. At least, that's what she had learned. Whatever had happened to that stone, that wasn't the way it should have been done.

Leah focused on the forest in front of her, unsure if anyone would chase after her. She had to find Serena. She had to find Sid.

"Leah!" Sarah's voice shouted behind her.

Leah slowed, holding the stitch in her side that had formed from running. "You guys don't need to follow me!" she shouted as Sarah and Isaac caught up with her.

Sarah took in a deep breath. "But where are you going? That was amazing!"

"I blew it, Sarah. There's no need to lie."

Sarah shrugged. "The first two phases sucked. You're not wrong. But the third pillar . . . you killed it."

Isaac raced to Leah's other side. "You turned the pillar

into a pile of sand while the rest of us were hoping to just make some rocks. Where did you even learn that from? "

Leah's arm twitched, and an image of Asmodeus grinning burned in her mind. "Uh, Alma, during one of her lessons. She'd mentioned a technique, and I felt like I could do it."

Sarah laughed. "Well, show us next time. I'd love to try that move. Don't mess with Sarah Turner. She'll blow you up with her mind."

Leah stifled a laugh. "Last thing we want is you with that ability."

They broke free from the woods and onto the primary fields. Isaac raced ahead and turned around. "But you still haven't said why you rushed out."

Leah looked past him, out to the academy. "I saw Sid leave right after Serena ran away. He's got to be up to something. Maybe he thinks she is easy prey after running away? Why else would he just leave right in the middle of the trial? Serena could be his next target."

Isaac shook his head. "But you saw Serena. What if he is just trying to talk her out of becoming the next runaway?"

Leah picked up her pace. "Serena wouldn't run. She'd fight to find Buck, even if that means failing the trial to figure out where he went." She picked up her pace toward the academy. "You don't understand. My dreams, or visions, they're as real as you and me talking. They're the reason I knew Asmodeus was coming after my family before it happened. I didn't know any better back then, but now I've got to trust my instincts. And those instincts tell me to follow Sid."

They reached the academy doors, and Isaac paused, his hand on the handle. "Fine, I get it. We look around and try to find either Sid or Serena. But then what?"

A door slammed to their left. Leah whipped her head

around, spotting Sid carrying a large duffel bag across his back, racing out of the Bishop and Knight dorms.

She waved Isaac and Sarah on, and they crept down the back sidewalk and peered past the corner.

He tossed his bag into the back of the red pickup and hopped into the driver's seat, revving the engine to life.

"Shit, he might have caught her already." Leah looked at Isaac, knowing full well he wouldn't like what she was about to say. "I've got to know where he's going. You two can stay here, but I'm getting in that truck."

"Are you nuts?" Sarah asked.

Of her two friends, Leah didn't suspect Sarah to be the one to call her that.

But Sarah grinned. "Of course I'm coming with you."

Isaac turned back toward the forest, spotting people emerging from the trials. He turned and sighed. "Yeah, me too."

Leah shook her head. "Guys, this is dangerous. If we make it out of here, there's no telling what the admins will do when they find out."

Sarah raised her hand. "Yeah, we get it. Now, let's move before we lose our chance!"

Warmth spread in her heart. "Fine, but getting on that truck undetected is going to be tricky. I have a plan, so trust me on the next part."

"Wait," Isaac said. "If you're thinking what I think you're thinking, then I don't think it's a good—"

"Shut up Isaac! It's too late now," Sarah hissed.

The truck backed up, and Leah grabbed both their hands and squeezed tight.

She focused on the feeling she'd had in the stairwell. The sense of cool water flowing over the top of her head, muffling sound and brightening colors to a sickly yellow.

She imagined that sensation flowing down her hands and up both her friends' arms.

Isaac's hand grew cold and sweaty while Sarah squeezed tighter. When the shroud settled on top of Leah, she opened her eyes. All three of them were invisible.

Sid backed up and stopped right beside them. Leah took a deep breath and walked toward the back of the truck, holding her friends tight.

"Leah, what are you doing?" Sarah asked, trying to pull away.

"Trust me!"

They reached the back, and Leah held up a hand, readying to pull herself up into the bed of the truck.

Sid looked back, although his eyes weren't on them. He looked *through* them, toward the students, teachers, and administrators coming back from the fields. Before Leah had a chance to move, he started drove down the driveway without them.

"Shit, there goes our chance," Sarah whispered.

Leah pulled Isaac and Sarah, gripping tight on both their hands. Movement caught the corner of her eye. She turned as saw the pale face of the ghost, eyeing them from the window of the cafeteria.

His voice carried, echoing loudly in her ear. "You brought me more like you? Wait. Where are you going? You can't leave."

Sarah stumbled over her words. "Who the hell is that?"

Leah yanked on their hands, cold sweat forming on her brow, and the ground beneath felt more like a ship than solid ground.

They reached the truck, and Sarah and Isaac used their free hands to pull Leah up and into the back, still under the shroud of invisibility. Leah turned and saw the ghost coming out through the wall. His translucent figure showed a young boy in an old Pawn's uniform.

"It's following us!" Isaac hissed.

The ghost levitated off the ground, trailing down the driveway, shouting, "Don't go! Please! I don't want to be alone anymore!"

The truck stopped at the gate, and the ghost reached the edge of the truck, looming over them.

His eyes turned completely white, and his face slowly elongated. His jaw widened, revealing rows of bloodied, razor-sharp teeth. "I'm so hungry."

Claws clutched onto the truck, and the ghost pulled himself closer to them. The three of them pressed up against the other end of the truck bed, cornered by the massive beast. The creature reached forward, scratching a single claw against Leah's legs, when the truck sped up.

Leah snapped her eyes shut and let the shroud of invisibility drop as Sid sped off. The creature popped out of existence, and the pale-yellow world transformed into a bright blue sky.

The three slouched down in the truck bed, out of Sid's sight.

"What the hell was that?" Isaac asked, his eyes darting left and right.

"I . . . I don't know," Leah said, wincing at a sharp pain pulsing in her head.

A paleness shrouded Sarah's face. "Where did it go?"

"We can only see him when we're invisible," Leah said. "I've seen him before. The little boy in the library and in the hall, but that thing he turned into—I don't know what that was."

"It was a fucking monster, that's what it was," Sarah said.

"I told you that invisibility thing wasn't a good idea!" Isaac protested.

"Shh! Sid might hear you," Leah whispered.

"Fine, but let's not do that again, okay? I don't think any of us can fight off whatever that thing was," Isaac said.

Leah bit her lip. "I don't know. Did you hear him? Before he changed into that creature, he was asking us to stay. And he was nice when I saw him in the library."

"Nice?" Sarah scoffed. "I'm going to have to agree with Isaac on this one. I don't want to see that thing again, even if you think it's nice."

The landscape changed from a few trees to fields, to buildings, and back to a forest over the course of an hour. Leah suspected they'd ridden through several small towns before Sid pulled off the road.

When Sid parked, Leah grabbed onto her friends and shrouded them once again, despite Isaac's efforts to stop her. The sensation felt worse this time, as if she were being thrown around by a current in the ocean. Yet, no creature seemed to wait for them this time.

Sid hopped out of the truck, reaching between Leah and Sarah to grab onto the duffel bag. It caught on Sarah's knee for a second, long enough for Sid to look at the bed of the truck, his eyebrow raised. Then he shook his head and turned, his footsteps trailing off.

Leah dropped the invisibility and peered over the truck bed. They were in a small parking lot with no other cars in sight.

She spotted the large arching sign, *Portside Warehouses.*

Her memory of Paige's abduction surfaced, and with it the numbers that had hovered above Paige's head.

"Guys, this is the place. This is where Paige is," Leah said.

She struggled to stand, falling back down onto the seat, the nausea still not done with her.

Isaac held Leah's shoulder. "You alright?"

"Yeah, I'm fine. Just a little sick, but it'll wear off."

Sarah hopped out from the back of the truck and stretched. "Maybe you should stay here, and we'll follow Sid."

Leah sat up, ignoring the spinning, and drew in several deep breaths. Isaac grabbed her arm while Sarah helped her hop out of the truck. After a few more deep breaths, the nausea subsided. "No. I'm coming with you."

Isaac hopped out. "Then let's get moving before I change my mind."

They started toward the warehouses as the sun dipped below the roofs and long shadows stretched across the parking lot. Passing beneath a sign, they rounded the corner.

Leah's chest tightened, and her feet froze, followed by the rest of her body. Her eyes, the only thing she could move, looked at Sarah, who seemed to be in the same predicament. She couldn't see Isaac, who was walking behind them, but he had to be right behind them, caught up in the same trap.

Before they could do anything, Sid stepped out from the shadows.

He pointed a gun at Leah's head. "What the hell are the three of you doing here?"

CHAPTER 36

THE BLACK BISHOP

Leah's heart raced, and she stumbled to the ground.

Sid pressed the gun to Leah's forehead. "Answer me!"

The serpent inside Leah uncoiled and pressed itself up against her chest, ready to strike. "We know about the kidnappings. We know you're involved. If you lay a finger on us, everyone back at the academy will know."

Sid laughed. "You think the academy would send kids to subdue a Bishop? Nice try. I guess it's a good thing you think I did it."

Leah frowned. "Why is that a good thing?"

"Because the real kidnapper would have killed you for getting in the way. I'm not who you're looking for. I've been working a case, figuring out if our missing Pawns are runaways or hostages." Sid holstered his gun. "I'll release *Hod* on your friends if you promise not to do anything stupid."

Leah eventually nodded, but her eyes remained locked on his gun. A wave of energy rippled past her, and Isaac and Sarah stumbled back, gasping for air.

Sid relaxed his stance and said, "I got the green light to

come investigate this place. That's why I rushed here from the trial. I didn't see anyone on my tail, so how did you three track me down?"

Isaac caught his breath. "We hopped in the back of your truck."

Sid scratched his head and laughed. "I thought my duffle got hooked on something. *Thagirion* . . . not bad. I didn't think to look out for that. Dangerous, though. You're lucky you didn't get trapped."

Thagirion. Leah had heard that name before. A ritual back at the outpost had been referred to by that name. That wasn't a name from the Tree of Life, though. Isaac was right. She'd been using the Tree of Death without knowing it.

Isaac stumbled over his words. "So, why do you think it's a mole? Why here?"

Sid looked over his shoulder. "There's been a slew of animal attacks around here. Pets missing or torn apart, and marine life is all in a frenzy. A couple of kids wound up dead nearby too. The news doesn't know what to make of it, but it all comes back to this place."

"And you think it's chimeras?" Sarah asked.

Sid furrowed his brow. "How did you know that?"

Isaac elbowed Sarah, but she shrugged him off. "What? He'd find out we snooped around his room, eventually. Yeah, we know you have basically all the books on chimeras from the library."

Leah cut in before Sid could respond. "I saw you the night Joanna went missing. You took that orange fur off the window. Why didn't you tell anyone?"

"I was on a special assignment," Sid said. "It's a need-to-know basis. Meaning, any damning evidence needs to be concealed until we have a case. We suspect a mole at the academy, working with chimeras."

Leah frowned. "So, you think one of the Bishops or Knights is behind this?"

He nodded and tossed his keys to Sarah. "I've told you all I'm going to. And you can't be here while I investigate. Wait by the truck. That's an order. Unless you want me to report this to the dean and push for you three to be expelled."

Sid turned without another word, heading to the dock buildings.

Leah bit her lip, a pit in her stomach growing heavier as she processed Sid wasn't the one they were looking for. "Do you have any leads on which warehouse?"

Sid turned around. "I don't, so get comfortable. This may take a while."

Leah recalled the numbers in her dream. "It's twenty-seven. Warehouse twenty-seven."

Sid frowned. "And how do you know that?"

Sweat formed on her brow, and she stumbled over a lie. "Joanna. She mumbled it over and over the night she came back. I didn't tell anyone then. Didn't know who to trust."

He smiled. "Twenty-seven then. Thanks. Now, get back to the truck."

Isaac ushered both Sarah and Leah back to the truck, where they sat inside while Leah let out a long sigh.

After an awkward silence, Sarah said, "Well, that was interesting. Good thing we were wrong about Sid. He held the three of us like it was nothing."

"Yeah, he could have shot all three of us, and there'd be nothing we could do to stop it," Isaac said.

The sun settled down past the horizon, and darkness shrouded the truck. Leah clenched her fists, angry at herself for thinking she could take on Sid and for being so sure of herself that he was the one behind the kidnappings. She still wasn't certain of that fact, but he gave no reason to not believe him.

Isaac cleared his throat and said, "Hey guys, I—"

Gunshots fired off in the distance, echoing from the docks.

Leah pushed open the door. "That has to be Sid!"

Isaac grabbed her shoulder. "What are you doing? He said to stay here."

Three more shots sounded, and Leah pulled away from Isaac's grasp. "What if he needs help? If he's on our side, then we can't just leave him to fend for himself, no matter what he says."

"I agree with Leah on this one," Sarah said. "If he dies, and we're just sitting here? I couldn't."

They raced past the arched entrance to the warehouses. After passing warehouse five, they heard another shot, but this time it came with a high pitch screech.

Leah guided them, turning left, then right, her memory of the night they took Paige guiding her in her mind.

They reached the twenty-fifth warehouse entrance and crouched behind crates stacked near an empty trailer.

Dull sodium lamps lit the way ahead. Sid crouched behind his own set of crates, one hand clutching his lower abdomen and the other pointed at a tall figure standing a couple feet away.

Dark liquid covered Sid's fingers and spilled onto the ground at his feet. It was blood; Leah was certain of it.

She looked at the figure, forcing her eyes to adjust to the light, tall and slender, with long pointed ears and a bald head. It didn't look human at all.

Images of an old black and white movie that she'd watched once with her dad came to mind: *Nosferatu*. Yet this thing looked worse, less like a human and more like a grey-haired bat stretched out to some semblance of a human.

Isaac tapped Leah's shoulder, pointing to the side of the warehouse. Leah had to squint, peering through the lights on the docks and into the entrance.

Another silhouetted figure stood in the dark with a clear path to Sid, who seemed none the wiser. They turned along the side of the building, away from the fight. They were tall, with short hair and broad shoulders that looked almost familiar to Leah.

Leah turned to her friends. "That's the mole. They're gonna get away. Unless . . ."

Leah forced pressure to build in her hands and flung a wall of *Malchut* toward the shadow. Before the energy hit them, the shadow figure jumped back, whipping their head toward Leah with an almost animalistic snarl while Leah's energy slammed into the brick wall behind them, crumbling bits of stone to the ground.

With the shadow figure now illuminated by the lights above, Leah made out a face she'd seen day in and day out, staring her down. Black Knight Ian Kim snarled, his eyes burning in the dim light.

CHAPTER 37

FAMILIAR FACES

"I told you three to stay in the car!" Sid said, briefly taking his eyes off the monster.

The bat creature smiled and grumbled, "Mistake," before leaping high into the air and soaring down on Sid, its clawed hands outstretched.

Sid had just enough time to turn around. Leah heard a clap behind her, and the creature froze in midair, its claws inches from Sid's face.

He leaped out of the way, his eyes now fixed on the creature.

Isaac stood behind Leah, his hands clapped together, holding the creature with *Hod*. The color drained from Isaac's face.

Leah turned back to the chimera, and Isaac's hold on it faltered, the creature dropping to the ground, claws sinking into the concrete like it was sand.

Ian whistled, and the bat chimera moved at a blink of an eye to his side. "Well, I'm surprised that someone showed up here. Didn't think you had it in you."

Sid aimed his gun at Ian, but the chimera moved to

stand in the way. "I'm not all that surprised it was you. What did they offer you to become a traitor?"

Ian feigned a sad look. "Ouch! It hurts that you think so low of me. If only you knew the truth! I've helped to make those students better and more obedient."

Sid winced, the gun in his hands lowering as more blood pooled at his feet. "Great, so you're delusional too. Just tell me where the kids are now."

Ian smiled at Sid. "I don't think you're in a position to be making demands. And your . . . backup? You think they stand a chance against us?" He waved his hand forward, and a burst of energy came barreling at them.

Leah lifted her arms and pushed out her own *Malchut* in time to clash with his.

Ian locked eyes with Leah, his eyes flashing yellow. "It seems you got rid of that little present we left on you. It's a shame; you would have made an impressive addition to the collection."

A phantom twinge shot up Leah's neck, glancing at the bat creature and wondering how close she could have been to becoming something like that. Rage bubbled up inside her. Capture her? Like he took Paige? She would have trusted him. A Knight, showing up and dragging her away before she could even realize. "Where is Paige, you bastard?!"

Ian snapped his fingers, and the chimera lunged at her.

"Leah!" Sarah yelled.

Leah was on her back before she could think, holding the creature's chest with her hands as it shrieked on top of her, flecks of spit hitting her face as she stared at its elongated fangs.

Energy washed over her, coating her as the creature's claw came down on her stomach. Sharp claws slid off her stomach, and she let *Malchut* throw the creature off her.

Ian snapped his fingers again, and the creature rushed back to his side, blackened eyes trained on Leah.

Ian looked at his fingernails. "You're all missing the bigger picture, the truth that your little minds can't seem to get a grasp on."

Sarah moved past Leah and sliced through the air. The chimera lurched between them and took the *Malchut* slice to the shoulder, a thin red line forming on its skin.

Sarah frowned and stared at her hand. Leah knew she had more than enough power to break skin, yet this chimera seemed to brush it off like it was nothing.

"He's just stalling!" Sarah shouted at Sid. "Talking nonsense until you can't hold up the gun. Shoot him already!"

Her words triggered the chimera into action. It launched off the ground, eyes now on Sarah. Leah threw herself at her friend, knocking her out of the way from the chimera's claws.

Gunshots zipped over their heads toward the creature. Isaac ducked down and out of the way while the chimera focused on dodging the bullets. One caught it in the arm, piercing right through.

The chimera grimaced as it touched the wound, stepping back.

Sid reloaded his gun. "I'll finish this one. Don't let Ian escape."

Isaac helped Leah and Sarah up, giving Sid one last look before saying, "We're on it."

Leah chased after Ian, trailing behind as he ran between two warehouses.

Ian swatted his hand forward, as if batting at a fly. Yet, with it came a wave of energy that slammed into Leah, and she landed on her back, the air knocked out of her.

Leah's chest grew tight, and her ribs creaked. Her vision

blurred, but she could see Sarah, her arms up, deflecting the blows coming from Ian.

She needed the upper hand and more energy than Ian had. Sarah and Isaac were shouting, fending off his blows, but couldn't last much longer. Leah could do it; she could pull on the Tree of Death for more strength—as long as it didn't take over.

The moment she thought about it, whispers filled the dead air between strikes, and an icy wind danced around Leah, leaving behind a light frost on the ground below her. Energy that hadn't been there before was now waiting for her, ready for the taking. She felt its strength, knew it would be more than enough. She just needed to take in a breath, and the power would be hers.

Isaac shouted out, and Ian landed a hit that cut into Isaac's thigh. Leah pulled away from the voices, away from the power, knowing that if she took it, she wouldn't be able to stop.

But her left arm moved against her will, and Leah gasped. The surrounding frost grew wider, and whispers echoed at the edge of her mind. Energy filled her, siphoning in through her left arm and coiling around the energy in her chest.

She didn't hesitate, instead aiming her hand at Ian and launching finely tipped *Malchut* through the air.

The energy tore through his calf like a bullet, blood splattering the ground.

Ian shrieked and then produced a wave of *Malchut* that sent her two friends tumbling to the ground. He stumbled back, resting against one warehouse, gasping for air.

Sarah launched off the ground with *Malchut* and aimed a fist at his face. Ian didn't move, the fist landing on his chest with a thud. But she couldn't defend herself fast enough, and Ian sent her flying back with a swat of his hand.

Drawing in a deep breath, Ian unleashed a deep, guttural growl. Energy came off in waves, forming a pressure in the air that made Leah's ears pop. He stepped forward, onto his leg that Leah had shot clean through, and put his full weight on it, as if she did not hit him at all.

Black veins surged up his neck, and he stared at them, ready to fight.

Leah launched off the ground, and Ian did the same. Their fists met in midair, and a loud crack rumbled in Leah's chest. She understood Ian was the master here, but she didn't back down.

They landed and raced toward each other again. A torrent of fists met Leah, one of which landed at her side. She didn't block in time, fumbling back for a second.

He was on her again, launching his second attack, and Leah couldn't do anything but block his fists before they did any damage.

Sarah and Isaac rounded behind him, sending kicks and punches that cut into his sides. He ignored it as blood splattered onto the ground and Leah watched as blackened veins crept further up his neck. He wasn't using *Netzach*, but whatever this was, it helped him ignore the pain the two were causing.

Ian glared at Leah, clearly expecting her to have dropped her defenses by now. He let out another wave of energy, sending everyone back and away from him.

A grin stretched across his face while he studied Leah. "My, oh my, they would have loved to have had you." He lowered himself down, readying to launch at her, hands balled into fists.

This was it. Leah wouldn't be able to stop him again.

He'd break through her defenses in seconds. She was going to lose.

His attack never came. Instead, he stood, semi-crouched, his eyes shifting back and forth.

Sid stepped into the alley, blood dripping from his forehead. He held his hands together, eyes locked on Ian.

"I've got you, friend."

Ian kept his eyes on Sid, his face turning red and his temples throbbing.

Sid held onto *Hod*, watching Ian's lips turn purple and his eyes roll into the back of his head. Sid turned pale, sweat forming across his brow. "We all trusted you."

Ian stared at Sid, blood vessels popping in his eyes.

Sid shook his head and dropped his hands. Ian collapsed to the ground, shallow breaths returning to his lungs. "He'll live." He nodded to the duffel back a few feet behind him. "There's rope in there. Grab it and we'll tie him up."

A shriek sounded near the front of the warehouses as they finished tying up Ian.

Rubble shifted, and the creature stuck out a long, clawed hand from the heap of bricks.

"That thing just won't die," Sid grumbled.

It stood at the end of the alley between the two warehouses, dark red blood dripping from its head and torso, silvery eyes glinting straight at them.

Something the color of straw stepped out from the shadows next to it. Shorter, with clawed hands outstretched and long blond hair covering half its—no, *her*—face. She was more human than animal, and Leah's heart sank as she recognized Paige's face staring back at her with shining eyes.

CHAPTER 38

TRAITOR

Isaac caught Leah as her knees buckled underneath her. Paige stood still, her eyes locked eyes on Leah with a gaze that tore Leah apart.

Sarah stepped forward, raising her hands. "Paige? Is that you in there?"

In a flash, both chimeras moved, the bat creature leaping into the air and Paige crouching down, ready to pounce across the concrete.

Mere feet away from Leah, a torrent of energy passed by her, freezing the chimeras. Sid gasped, his face pale, holding his hands together, eyeing the creatures. "I can't hold them for long. The keys are in my pocket. Take Ian, get back to the academy, and tell Nykima this is an Amar opening. Don't let him out of your sight until you find Nykima. She'll know what that means."

Leah took a step back. "Amar?"

Sid's knee gave, and he slammed into the ground, grunting from the pain. His hands remained together, but in that split second, the chimeras had inched closer. "Just do it! Go!"

Leah raced forward and fished the keys out of his pocket, then grabbed Ian's feet. "Does someone want to help me?"

Her friends rushed to her side. They paused, eyeing Sid once more before lifting the body.

They heaved Ian's body into the bed of the truck, and he let out a quiet moan.

Sarah held out her hand. "I'll drive. You two stay with him. He might wake up and both of you will be better at holding him without blowing the truck in two."

A howl pierced their ears, a strange mix between a person screaming and a wolf.

Leah nodded and handed Sarah the keys. "Sid's done holding them off. We need to go, now!"

She pulled Isaac up into the bed of the truck while Sarah hopped into the front, squealing tires as they tore out of the parking lot.

Leah stared back at the warehouses, seeing two shining eyes staring back at her in the distance.

They raced back to the academy. Sarah followed the GPS while the ropes kept Ian restrained. The bumps in the road, however, added a few more bruises to his head.

Once they got off the highway and back into the woods near the academy, Leah asked Isaac, "What do we do now? Just turn him in and hope for the best?"

"We tell everyone what we saw, and we make sure they know we aren't sitting on the sidelines while they take their sweet time," Isaac said.

Leah peered off into the woods, half expecting to see

those silvery eyes looking back at her. She focused on the cool breeze, trying to get her mind away from the thought of them chasing after her.

"Why aren't the chimeras following us?" Isaac asked. "They got past Sid in time; they could have reached us."

Leah stared at the road. "Who knows? But I'm glad they didn't."

"It just doesn't add up."

Sarah stopped the truck in front of the large metal gates to the academy and laid her hand on the horn.

They sat in the dark of night in silence for a long while, their only source of light being the headlights bouncing off the metal gate.

From the tree line, a tall man dressed in all black approached, a pistol fastened on his side. He eyed Leah and Isaac sitting in the back of the truck. "What are you three doing in a stolen truck? Explain yourselves. Now."

"We need to speak to Nykima," Leah said. "Let us through. It's urgent."

The man put his hand to his ear and approached the truck, eyeing the back seat and then the bed of the truck, spotting Ian. He stepped back and aimed the gun at Sarah. "Exit the vehicle and keep your hands where I can see them. All of you."

Isaac shook his head, his voice shaking. "Black Bishop Gunn told us to speak to Nykima. We aren't letting him out of our sight until we do. Got it?"

The man whistled and floodlights pooled onto the truck. In seconds, Knights carrying assault rifles surrounded them.

A woman with short black hair approached, holding an assault rifle pointed straight at Leah, and peered into the bed of the truck. "As third in command of security, I'm commanding you, Pawns, step out of the truck, or we will use force."

"No!" Isaac shouted. "Sid gave us direct orders to not leave Ian's side until we speak to Nykima."

The woman pursed her lips. "Pawn, this doesn't concern you anymore."

Leah scoffed. "Doesn't concern us? Do you even know where we found him, or who we found with him? We know where the abducted Pawns are. We know what happened to them, and it will happen to more if you don't let us speak to Nykima right now as Black Bishop Gunn demanded of us."

The woman pursed her lips and clenched her gun. "You insolent little—"

A familiar voice cracked over the radio. "Why wasn't I notified of this sooner? Black Knight Harris, this is B1, authorizing the Pawns to be escorted up the driveway in the truck. I want two Knights in the truck securing the prisoner."

Black Knight Harris glared at Leah, then pointed to two of the others. "You heard her. Secure the truck, and let them through."

Two Knights jumped into the back of the truck and looked over at Ian, checking the ropes before nodding back to the woman. She snapped her fingers, and the gates opened.

Sarah drove the truck up the winding path and up to the front of the academy, where Nykima waited in front of another group of Knights and Bishops. She eyed the back of the truck bed before looking at the three Pawns. "Come with me. I want you to tell me exactly what happened."

"Sid said this was an Amar opening. He wanted us to be sure that you heard it," Leah said to Nykima.

She nodded. "You all heard it. Take him to the cells.

Maximum security. This does not get out, under any circumstances, to anyone but the gate crew. No one, and I mean no one, shares this information but me. Let me know when he's conscious." She turned and pointed at the others dressed in black behind her. "Wake the admins and tell them to meet me in the dean's office. Now."

CHAPTER 39
ADMINISTRATIVE DUTIES

Leah, her friends, and Nykima stepped into the dean's office, Dean Wright already cramped inside with Grace, Constance, and Reginald.

Constance stood with a housecoat wrapped around her, bags visible under her eyes. "What is the meaning of this?"

Nykima stood at attention. "I have secured Pawn Ackerman, O'Connor, and Turner with me. They've returned in Black Bishop Gunn's truck. He informed these Pawns of an Amar opening, for me to hear specifically."

Grace cocked her head. "Amar? Who would have done this?"

"We found Black Knight Kim bound in the truck's bed."

William's eyes widened, and he shook his head. "He told me he wasn't feeling well." His face hardened, and he stared at Reginald. "I assure you; I knew nothing of this."

Reginald held a hand up. "We'll address that in a minute." He turned his gaze to Leah and her friends. "May I ask what you three were doing? We thought you'd run away."

Isaac stepped forward. "Black Rook Platt, we followed Bishop Gunn out this evening. We suspected he was the one behind all the disappearances, but we were wrong. We found Black Knight Kim with a chimera. Paige was there too, and I bet if you investigated it, you'd find evidence that Theodore, Joanna, and the others have been there too. But Paige wasn't herself anymore. She's a chimera."

Constance frowned. "We hunted chimeras to the brink of extinction centuries ago. There's only a small group of lycanthropes left in Tasmania, last I checked. How can they be here?"

Leah looked at Grace. "You assigned Sid to research this. There was a pile of books on the subject in his room. There's evidence there too. Orange fur from the night one of them took Joanna."

"He hadn't come to me with anything yet. But yes, I had asked him to investigate the disappearances," Grace said.

Constance tightened her grip on her housecoat. "If the disappearances are linked, and students are undergoing these forced transformations, then someone on the Board would have to be helping. And that would mean there's a chimera out there with enough willpower to transform many creations at once."

William paled. "Especially if we kept all the historical texts of chimeric transformations. Someone from the inside had to be feeding them information. Ian . . ."

Nykima cleared her throat. "We need to send a unit out to Black Bishop Gunn's location now."

"He's at the Portside Warehouses, number twenty-seven," Sarah said. "About one hour west of here. He needs help. He was shot."

Grace nodded. "Nykima, get on it. Prepare a second wave in the event they need backup."

Nykima bowed her head. "At once, White Bishop John-son." She turned and gave Leah a nod, the first genuine look of approval that she had given her since coming to the academy. Nykima pulled a radio from her side. "I want a full squad ready to head out in five. I'll meet you at the gate."

Reginald tapped on his cane. "William, why don't you take a seat? And put your hands where we can see them. Now that we've addressed any immediate concern, I'd like to hear from these three what exactly they've been up to."

William obeyed, sitting down in his chair, hands on top of the desk, while the administration stood around him.

Isaac and Sarah recounted the events, leaving out Leah's invisibility trick but ensuring that they covered everything else leading up to tonight, including breaking into Sid's room. Leah could barely keep herself on two feet, the exhaustion washing over her.

When they finished, Reginald leaned against the book-case behind him and crossed his arms. "I can see why he called for this Amar opening, then. But Ian Kim? He alone doesn't fit the bill."

William steepled his fingers. "He is my bond, and my responsibility, but he barricaded this side of himself from me. Even now, the bond between us is silent, but one thing I am certain of is that there is no corruption stemming from him."

Grace's eyes flashed yellow, and she stared at William. "Once he's awake, we'll need to interrogate him."

"I agree," the dean said. "And I don't expect you to hold back because of me. I'll be there by your side. I want to know why he did this as much as you do."

"And what about Paige?" Leah asked. "Can we change her back?"

Constance sighed. "I don't know. Chimeras were things of the past. The texts we have describe some of their rituals, but no one here has seen them in action. From what you've described, the person behind this knows what they are doing, and they do it well. I'm afraid that anything else on the matter that could help us would come from one of two sources, Black Bishop Gunn or Black Bishop Kim."

"From your descriptions of the chimeras," Reginald said. "You described one like a bat and the other like a wolf, signature chimeras that are remembered throughout history as vampires and werewolves. I think what my colleague was alluding to was that if this chimera ringleader could produce such an array of chimeras, then there is some level of skill and finesse with a blade and depth of connection to the Trees."

"But if we get Paige, we can turn her back, right?" Sarah asked.

All three admins eyed each other until William broke the silence. "Perhaps. We need to capture Black Pawn Jones and any other student entangled in this mess. Once we have them, we can see what we can do about their condition."

The door behind Leah burst open, and everyone jumped to their feet as Eric rushed in, his face white and eyes wide. "Apologies for the intrusion. Black Knight Mizrahi, sir! Permission to approach my niece?"

"You could have knocked," William said, holding his hand over his chest from the startle. "What is this about?"

"Our bond, sir. I felt a disturbance."

William raised an eyebrow. "Seems that distance can only work so much. Permission granted, Black Knight. In fact, could you please escort the three Pawns back to their dormitories? I think we are done here."

Eric rushed over and hugged Leah, whispering in her ear. "Where were you? The bond. I couldn't feel you again. It's like you vanished."

Leah didn't respond, feeling the waves of fear, happiness, and guilt coming from Eric.

"You want us to sleep?" Sarah protested. "But we can help!"

Grace shook her head. "You three have done more than enough, and we're already on the case. Even soldiers need rest, and I can tell the three of you are ready to topple over any minute. Rest now, Pawn Turner, and we'll keep you informed."

Constance stepped forward and raised a hand. "On second thought, take these three to the infirmary. Grace made an excellent point I overlooked. These three have overextended themselves, and I'd like to keep them under observation, just in case."

Reginald and William nodded together.

Eric stood at attention and gave a slight bow. "Will do, right away."

He ushered the three of them toward the door.

"Just one more thing before they go." William said. "I know my Knight wrapping himself in all of this reflects on me, but I am still the dean of this academy. For what it is worth, the three of you have gained points this evening. I'd say twenty a piece. Thank you for your efforts in keeping the Infinity Board safe."

He gave an enormous, sincere smile before they turned and left his office.

CHAPTER 40
DEMON KNIGHT

Eric closed the doors to the dean's office and turned, noting Leah already several feet ahead of him, heading to the stairs. "Leah, wait, we need to—"

Leah turned, sadness flowing into her. "We know where the infirmary is. We don't need an escort."

Eric bit his lip. "Leah, don't be like that."

"I can't help it. I told you from the start that something was off. Just because you now believe me and want to flood me with all your guilt and happiness doesn't excuse you from not helping. I may have been wrong about who, but with your help, we could have . . ."

The rest of the words couldn't come out, but she knew he felt what she did.

Eric looked at Isaac and Sarah for support, but Isaac shook his head. "Just give us some space. Some time. We know our way, Black Knight Mizrahi. Goodnight."

Isaac and Sarah stepped to either side of Leah and proceeded to the infirmary.

"I'm sorry," Eric croaked behind them.

But Leah never looked back.

They arrived at the infirmary. Each took a bed, and

before Leah could even get the blanket all the way over her, she was fast asleep.

Colors flashed in Leah's eyes, ribbons of violet, blue, and green dancing above the night sky, passing through her as if she weren't even there. Her body descended from the skies and onto a dark plain. The wet grass squished beneath her feet, and when she looked up, she could see a pair of shining wolf eyes looking back at her.

"Paige? Is that you?"

A heavy metal door unlocked behind her. As she turned, her vision blurred and reshaped itself into a dimly lit corridor. Gray stone walls stretched to either side, and a large metal door stood in front of her, lit by old, yellowed lightbulbs. Two men wearing black lay at her feet. They were Knights by the look of it, still alive, but unconscious.

A voice echoed from the door. "I'm sorry. There . . . there must be something. I've given everything to this."

Another voice, deeper and melodic, spoke. "You gave up your life the moment Pawns captured you."

Leah stepped forward, passing through the door as if it were an icy waterfall. Inside, she spotted Ian, bloodied and tied up to a chair. His head down, he muttered inaudibly to himself.

Two figures stood at his side, shadows wrapping unnaturally around them, covering their faces from Leah's eyes. She held her breath, but neither of the figures acknowledged her presence.

One crouched next to Ian, speaking just loud enough for Leah to hear. A familiar male voice from her memories that she couldn't quite place. "I'm sorry, my friend. The risk is too high."

Ian jerked his head up, his eyes searching the shadowed man's face. "But I did everything you asked. You promised we'd change the world. You promised I'd see the day it all changed. I did what you wanted, didn't I? Please—"

The other shadowed person, more androgynous, waved their hand. Their voice came out distorted, rising and lowering in a strange pitch. "Just get it over with. I don't have all night."

Leah took a step back, against the cold and now very solid metal door. She didn't want to be here, not for what was about to happen next. Yet, she couldn't move, trapped, watching whatever played out.

The shadowy man next to Ian stood back up and stepped behind him as he pulled a slender box from his jacket pocket. He cracked the box open and pulled out a syringe. Standing behind Ian and resting a hand on his shoulder, he continued. "For what it's worth, losing you will hurt me, and our plans, much more than it will hurt you." The man slipped the needle into Ian's unflinching neck and depressed the plunger.

Ian's eyes widened, and his pupils dilated as his breathing slowed. He kept his eyes on the shadow, tears forming in the corners of his eyes, until finally, his head fell forward and his breathing stopped.

Leah stepped forward, focusing on the executioner's face. The more she squinted, the more the shadows seemed to lighten, and the more the face came into focus.

A clawed hand wrapped around Leah's neck and pinned her up against the wall. The other figure was on her, a collection of voices intertwined with a melodic chittering spoke in her ear. "You've become quite the nuisance, Leah Ackerman. Always poking your head around."

The clawed hand tightened, cutting off her airway, and the man behind Ian looked up and crossed the room.

The creature that held her spoke back. "You know what you must do now. Leave us."

The man left as commanded.

Leah stared at Ian, slumped over and dead. He'd been the only lead the Infinity Board had to getting Paige and Theodore back.

She grabbed at the hand around her neck, scratching at the claws while she attempted to gather *Malchut* to rip them off if she had to. But the energy didn't flow. Nothing stirred from her chest.

The thing spoke once more, its hot breath spreading across Leah's neck. "Don't bother. The Tree recoils from my touch."

Leah tried to speak, but nothing came out.

The creature snorted. "You are asleep, girl. Do you think you need your breath to speak?"

She focused on the sound of her voice, feeling the words form in her throat. "Who are you?"

"We've already met. Several times." The creature let out a high and piercing laugh that sparked a memory in Leah's mind.

That laugh had echoed many times in her head. A laugh that hid in shadows that moved of their own accord.

"Legion," she said.

Heat billowed onto her ear as he spoke. "Yes."

"What do you want?"

The creature paused for a moment, running a sharp black finger back and forth on Leah's clavicle. "You're a Mizrahi. And one who meddles too much. I want you dead."

A twitch in her left arm sent a numbing sensation up around her throat, like a barrier between her and the creature. Energy blossomed to life inside her chest in response.

Leah felt Asmodeus helping her, taking partial control of her body as he smiled through her, and her left hand tightened around the claw. "I'm not so easy to kill."

A wave of *Malchut* pressed through her hand, ripping off the creature's fingers while it tumbled backward.

She landed hard on the tiled floor, sheets wrapping around her. She looked up to see the ceiling of the infirmary and gasped for air, relieved that she finally woke.

A chuckle sounded from the foot of her bed, and the familiar voice of the shadowed man spoke. "Even he can't hold you, clever girl."

Dean Wright stood over her, reaching a hand toward her head, and everything went dark again.

CHAPTER 41
THE CHIMERA'S LAIR

A dense, foul odor that Leah could best describe as a wet dog riled her from sleep. Her mind and thoughts waded through thick gel, screaming at her body to move.

Steps sounded beside her, creaking along the wooden floorboards. Where was she? The last thing she remembered was Dean Wright standing at the end of her bed, the man who'd fooled the admins and was in on whatever sick trafficking scheme Ian had enacted. Was Dean Wright the one who'd murdered him?

She strained her mind again, focusing on her eyelids. They twitched and cracked open, just enough to let her peek.

Wooden rafters supported the roof above her. An old structure, by the look of it, and not something she'd seen at the warehouses.

Flood lights stood on long stands, illuminating the room and the set of shiny metal medical instruments next to her. Her eyes swept up, and she spotted the IV bag, connected straight to her arm, and she knew right away that was the source of her semi-paralyzed state.

She focused on moving her hand, bringing it closer to the needle, but it was useless. Her hand didn't move.

A buzzing sensation formed in Leah's arm, numb and distant. The voice Asmodeus of sounded in her head. *I can help.*

She tried speaking, but the words didn't come out of her mouth. Yet Asmodeus still heard her question. *Why are you helping me?*

We have a mutual enemy. One that poses a significant risk to both our worlds.

Legion? Leah asked, but Asmodeus didn't answer.

Pain shot up from the inside of her elbow. She saw the needle pushing itself out and away from her body, pulling the tape along with it. In seconds, her arm was bare, only a small dribble of blood pooling where the needle had been.

Sensation returned. First, the uncoiling in her chest as *Malchut* came alive inside her. A great weight lifted off her head, like someone had pulled a weighted blanket off her.

Leah turned and saw another gurney several feet from her. Sid lay still, only his head protruding out from under a white sheet, an IV sticking out of his arm.

Before she could sit up, a door behind her opened, and cool air rushed in along with the sound of water lapping up against a shore. The door squeaked closed again, and footsteps approached.

The wet dog smell all but vanished, replaced with the scent of a lake with a tinge of something fishy.

As the person approached, Leah focused on building up energy against her skin. The energy would build for a second, and then vanish, as if something had yanked it away from her. At first she thought it was Asmodeus, collecting energy again. But it couldn't have been him; the energy didn't move to her arm. Instead, it simply left her body.

She opened and closed her hands and tried moving them against the restraints, testing how well they held her before going limp again and shutting her eyes.

"Don't bother. The restraints are better than any medical grade ones I've used before, marked with sigils that absorb any force applied to them. Interesting, though, that you could get the IV out."

Leah swallowed, her throat going dry as she heard the familiar voice. Leah opened her eyes only a sliver to see Dr. Toppen pass beside her, holding a cotton swab to Leah's elbow before applying a bandage.

Dr. Toppen adjusted her black coat. "I know you're awake. You can open your eyes." She walked to a sink, turning on the faucet and washing her hands.

Leah worked her jaw and spoke, her voice hoarse and weak. "Why are you doing this? What did you do with Paige?"

She dried off her hands and approached Leah. "How about this? You answer my questions, and I'll answer yours. Deal? We'll start with how you got the IV out of your arm."

"I . . . I don't know how I did it."

Dr. Toppen sighed and tossed the towel in the sink. "You Mystics. So much power and not enough understanding. Pity. That might have been interesting. My turn then? I freed Paige from a life she didn't want. I gave her the keys to advancing her knowledge on what we know and believe to be true."

Leah strained against her restraints. "Liar! She wouldn't want that!"

Dr. Toppen unbuttoned her coat, and as she did, her sides bloated and shifted. "I suppose now is as good a time as any to show you my commitment to the cause."

Underneath, large tentacles unwrapped around her

stomach, reaching out and pushing back her coat to show the full extension of the appendages.

"We were never meant to be constrained by the forms of man."

Leah couldn't believe her eyes. As strange as the other chimeras were, her changes were distinct, contained to her sides.

Dr. Toppen turned to the corner of the room and snapped her fingers. A large man, covered with ginger fur, stepped out from the shadows. His jaw was unnaturally long, slightly distorting half of his face, and his eyes looked at her as if she were his next meal.

His eyes shone, and it took Leah back to the night at the library, where she'd last seen this creature. Now, in the light, he appeared more human, and more familiar.

"Theodore?" Leah asked Brandon's lost brother, but the chimera ignored her.

He approached Dr. Toppen, handing her a pair of gloves while she caressed his face with a wet tentacle and smiled. "I told William that memory wipe wouldn't stick. You were too . . . different. Yes, my dear Theodore worried me when he went on his brief escape. Poor thing was confused. Lucky that William found you three in the library when he did, before anything unfortunate happened to him."

Leah's heart raced. The gloves, the instruments next to her, and the drugs. All of it was too much. "What are you doing? What do you want with me?"

Dr. Toppen approached the table, her tentacled arms brushing over the metal instruments. "You know too much. Poked your nose where it shouldn't have been. Even when they tried their little parasites on you, you persisted. You've made yourself a nuisance to some powerful people. But me, I am in awe of you."

"What are you talking about?"

"The Infinity Board doesn't have a place for you. It doesn't cherish women like us, willing to forge our own path and fight against the grain. They're archaic, and we're creatures of chaos, something they'd snuff out in an instant if they could. You asked, why am I doing this? I'm on the verge of something beautiful. Something that my colleagues couldn't see."

Leah shifted her gaze. "Theodore, do you remember your brother? Brandon? He misses you. He wants you to come back. Help me out of this, and I'll help you get back to him. Please, you're one of us, a Black Pawn!"

Dr. Toppen extended a tentacle over Leah's lips and waved her hand. "Save your breath. He's with me now. And he knows what would happen if the Infinity Board got hold of him. There hasn't been a chimera for centuries; they'd be over the moon to check what's on the inside."

The doctor's tentacle picked up the needle from the ground, still dripping clear liquid, and wiped it off with an alcohol wipe.

Leah's eyes widened, and she pressed herself against the bed, trying to fight off her restraints. "No! She's lying, Theodore! Do you think your brother would let that happen? We need you!"

Theodore approached Leah, his fanged face inches from hers, his hot breath rolling over her. "Enough! Do you think I wasn't there when that Black Bishop attacked my friends? They're the danger. They want to cow us into what they believe is right. I have a new family, a pack, that I need to protect. Something Brandon and the old Theodore lost a long time ago."

He held her down with one hand as Dr. Toppen approached. Every attempt to build energy was foiled as *Malchut* vanished into the restraints.

Asmodeus spoke again in a quick whisper. *Let me help.*

She nodded, unsure if that was enough of a signal to him.

Warmth billowed in Leah's stomach, and she felt the *Yesod* bond between her and Eric. Sensations that weren't hers, a mix of fear and terror, shot from her end of the bond like a bone curdling scream.

Then the needle slid in with ease, and the sensations within her disappeared altogether, her limbs falling numb and distant. Words fell out of her mouth, a fear and anxiety that she had been holding on to. "I don't want to be like you."

Theodore looked at her, his wolffish face forming a slight smile. Was that sadness she saw in his eyes? "Don't worry, you won't."

Dr. Toppen held up a scalpel and started unbuttoning Leah's shirt with her other appendages. "They gave us different instructions for you, as part of the agreement."

Leah's mind slipped away, and her eyes fluttered closed.

"You'll wake up in a few hours, none the wiser, trust me. Now sleep." A cold tentacle brushed against her cheek, and darkness overtook her.

CHAPTER 42

GHARAB TZEREK

A loud crash jostled Leah awake from her dreamless sleep, the sound of wooden beams snapping like toothpicks. Through the medicated exhaustion, she forced her eyes open, seeing two blurred figures standing in front of her: Theodore and Dr. Toppen.

The doctor raced around the room in a flash, wrapping her arms and tentacles around the instruments and a small pile of books. She turned to Theodore. "Keep an eye that no one follows."

He nodded, and Dr. Toppen fled out the door opposite Theodore, who leaped through the hole in the wall.

Alone again, aside from Sid who lay there unconscious, Asmodeus spoke, his voice even more distant. *Good, he got the message. Now let me do this again.*

Energy flowed back as the needle fell to the floor, her senses flooding back into her, faster and stronger than before. She focused on the restraints on her arms and let the *Malchut* flow.

Help me, she thought to Asmodeus.

She took in a sharp breath, and frost formed on the

floor. Energy surged into her, and she let it flow through her, directing it into the restraints. Pressure built between her and the cuffs, growing until Leah was certain her wrists would crack. Then the restraints snapped, busting in half like a bomb had detonated them.

Her vision returned as her eyes settled on the massive hole in the wall and the surrounding rubble. Through it, the moon, momentarily breaking free from the storm clouds, shone on a river, a familiar sight she'd seen many days running by it. She was still at the academy, up in the attic of the dock house.

Leah rushed to Sid's side. Cuts and bruises lined his face and arms, and he looked worse off than when she'd left him at the warehouse. She slid the needle out of his arm, but he didn't wake. She backed away. "I'll come back; I promise."

Leah jumped off the attic platform, using *Malchut* to break her fall and land on her feet. Outside the boathouse, she saw Eric dealing a massive *Malchut* punch to William, who stood still as the punch grazed off him. She stepped forward, ready to help, but a blur of orange fur rushed behind Eric.

She threw a wave of energy toward the mass of fur, which hit Theodore square in the chest, sending him spiraling into a tree at the edge of the woods with a yelp. Leah stepped forward, focusing on William.

Eric turned and shouted. "Leah, stay back!"

William moved quick, using Eric's distraction to close the distance and collide into Eric's side, sending him off near Theodore.

Leah pointed her fingers at William and flung piercing bullets of *Malchut* his way. He didn't even look at her, his eyes locked on Eric while he dodged her attack with ease.

Theodore pounced on Eric, tearing into his shoulder with his claws.

William shifted his gaze toward Leah and cracked his neck with a grin. Before she could even think, he flew forward, landing a knee in her stomach.

All the air rushed out of her body, and she fell to the ground. He aimed his leg again, ready to slam his foot into her side.

Her arm moved without warrant, reaching for his leg, but it was too slow. *Malchut* flung her into the air, and she heaved as she landed hard on the grass.

He sauntered over to her. "You are quite the nuisance. Idiocy doesn't fall far from the tree."

Leah turned to her side, ready to stand and take on William with newfound anger. But he moved faster. His foot rested on her head, pushing it to the wet ground, her head sinking into the mud. Pain seared through her as he pressed his foot harder. She grabbed for it, but he didn't move.

She built up *Malchut* in her left hand, ready to tear off his foot, but he held out a hand above her, unleashing a wave of *Malchut* that pushed down on her as if gravity had increased tenfold. Leah's arm went limp, and the energy vanished. William's boot slipped to her neck, and her head throbbed as her breathing strained.

A new fear rose. Not hers, not Eric's, but something inside her, worried that this was the end. Asmodeus.

Gunshots echoed from the tree line, whizzing above Leah. William stepped off her.

Air blossomed back into Leah's mind, and she lay for a moment gasping for breath.

"Get away from her!" Eric shouted.

Leah pushed herself up off the ground, expecting William to be on her any minute, but he remained standing next to her, facing the woods.

Her eyes traced up to him, and she spotted the holes in

his white coat, now filling with bright red stains. Cold energy whooshed past Leah, William's mouth agape and jaw moving with soundless words. The energy stopped, and his knees gave, slamming into the ground as he fell face first into the grass.

Leah stared at the dead dean, backing away as Eric caught up to her, his gun pointing at William.

She clutched her left arm as it throbbed over and over. Eric turned, pushing Leah behind him as he aimed his gun toward the forest. Theodore emerged from the bushes and headed right toward Eric.

Leah darted out from behind Eric and placed a hand on the gun. "Wait! That's Theodore! He's one of us."

She pushed past Eric and held up her hands. "You're still a part of the Infinity Board. Theodore, please."

He growled, and the fur on top of his head rose. "It's too late."

More leaves moved behind Theodore, and two other figures appeared at his side. The bat-like creature sported a fresh scar across its face while Paige bared her fangs at Leah.

"Paige," Leah started, but then her sense of balance flew into a frenzy. The world moved like waves while her stomach turned.

Her uncle backed into Leah, his gun no longer pointed at the forest. "Someone is using the Tree of Death."

Leah frowned, her eyes still on Paige. "Who? The chimeras?"

Something cracked behind her, and she looked over her shoulder.

William's body twitched and contorted, flinging itself upright as if it were a rag doll on puppet strings. The sporadic movements shifted into smooth ones as Leah watched in horror. The White Knight stood, brushing wet dirt off his white coat, and smiled. "I haven't had the chance to practice that one yet in a real-life situation. Thanks for the opportunity to test it out."

CHAPTER 43
TREASON

Leah stumbled back, nausea carrying bile to the back of her throat. "But how?"

William looked past Leah to Eric. "I wouldn't bother with that again." He flicked a finger and sent Eric's gun flying out of his hand.

His expression changed, returning to the face Leah was used to, the warm dean she knew. "*Gharab Tzerek*. Opposite of *Netzach*. While one uses energy to protect and make you invulnerable, the other takes injury, pain, and even death to make you immortal and full of energy while using it. At least, if one were a sage. The only unfortunate side effect is the scarring. The well doesn't make for a gentle touch."

Eric clutched at his side, pointing to the blackening earth around William's feet. "And you poison everything around you when you use it."

William's smile grew wide. "Ah, I'd say I'm reshaping it. Giving it a chance to start anew."

He propelled forward toward Leah. From the corner of her eye, Leah saw the bat-like creature leap into the air, and Paige and Theodore lunge forward. They surrounded Leah and Eric, who had no place to go.

Eric wrapped his arm around her waist and pulled her in, sending a *Malchut* wave into the ground that propelled them through the air. They landed hard on the gravel at the edge of the river.

She glanced behind them, William and the chimeras closing in.

William glared at the chimeras. "Well, what are you waiting for? Kill them!"

Eric pushed Leah backward. "Jump into the river. The current will take you away. I can buy you some time to build some distance so you have a chance."

Theodore stepped closer, drool streaming out of his mouth.

Leah frowned. "Did you not call for reinforcements?"

Eric shook his head. "Came alone. That message you sent me, through the *Yesod*, was clear. *Don't trust anyone.* Rightfully so, too."

Her uncle kneeled and sent waves of *Malchut* forward, hitting Theodore and Paige, knocking them back while William and the bat creature closed in.

Leah focused on the chimeras, mimicking what she had seen Isaac, Sid, and Eric do before. She closed her eyes, and Isaac's words resonated in her head.

. . . When I clap, it's like the energy inverts before projecting out, if that makes sense . . .

Pressure formed in her hands as the chimeras closed in. She clapped and drew the energy inwards. As she did, a balloon of energy stretched out around her, expanding toward her targets.

Hod spread over the chimeras, slowing but not stopping them. Each one of them pushed forward, fighting against *Hod* and sending Leah's mind reeling to keep control. Sweat formed on her brow, but she held her hands together, keeping them stuck in this slow state.

Eric sent another push, one that the chimeras couldn't brace against, and they both went flying back as William withstood the blow. He huffed, glaring at Leah. "Get out of here!"

Leah let go of *Hod* and launched a *Malchut* push forward against William. "No! I won't let anyone else die protecting me."

William launched another blow of *Malchut* that Eric fended off.

As he did, Theodore erupted from the woods and raced along the edge of the water.

"Don't do this!" Leah yelled, raising up a hand.

The chimera leaped forward, mouth wide open, fangs ready to sink into her.

Alma's training kicked in, and Leah raised her left hand. She let out a single energy push, refined down to a point that collided with Theodore's skull.

She heard the crack of bone, and his eyes rolled up into the back of his head before he crumpled to the ground next to her. Leah stared in horror, waiting for his chest to move up and down, to see that he was still breathing, but it didn't come. In an instant, he was dead. She'd killed him.

Paige and the bat creature broke from the treeline. They looked at Theodore's body, and Paige's eyes reddened as a snarl escaped her. She rushed toward Leah, but the bat creature grabbed her, sniffing the air. He shook his head and pulled her back into the woods.

William shouted after him. "Where do you think you're going? We had an agreement!"

Bright lights filtered through the trees opposite from where the chimeras had left, as engines roared up the path and SUVs tore through the mud, stopping feet away from William.

Two glowing lights shone from inside one of the SUVs,

moving with every bump in the road. A seer, burning *Tiferet,* sat in the passenger seat.

A squad of ten Knights and Bishops rushed out of the SUVs, aiming their weapons at William. He raised his hands.

Nykima's voice sounded over a megaphone. "Keep your hands where I can see them and get on the ground!"

William took in a deep breath, and with it, Leah sensed a massive pull of energy. The air turned to ice, and his hands dropped, releasing a *Malchut* push that shoved the SUVs back and crashed into the Knights and Bishops. When the energy reached the treeline, trees snapped in half, and another part of the boathouse tore off, flying off into the woods. The amount of energy he could wield was unlike anything Leah had ever seen before.

Leah stepped toward the boathouse and screamed, "Sid!" She turned to Eric. "He's still in there!"

Gunshots fired, and Eric yanked Leah down flat onto the ground, manifesting *Netzach* to deflect the bullets. The bullets pierced William's body, forming a mist of red around him and tattering his coat even more.

Nykima shouted over the megaphone again. "Stop!"

The sound of gunfire ended, but William didn't seem phased. He stared at the remains of his coat and tore it off. Underneath, his skin seemed more like black-and-white marble than flesh. Obsidian scars webbed their way through his torso, turning any nearby veins black. William looked at the SUVs, raised one hand, and shot off a torrent of *Malchut* bullets.

Metal tore apart, and the barrier between him and the Knights and Bishops faltered, his energy piercing through several Mystics who fell to the ground, dead.

Once the bullets stopped, Nykima flew out from behind the SUVs and collided with William. Energy ebbed and flowed through the air as *Malchut* collided. Constance, Grace, and Reginald all stepped out of the farthest SUV and raced into battle as well.

Gharab Tzerek and *Nehemoth* fed him more energy than he should have. His energy permeated the air like a noxious gas. It washed over Leah, burning her skin and causing her insides to twist in knots.

Constance formed a clawed hand over the ground, sending a shockwave that cracked the earth and raced toward William, knocking him off balance. Grace flung a wall of fire at him, and he was set aflame.

William took in a breath, and the flames on his skin died out. His charred flesh healed and charred black, and he laughed, raising his arms up into the air.

Heat billowed through the air, and the ground around William burst into a blue flame, the stones glowing red hot.

Eric pulled on Leah's arm. "We have to get out of here!"

They stumbled away from the fight, moving toward the SUVs, and finding refuge at the side of the boathouse.

Leah looked up at the hole in the wall. "Sid's still up there! We can't just leave him."

Eric sighed and followed Leah up the stairs and into the attic of the boathouse.

When they got up there, Sid lay on the ground, unconscious. He lay fastened to a gurney similar to Leah's, with an IV bag hanging at his side.

The building rumbled, and a kayak hanging from the wall fell to the ground.

Leah raced over to Sid's side and pulled his restraints loose. "We need to hurry!"

Eric nodded, rushing as he pulled the needle from Sid's arm and heaved his unconscious body over his shoulder.

They broke free of the boathouse and propped Sid up against a tree, away from the battle.

The dean turned to Reginald, tearing through the space between them in an instant and launching a fist toward his side.

Reginald lifted his cane, centering it with William's fist and bracing for the impact. It should have snapped. Instead, it held solid. All of Reginald held solid, as if the punch from William had never come. The dean leaned back, but the Black Rook was faster. He didn't even clap his hands together, but William froze, held in an awkward stance, balancing on one foot as the other was preparing for a kick.

Reginald inspected his coat, straightening it before turning to William. "Pity that it has to end this way."

The air seemed to vibrate as William strained against *Hod*. In the seconds that Reginald slid the sheath off his cane, revealing a sword that he swung toward William's neck, William cracked through *Hod*. He ducked out of the way, the sword slicing his cheek before he flew backward.

He stood, blood dripping down his now black-scarred face, and roared. Energy rushed toward him, forming ice crystals on the ground and a mist in the air. Voices filled the void, shouting and whispering obscenities in Leah's ear, telling her how worthless she was. William paused and threw out his hands, bursting with *Malchut*, tearing at the ground and forming a barrier between his opponents.

Blood poured from his face, and his eyes shifted wildly. "You don't know what's coming. None of you can stop it."

Constance stepped forward, her hands out in front of her, fingers spread wide. "Enough, William. Surrender, and we will show mercy. There's still time for you to do the right thing."

The others, Grace, Reginald, and Nykima, stepped behind Constance, at the ready to attack.

William spat blood on the ground between them.

"Mercy? Ha! I'm bonded to you, Constance. I know what your twisted version of mercy is."

He drew in a sharp breath, more ice forming around him. Before he could attack, though, Constance's hands shook as she curled her fingertips into clawed hands. Massive roots burst out of the ground and wrapped themselves around William in an instant, squeezing around him like snakes. He screamed as roots tore through flesh and wriggled into cuts. The more he moved, the more spaces they found to tear into.

Constance stepped up to him, tears forming in her eyes, brushing a hand against his charred face. "Why, William?"

He mustered up a slow laugh, muffled by the blood streaming from his mouth. "The apple doesn't fall far from the tree, Master. And our tree is rotten. It's time for a new one to take its place. I won't go silent."

She took a step back. "I know."

Before she could say anything else, blue fire burst from his hands. The heat burst the roots into flame in an instant and engulfed William in a tower of blue fire. His sickly laughter sounded, William still somehow clutching onto life.

Constance shook her head, holding up her hands. "I'm sorry." She pulled her hands apart, and with it, the remains of the roots cut into William, tearing him into pieces.

CHAPTER 44

REPERCUSSIONS

Eric stayed by Leah's side as they were escorted to an SUV. Leah tried to stay behind while the Bishops aided Sid, but try as she might, she was too exhausted to protest for long.

When they arrived at the SUV, two Bishops took their vitals and passed Leah and Eric bottles filled with a dark purple ooze. Leah uncorked hers, smelling the foul contents within.

Eric downed his in an instant, his face verifying that it tasted as bad as it smelled. He pointed to the bottle. "Hurry and drink up. We were close to William. You don't want any long-term effects."

She frowned. "From the corruption?"

He nodded. "*Gharab Tzerek* poisons everything around it, sort of like radiation."

He didn't need to say more. She downed the bottle, which tasted like the smell of rotting garbage, and spent the next hour focusing on not vomiting it back up.

She rode back to the academy with Eric and two Bishops who monitored them on the way. The radio confirmed seven casualties, and rage boiled over her as she clenched her fists. *How could the dean, of all people, betray them?*

In the infirmary, they were treated for their physical injuries. Leah had two cracked ribs, while Eric had a broken arm and a dislocated shoulder. Constance, who took on the role of lead medic without Dr. Toppen around, instructed them to stay the night. She couldn't treat everyone, forcing her to limit her use of *Chesed* to only the most severely injured of the surviving Knights.

As soon as her head touched the pillow, Leah was off into a dreamless sleep that carried her on into mid-afternoon the next day.

Her eyes were barely open when Eric spoke. "How are you feeling?"

She stretched, a warm sensation building in her navel. Relief, maybe? "Much better." She looked over at her uncle. "Thanks for finding me. If you didn't, I don't know what would have happened."

He smirked. "You contacted me. Hell, I didn't even know you could do that. That's not a common thing people can do with *Yesod*, especially at your age."

Leah frowned. She'd contacted Eric? A tingle shot up her left arm, and a voice echoed in her memory.

I've brought reinforcements.

She wondered what else Asmodeus could do, and more importantly, what else he could make *her* do.

Eric swung himself up off the infirmary bed, his arm wrapped in a cast and pointing to a pile of clothes beside Leah's bed. "The administrators wanted a meeting once you were up. Best get it over with."

They walked past the dean's wide-open office. Inside, Bishops inspected every corner of the room. Leah spotted an enormous pile of books on top of the desk and paused for a moment as her eyes landed on a familiar black book. The same black book Leah had used to get into the Astral Realm back at the outpost.

The room next to it was simple, no bookshelves to clutter the space, instead just a single long table, which held Grace, Constance, and Reginald as they waited for them to enter.

Reginald stood and nodded at Leah. "Good day, Black Pawn Ackerman. I hope you're feeling better after some much-needed rest. Please, have a seat."

Leah took a seat, placing her hands in her lap.

Constance, seated in the middle of the other two admins, leaned forward and folded her hands. "We wanted to begin by expressing our gratitude. Both we, the administrators of this academy, and members of the Infinity Board at large, owe you and your friends many thanks." Both Grace and Reginald nodded in agreement, and Constance carried on. "As we continue to collect evidence, your testimony leading up to your encounter with William Wright yesterday will be crucial in our investigation."

Leah stared at her hands, knowing that this would come at some point, but still not excited to retrace her steps. The image of Theodore, dead at her feet, flashed in her mind. She'd failed to save him.

She'd also failed to bring Paige back. Could she ever face Emma or Brandon again? She took a deep breath, staring at the top of the table, and started from the beginning, including the dreams, and they listened without stopping her.

When she'd finished, Constance looked at Reginald.

"Her *Malchut* failing when she was tied up at the upper level of the dock; that would explain how the students couldn't fight back. Any ideas?"

"I know of one ritual, known as Ayin," Reginald said. "It takes parts of *Nehemoth* to dispel and absorb any residual energy. They must have marked the restraints with it first. This move is dangerous to perform, which is why the Queens instruct us Rooks to keep it secret. One could lose connection to the tree altogether if they do it wrong. I wouldn't be surprised if William found it in one of the books he's collected over the years."

Grace crossed her arms. "He likely learned to perform *Gharab Tzerek* from one of them as well, no doubt. We must keep an inventory of his collection and review everything he has been up to."

Reginald turned his raven-headed cane over in his hands. "Yes, but I'm still curious what interest Ian and William had in Dr. Toppen's work. Trafficking students to make a small chimera army doesn't seem to benefit them."

Grace nodded. "Yet some students returned to the academy unharmed. Joanna Morales, for example. And from Leah's testimony, they were not planning on converting her into a chimera."

Constance scrawled down a note. "I examined her myself when she returned, albeit with Dr. Toppen at my side. We'll need to perform additional tests on Joanna at once. Reginald, I presume you can request some texts that are above my clearance? We'll need to dig deep. I'd rather not leave a stone unturned, only to discover a viper when it's too late."

"Not a problem," Reginald said, taking note.

Eric scratched his chin. "But what could they have done to her? From your initial examination, you cleared her corruption, and from Leah we know she appears to be stronger."

"All the more reason to think she is fine now," Grace said. "Which forces me to suspect she could be some kind of Trojan horse, waiting for the right moment."

Constance shook her head. "I wouldn't go that far, Grace. She had no markings or signs of possession. Perhaps they used her to test something they were too afraid to try on themselves. Either way, additional tests and continued observation are in order. She escaped, remember? She may have fled before they did anything untoward to her."

Reginald clasped his hands together. "We shall take extra precautions with that Pawn. You also mentioned an entity that pinned you down. You said his name was Legion?"

"He was leading them, I think," Leah said.

"That name isn't familiar to me," Grace said. "We'll need to do a thorough check on everything we have. See if we can find anything on this Legion."

Reginald's pen scratched in the otherwise silent room.

Leah cleared her throat. "And what about Paige?"

Reginald peered into Leah's eyes. "The Infinity Board has a vested interest in bringing back both Black Pawn Turner and this unknown chimera if they were a prior student. I've already sent several squads of Knights and Bishops out to determine their whereabouts." He leaned in closer, his eyes still locked on Leah. "What interests me most is the contents of your dreams. You seem to have a unique talent that could offer more insight into tracking down your lost classmates."

Goosebumps rippled across Leah's skin. She knew she had to tell someone about the dreams, but she had hoped they'd gloss over them. "So, you believe the dreams are real?"

Reginald leaned back, clasping his hands together. "There are theories, old tales from past Mystics, but nothing more. What I am more curious about is how someone can shadow themselves from your vision. It may be this Legion who is behind it, but I would be careless to not think that someone more powerful than a White Knight may be involved."

Constance cleared her throat. "I believe that would be all for today, don't you agree, Reginald?"

He nodded.

Constance smiled at Leah. "Again, we thank you for what you have done for the Infinity Board. We'll carry on with the investigation. Until further notice, know that any further discussion on this matter, including talk of the former dean, former Black Knight Kim, chimeras, and any other discussion, is confidential. You have no clearance to discuss these matters outside this room, and doing so will cause swift action to ensure the confidentiality remains intact until we conclude our investigation. Do you understand?"

Leah wanted to speak, but a weight settled in her throat. Instead, she stared at her lap and said, "Yes, White Bishop Berkenshire."

"In the coming days, we'll inform you about what you can and cannot discuss on the matter. You and Black Knight Mizrahi are dismissed."

Eric stood, pulling Leah up to stand at attention with him in front of the administration before he escorted her out of the room.

In the hall, Leah mumbled, "I'd like to see my friends . . . alone, if you don't mind."

Eric frowned and peered down the hall. "Yeah, I need to speak to someone too." His eyes flicked over to the former dean's office, where Nykima stood.

She stepped over and hugged him. "Thank you."

Eric hugged her back. "For what?"

Leah imagined herself back on the table, Dr. Toppen hovering over her with a knife in hand. "For saving me."

CHAPTER 45

BROTHERS

Leah rounded the corner, peering out of the stained-glass window to the sunny lawn. Students were out there, practicing forms, unaware of the events that had taken place in the last twenty-four hours. She descended the stairs to the first floor and found the results of the second trial displayed on the scoreboard. She bit her lip and drew in a deep breath as she read it.

Leah Ackerman – 81
~~Serena Bacchus~~ – 61
~~Paige Jones~~ – N/A
Emma Mitchell – 79
Isaac O'Connor – 82
Gabe Tate – 83
Sarah Turner – 89

Serena was gone. She winced at the thought, but hoped she'd be with her brother now, at least. Seeing Paige's name also hurt, knowing that she wasn't coming back. Not anytime soon.

Leah didn't know how long she stood there, but when she turned, she was staring at Brandon, only inches from his face.

"I've been calling your name."

She could see it in his eyes, the same eyes Theodore had. Those eyes were dead, laying in front of her, staring up from beside the river. She'd killed him. She'd killed Brandon's brother.

"Something went down last night, and no one will tell me. I heard a rumor you saw him. You saw my brother?"

Leah took a step back. How did he know?

He reached out and grabbed her arm. She tried pulling away, but his grip tightened. "You know. Please, just tell me. I have to know. Where is he?"

Theodore's dead eyes stared back at her, moonlight gleaming off them. Words fell off her tongue. "I . . . I don't . . . I can't . . ."

"Pawn Roe, remove your hand from Pawn Ackerman at once!"

Nykima walked down the steps, Eric right behind her. She stared expectantly at Brandon, arms crossed.

Brandon squeezed tighter on Leah's wrist and pulled her in. "No! I know you found him. Tell me where he is! She knows what happened. I'm not letting go until I get some answers."

Eric reached past Nykima, but she put a hand on his chest and stopped him. She descended the stairs and raised a hand to Brandon. "That poor girl has had it rough. I know what happened to Theodore. So, let her go, and we'll talk. I'll tell you what I know."

He squeezed tighter, his breathing intensified, and Leah winced as heat billowed from his hand.

Nykima spoke again. This time, her words were sharp. "If you choose to harm her, I will have to act. You won't only be losing points, do you understand?"

Brandon slowed his breathing, and the heat in his hand vanished. He let go.

Leah stepped away from him, rubbing her wrist. Eric rushed to her side.

Nykima pointed up the stairs. "You know where my office is. Wait inside. I'll be in shortly."

Brandon stared at the floor and brushed past her, heading up the stairs without another word.

Nykima waited until he was out of earshot. "That damn boy makes it hard to care for him." She raised an eyebrow. "It seems like trouble follows you everywhere you go."

"It's not like I ask for it, do I?"

"No, you don't." Nykima rested her hands on Leah's arms. "You did what needed to be done. No one holds that against you. Understand?"

Leah felt the warmth of Nykima's hands. In that moment, some unspoken bond formed between the two, a knowing that both were fighters who'd do whatever it took to protect the ones they loved. "Thank you."

Nykima let her go and looked over her shoulder. "I'll take care of Brandon. Why don't you enjoy the rest of the day with your classmates? Maybe take a break from being a detective for one day." She paused, raising an eyebrow at Eric before focusing again on Leah. "It's a shame you're already bonded. I could have used someone with as much passion as you."

CHAPTER 46
FRIENDS REUNITED

Leah opened the doors to the third-floor common room and found Sarah and Isaac hanging out on a couch. They smiled and jumped out of their seats, racing over, arms outstretched for a hug.

Being by their side felt safe and right. It reminded her that, after all that had happened, she still had these two to lean on. They ushered her to the couch, and Leah noted how empty the common room was. "Is everyone else outside?"

Sarah plopped down on the sofa. "Yep. No classes today since they announced the results of the second trial. Some Black Bishop escorted them outside to enjoy the weather. But we left the infirmary just in time to hide and wait for them to pass. We weren't in the mood to enjoy the weather when we didn't know what happened to you."

Isaac found a seat next to Sarah and leaned back. "We heard some rumors. Is it true what they are saying? About Dean Wright?"

Leah sat across from them and crossed her arms. "I've been told to not tell anyone anything. But that specific rumor . . . how did you hear about that?"

Sarah smirked. "Well, Isaac here woke up and saw you missing from bed. We snuck out of the infirmary, and that's when we heard it over the radio from one of the Black Knights as they did their rounds. Something about reporting to the boathouse to contain the dean."

Isaac bit his lip. "We tried to get out there, but they locked down the academy. Full lockdown, like an automated system that blocked all the doors and windows."

"We stayed up," Sarah said. "But someone found us and sent us back to the infirmary. Then they discharged us right after sunrise as we started seeing some Knights race into the infirmary. They were trying to rush us out while looking for something, kept calling it an 'antidote.'"

Leah looked back toward the doors to the common room, then leaned forward. "William used a well from the Tree of Death. It stopped him from dying, but it was like a poison to anyone around him, almost like radiation."

Leah did her best to recount the events, checking on the doors every few minutes, expecting the administration to come bursting in for her disobedience. They didn't, and instead, Sarah and Isaac listened to every detail and came to her side to offer comfort.

Moments of silence passed between Leah and her friends until Isaac spoke. "What about Paige and Theodore? Do you think they'll look for them still?"

There was his name again, and his face, dead in on the sandy shore, eyes looking up at her. She couldn't face it, couldn't face telling them the truth. Not yet.

Leah shook her head. "I don't know. I saw them run before backup arrived. Knowing that chimeras must have been in hiding for centuries now doesn't give me much hope."

"That and they wanted us to keep quiet about chimeras," Isaac said. "I guess we can keep looking for them in case the Infinity Board does nothing. And if they do, then maybe it'll restore a bit of my faith in them."

"Amen to that," Sarah said.

They stayed in the common room as the day carried on, relaxing and enjoying each other's company. At one point, Sarah went down to the cafeteria and came back with a massive plate of cheesy mushroom pizza for the three of them. Leah had a moment of calm, a moment to feel herself again, and felt thankful for the friends she had.

A few hours later, a voice sounded over the intercom. "All Black Pawns report to field three, in full uniform, at three p.m. I repeat, all Black Pawns report to field three, in full uniform, at three p.m. Thank you."

Leah frowned and sat up. "Why do they want us in uniforms?"

Isaac shrugged. "Guess we'll find out. Hopefully, they tell everyone what happened."

Sarah locked her arm around Leah's and pulled her off the couch. "Either way, we need to get dressed." She smirked at Isaac. "And no boys allowed."

He blushed, and the doors to the main hallway opened as other girls entered the common room. "Right. Uh . . . I guess I'll just be going."

Sarah giggled and turned to Leah. "Look, whatever happens, you did what needed to be done. No matter what they say, I'm by your side." She pulled Leah along to their rooms.

CHAPTER 47
BONDING

They found Isaac again, waiting for them out on the field. Leah shifted uncomfortably in her black uniform as the afternoon sun, on a mild spring day, beat down.

The Pawns assembled a platform on the field, where all three administrators stood in full uniform. Both Constance and Grace wore the same white button up blazer and white gloves, but Constance wore a white skirt and flats, while Grace had on white pants and high heels. Reginald stood in a gold-buttoned black military coat that matched his black cane and golden crow head cane topper. Behind them, Knights and Bishops of the academy lined up in an array of white and black uniforms.

The Black Pawns took their positions in front of the platform.

Nykima stepped forward. "Attention!"

All the Pawns shifted and stood straight-backed, awaiting further instruction. It surprised Leah to see so few still around. Out of the forty who had started, less than half had made it through the trials.

"At ease," Constance said.

The Black Pawns relaxed but kept their attention on Constance.

"Good afternoon. By now, you all know that last night was eventful, to say the least. To cease the urge to spread rumors, we'll be as transparent as possible. The Tree of Death corrupted Black Knight Ian Kim and White Knight William Wright. We suspect Dr. Toppen was involved somehow. However, she vanished before we could question her. We've taken swift action regarding Black Knight Kim and Dean Wright to contain the corruption, and as a result, we have executed both."

Pawns around Leah gasped. Others whispered around Leah, asking questions like, "What does that mean?" and "How can they be corrupted?"

Constance raised her hand, commanding silence. "I know this news comes as a shock, but as future members of the Infinity Board, you must keep yourselves in check." She paused, waiting for the Pawns to silence themselves before continuing. "With such a stain on this academy, the first in this country, we've decided to close this establishment."

None of the Pawns spoke, but Leah felt the tension buzzing about as they tried to contain themselves.

"The Infinity Board is committed to investigating the cause of the corruption and tackling it head on. As for the current class, know that we are invested in your futures. While the closing of this academy will occur this week, that means that we have concluded your trials early. We have more than enough information to determine your future within the Infinity Board. The Knights and Bishops who have come to the trials have selected you, and training will resume within your assigned units from here on out."

Constance rejoined the administration while Grace stepped forward and opened a booklet. "I will call the Knights and Bishops who have requested bonds. They will choose which Pawn, or Pawns, are best suited to join their unit. Knights and Bishops take into consideration your skills, intellect, and personality to determine what will most suit you and the Infinity Board."

Reginald cleared his throat and stepped forward. "If I may, White Bishop Johnson, I'd like to take care of one thing before leaping into the bonding."

Grace nodded and stepped back.

"Black Pawn Ackerman, please come to the platform," Reginald said.

Leah swallowed and her heart raced. She approached the administration, feeling the eyes of the remaining Pawns burning her back. Reginald guided her to stand next to him, facing out to her peers.

"Pawn Ackerman came to this academy already bonded, a divergence from tradition. I was skeptical but swayed into allowing her to proceed through the trials to prove that the bond was worthy of being kept. We adjusted several bits of tradition to accommodate, and even then, the points she earned and lost were questionable."

Cold sweat formed on her brow. Did she fail Eric? Was their bond going to be severed?

Reginald rested a hand on her shoulder. "Yet, she persisted and kept fighting. While this may not be customary to announce, we've already broken many tradi-tions this term. Black Pawn Leah Ackerman, I want to state my gratitude, publicly, for your help in uncovering the actions of our former Knight and Dean. You persisted when we turned a blind eye, and for that, I owe you a debt. Your bond with Black Knight Eric Mizrahi will remain. You may stand beside him while your fellow Black Pawns are assigned."

Warmth shot through Leah's bond, a happiness that reverberated with her own. She met Eric's smile and shook

Reginald's hand in gratitude, forcing herself to remain collected as she walked over and stood at Eric's side. She turned to see Isaac smiling up at her and Sarah giving her a thumbs up. Even Gabe half smiled before turning his attention back to the administration.

Reginald stepped back and bowed to Grace, who eyed her list. "First up, Black Knight Abercromby."

A short, broad-shouldered bald man with a massive reddish beard stepped forward. In a thick accent, he spoke. "Black Pawn Sediki and Sarkar, I pick ye two as me bond."

Omer, his bulky frame only shadowed by the Knight who called him, stepped free from the Black Pawns and up to the Black Knight's side. Deepak, shorter but still as muscular as the other two, joined them as well, the trio forming a seemingly formidable team.

Grace continued shouting names of Bishops and Knights in no particular order that Leah could discern. She watched as others joined their Knights and Pawns. Emma was the first to be called from her original outpost, chosen by a tall Black Bishop who seemed like he belonged at a metal concert more than at the academy, his arms tattooed, his hair long and black and his eyes covered by aviators.

"Black Knight Gunn," Grace called.

Sid limped forward, his arm in a sling and a few bruises across his face.

"Black Pawn O'Connor, Tate, and Lopez. I pick you three to bond."

Leah smirked. Sid was a perfect choice, now that she knew he wasn't evil. Intelligent and resourceful, the qualities she liked best in Isaac and Gabe.

She noticed Ricardo and Gabe stepping forward from the group up onto the platform. She looked for Isaac and saw Sarah push him, pulling him out of shock. He raced forward, meeting Sid and smiling at his side.

Grace continued. "White Knight Amana."

Nykima stepped forward, her white uniform cinched to hug her waist, and her white pants flared at the bottom.

She peered into the crowd of Pawns. "Black Pawns Roe and Fogle, I pick you two to bond."

Everyone stared at Brandon, except Leah, who realized now why Nykima had seemed to have a vested interest in him before. She also realized why she'd picked Miranda, the most technical student, and the most reliable.

The group of Pawns awaiting their assignment dwindled, and Leah shifted uncomfortably when she noted that Sarah and Joanna had yet to be selected.

Leah eyed the row of Knights and Bishops, seeing that Grace had called on all of them. She could see the look of defeat on Sarah's face. She and Joanna were the only ones left to be assigned, but there weren't any Knights or Bishops left to claim them.

Grace looked up. "There is one more Bishop who will take on Pawns. Myself. Black Pawns Turner and Morales, I pick you two as my bond."

A grin spread on Sarah's face, and she rushed up to the platform to greet Grace, Joanna right behind her.

Reginald cleared his throat and said, "Knights, Bishops, bond with your Pawns."

One by one, the Knights and Bishops grabbed the hands of their Pawns, muttering words under their breath before taking their Pawn's hands and placing them on their chests. Leah stifled a laugh when she saw how Brandon's face turned red when Nykima placed his hand on her chest, yet he didn't flinch or say anything.

Heat rose around them as the bonds formed. Energy crackled in the air, and she turned and looked at Eric. He smiled and gave Leah a gentle pat on her head, shocking her with static.

Once everyone had formed the bonds, Reginald clapped his hands together. "By forming your bonds, you have deepened your connection with the Tree of Life. Each one of you will leave the platform as White Pawns, free to set out with your units on missions and assignments from the Infinity Board." He stared at Leah and gave a slight nod of approval. "Do us proud."

CHAPTER 48
QUEEN'S GAMBIT

Days passed, and Leah watched the academy empty. Each unit got their assignment, and no two groups went to the same place.

She feared the day they would call on Eric, so instead, she spent every waking minute with Isaac and Sarah, scanning over books as they packed them into boxes or practicing with Sarah and Isaac's newfound strength in the sparring ring.

She told Emma everything about Paige. That she saw her, fought her, and that she was a chimera. The last bit took some convincing, but by the time Emma left on assignment, a newfound life was in her eyes. She'd search for Paige, knowing that Leah, Sarah, and Isaac would do the same.

After a week, all the departures ended. All who remained were Constance and the units led by Grace, Nykima, Sid, and Eric.

Joanna and Gabe found Leah and her friends out at the boathouse, still damaged from the fight and barricaded off by boards.

Joanna caught her breath while Gabe spoke. "We've

been running all over the place. Constance called a meeting. We're to report to the classroom now."

Sarah took aim and launched a rock at the river's
surface, skipping it clear across and onto the other shore.

"Did she say why?" Isaac asked.

Gabe shook his head. "Nope, but it's for all of us."

Joanna stood and clutched her side. "I . . . don't . . . want
. . . to run . . . anymore."

Leah eyed the spot where Theodore had died, feeling
the pain bubble up inside her. She had killed him. It was all
her fault. And now she got to be here, among friends, while
he lay rotting in an unmarked grave.

She pushed the feeling down, forcing the pain somewhere deep inside her, and glanced back at Sarah. "Last one
back has bathroom duty."

Sara grinned. "Oh, you're on. Good luck Joanna!" She
launched herself forward with *Malchut* and Leah followed,
leaving the pain behind while Joanna shouted behind
them.

Chairs lined up where their desks had been located,
everyone else already piled into the room, waiting, when
they all walked in.

Constance stood at the front of the room, eyeing them
until they found their seats behind Eric, Sid, Grace, and
Nykima.

"Now that everyone is here, we can begin." She turned
and closed the door to the classroom. "We have deployed
the other units with no awareness of what is happening
here, within these academy walls."

Leah looked at the other White Pawns, each with the same expression of confusion.

"This group right here will be part of a special operation, led by me, based out of this academy. Black Queen Nielsen has given us a special set of assignments."

Leah moved to the edge of her seat, holding onto every word from Constance.

"We are to locate all chimeras, including our lost Black Pawns, so we can discover their plans and put an end to them."

Brandon sat up and let out a quick. "Yes!" before catching Nykima's glare and calming himself down. Leah frowned at his reaction and wondered what exactly Nykima had shared with Brandon.

Constance paced the front of the room. "That's not our only mission." Her tone took a more serious turn, and the air grew heavy once again. "Considering the actions of Mr. Wright and Mr. Kim, we have caught wind of an entity that poses a threat to the Infinity Board." She shot a quick glance at Leah before continuing. "Through recent evidence, we learned William was under the command of a being named Legion."

The Knights and Bishops frowned. Nykima leaned back in her chair. "What do we know about this, 'Legion'?"

"Very little. We don't even know if it's a human, chimera, demon, or something else. The evidence, although scarce, was enough for Black Queen Nielsen to form this unit."

Leah stared at Sarah and Isaac, excitement bubbling up inside her. They wouldn't be separated. At least, not yet.

"Given Black Queen Nielsen's direct command to form this unit, and her full support, we are now known as the Queen's Gambit."

Leah looked around the room and grinned. She

wouldn't trust any other group of people to help her track down Legion, the thing that had ordered Asmodeus to kill her parents. She felt a small pulse from her left arm, as if Asmodeus noted his approval.

"Any other questions?" Constance asked.

Silence overtook the room. She nodded, heading to the door. "Good, then let's get to work."

A Small Request From Us, The Authors

Thank you for continuing Leah's journey. We hope you've enjoyed it, so far.

As independent authors, reviews are so important to spread the word and reach new readers.

If you have a few seconds to spare, would you please consider leaving an honest review on the website you bought this book?

Your support helps so much in continuing Leah's story and the many others we plan to write in this world.

All the best,

A.B. Cohen & JP Rindfleisch IX

DECEIVED BISHOP
LEAH ACKERMAN SERIES BOOK THREE

The story continues:

https://abcohenwrites.com/deceived-bishop

CURSED JADE
AN ERIC MIZRAHI NOVELETTE

Get it free using the link below:

https://abcohenwrites.com/cursed-jade

Acknowledgments

Thank you so much to everyone who has helped Demon Knight cross the proverbial published finish line. Who knew that two strangers could spend a weekend together in a haunted mansion back in January 2020 and craft an entire story universe?

To our editors and proofreaders, J. Thorn, Zach Bohannon, and Lori Diederich, thank you! Your advice helped make this story what it is today. You all have been amazing at supporting our vision while helping us button up the story and teach us how to improve our craft.

We also want to mention our Beta readers, who gave us excellent feedback. Thank you for helping us expand on the relationships and tease out the confusing bits.

Shout out to our awesome cover designer, Getcovers.com who has knocked it out of the park with another superb cover. We appreciate everything that you have done for this series!

JP here, thank you to my local bookstore, Maze Books, in Rockford, IL, for becoming a community hub for local authors to network and showcase our work. You were the first bookstore I reached out to and what you have been doing for the local author community is amazing. For all those reading, check out and support your local libraries and bookstores.

Last, thank you, our wonderful readers. We hope you enjoyed Demon Knight, and that you are just as excited as we are for what is to come.

Thank you all.

A.B. Cohen & JP Rindfleisch IX

ABOUT THE AUTHORS

A.B. Cohen is an author of freaky stories for weird people. He focus mainly on thrillers, horror and urban fantasy tales. Originally from Caracas, Venezuela, today he lives in Berkeley, California. Along with his passion for writing, he also loves dancing, soccer, and traveling. You can find out more about A.B. Cohen's upcoming writing projects using the link below:

www.abcohenwrites.com

JP Rindfleisch IX is a horror, urban fantasy, and science fiction writer. They live in Rockford, Illinois, with their partner of eleven years, and a menagerie of animal children including a Siberian husky, miniature dachshund, African grey parrot, Quaker parrot, and a run of the mill cat. They love creating art, nerding out over science, video games, tabletop RPGs, and spending hours in the kitchen crafting delectable vegan grub. You can learn more about JP Rindfleisch IX by following the link below:

www.jprindfleischix.com

www.ingramcontent.com/pod-product-compliance
Lightning Source LLC
Chambersburg PA
CBHW051126190726
48290CB00006B/1705